BURIED

Also by Marissa Farrar

The 'Serenity' Series

ALONE
BURIED
CAPTURED

Book Four, DOMINION, will be published late 2012.

THE DARK ROAD

UNDERLIFE

BURIED

Book Two in the Serenity Series

Marissa Farrar

BURIED
By Marissa Farrar

Paperback Edition
ISBN 978-0-9571524-2-7

Copyright © 2011 Marissa Farrar

Warwick House Press

License Notes

This eBook is licensed for your personal enjoyment only. This eBook may not be re-sold or given away to other people. If you would like to share this book with another person, please purchase an additional copy for each recipient. If you're reading this book and did not purchase it, or it was not purchased for your use only, then please purchase your own copy. Thank you for respecting the hard work of these authors.

Publisher's Note

This is a work of fiction. Names, characters, places, and incidents are either the products of the author's imagination or are used fictitiously, and any resemblance to actual persons, living or dead, business establishments, events, or locales is entirely coincidental.

To my husband, who has put up with an unsociable wife and a dirty house while I tapped away on my keyboard, fulfilling my dreams. I will always appreciate how hard you work for us.

BURIED

Acknowledgments

Two editors worked on this novel. The first, Danielle Gavan, was unable to complete the book due to illness, but the job was taken on by Sydney C. Jelinek. Thank you Sydney, for working hard to keep to my deadlines. Without your hard work, I wouldn't have been able to give my readers the book when I promised.

BURIED

CONTENTS PAGE

BURIED

Prologue

It woke to the sense of drowning; of lungs so full it was unable to take a breath. It woke to claustrophobia; compressed on every side. It woke to panic and fear.

Though the creature's eyes were wide open, only darkness filled its sight. Its natural instinct was to take a breath, feel its chest rise and fall, but despite its struggle, nothing happened.

Its mind was a blur—a mess of darkness, pain and anger. It had no idea who it was or what had happened. Negative emotions filled the creature; fury, fear and an overwhelming desire.

Something was wrong.

The creature opened its mouth to roar in frustration and fear, but dirt poured into its gaping maw. The grainy taste of earth filled its mouth and the particles crunched between its teeth, clogging its throat.

Panic took hold and it fought against the confines. It clawed and scratched, pushed and fought until something above gave way.

With increased vigor, it burst from the earthen tomb. Dirt flew upward, spattering around in clods, as though an explosion had occurred beneath the ground.

The thing sat up, the last of the earth falling from its body, and blinked against the sudden light. For a few moments it sat, waiting for the burst of fire in front of its eyeballs to subside, waiting to adjust. Soon enough, they did and the creature looked around with wary curiosity.

Trees towered above, creating a canopy of dappled green light. Lifting its dirt encrusted fingers, the creature shielded its eyes again, seeing none of the beauty. All around was silence. No birds sang, no insects buzzed in the air, even the wind seemed to pause in the leaves, holding its breath against the horror beneath.

Pain ripped through its body, and the thing shrieked, curling over upon itself. Every nerve ending burned. It wanted to rip the flesh from its own body, tear at itself with its teeth.

A need overwhelmed it, a thirst, something that would stop the pain. With wild eyes, the creature lifted its face to the sky and sniffed the air. What it needed was out there; it smelled it on the air like smoke from a bonfire on an autumn day. Though the thing's muscles burned in agony, they also twitched with strength, an energy needing to be used, and it itched to get moving.

The creature unfurled from the earthen hole that had been its resting place and stretched, flexing stiff muscles. Clothes hung from its limbs in tattered pieces; the years spent buried beneath the earth decomposing them beyond recognition.

As it took the first tentative steps, flashes of thought jolted its mind like lightning strikes, memories of a life once lived. The thing stopped in its tracks, clutching at its head, confused.

But need drove it on.

Pushing its way through trees and bushes, it paid no attention to the branches whipping at its head or the brambles hooking its flesh. External pain meant nothing.

The flashes came again and it screamed at the thoughts, battering at its head with its hands, trying to drive away the images. Nothing could keep it from what it needed.

As it pushed its way through more undergrowth, the scent became overwhelming. Ahead, the thing noticed two figures, one larger than the other, both with bags strapped to their backs.

Out of an instinct coming from somewhere ancient and dark, it went for the larger one first, knowing the smaller one would do little to defend itself or its mate. The larger one— the male—didn't even have time to scream

Sharp teeth sank into the male's throat, tearing and biting and devouring. Overcome in its frenzy to feed, not only on the blood, but on the flesh and the fear, the creature forgot the pain for a moment. The smaller one, a female, screamed in a pitch that hurt its ears and it turned to see her eyes wide with fear.

Filled with its own sense of power and strength, its face and chest covered in warm blood, it lifted its head to the sky and roared.

The smaller one turned and ran.

The creature leaped, soaring through the air, landing directly on the smaller one's back, knocking her to the ground. The air crushed from the female's lungs and she didn't get the chance to take another breath. The thing buried its face in the sweet warmth of her throat and slowly sank its teeth in, relishing every moment as she lay beneath, defenseless and fragile as a bird. The blood came in like mother's milk and it fed—tearing, lapping and swallowing, until only a carcass was left.

It lifted its head and sniffed the air. It could kill again if it wanted, but for the moment it needed to rest.

Something beyond the trees drew it—the noise of the city in the distance—but it would wait. It needed to grow strong, and so needed to go back beneath the ground. Using its bare hands, the creature dug its way back into the comfort of the earth, pulling the dirt back in over itself. Despite its earlier panic, the cool dark of the ground now offered peace.

As it lay down to rest, one name formed in the thing's deranged mind.

Serenity.

Chapter One

Rumors in the underworld worked in much the same way as they did amongst mortals. A hushed breath upon still air, followed by a whisper, and finally a spoken word. Confirmation that something was out there, something to be feared—even amongst their kind.

Sebastian knelt on the cool stone floor of a cave once used as a church for over a thousand years. A mural depicting the body of Christ in a ruthless parody of ecstasy, hanging from the cross, was painted on the wall above.

In the presence of such an image, Sebastian felt vindicated. How could any religion talk about forgiveness when its followers were asked to pray under this horrific gaze of a dying god?

Sebastian wanted to be here; he wanted to be judged. He deserved nothing more. He only wished he believed in the entity enough for the retribution to be real.

He'd thought himself cut off from the rest of the world. Since leaving Serenity, he had wandered across the earth trying to find the perfect place to nurse his wounds. Desperate to leave America far behind, he'd traveled across Europe for many months, searching for a somewhere to hide.

Eventually, he happened upon Goreme in Turkey. The few people living in the area had dug themselves into the rock, hiding from the intense sun scorching the area, leaving only a few traditional buildings visible above ground.

The strange, almost alien landscape matched his tortured soul. Fairy chimneys—huge stone structures, like giant termite mounds—rose from the ground. Single rounded rocks balanced on the tops of the mounds, eroded by the sun and wind. Goreme looked as though it belonged on another planet. No trees or grass grew, instead the uniform color of sandstone and rock stretched as far as the eye could see.

Goreme's scenery wasn't the only thing to capture Sebastian's attention. A system of disused tunnels ran beneath the rock, running hundreds of feet into the bedrock, as many as nine levels deep. He took to these tunnels, living below ground in the daytime, hunting at night. Sebastian lived as he believed he should, as a monster, hiding in the dark.

He was aware of the other vampire standing in the doorway before he even spoke.

"Surely you are not praying?" The vampire laughed, but any mockery dropped off his young, pale face as soon as Sebastian turned to him.

"How can I pray to something that cannot possibly exist?"

The other vampire raised his eyebrows. He was young and handsome, with fine, jaw length blond hair and a slender frame.

"How do we know?" he said. "We never die. If a God does exist then it will not be for us to find out."

Sebastian growled. "If a God existed then we would not."

He fought his own demons daily. Pining for Serenity, heartbroken at staying away from her, he remained in the darkness and shied away from contact with others—mortal or immortal. Yet, despite his isolation, from time to time Sebastian happened upon one of his own. These vampires hadn't found a place to call home and wandered the earth.

This was one such vampire.

As nomads, they believed their presence in any one place would bring about the end of their species. In truth, this would not happen. The human species was cruel; people vanished, people were murdered all of the time. If someone mentioned the possibility of such disappearances being linked to his kind, they would be dismissed as crazy. Yet still these vampires preferred to be alone. Though solitary beings, they desired the chance to talk with their own kind.

The young vampire leapt at the wall, settling himself into one of the nooks carved into the rock as a seat.

"Maybe not," he said, pushing his hair away from his face. "Perhaps we're not the most terrible thing out there. Perhaps your God created worse."

"Nothing is more despicable than what we are." Sebastian watched his visitor coolly. He hadn't wished for company. "We murder so we can survive. We are destined always to value our own lives above others."

Sebastian killed; out of pain, anger, a need to forget the life he might once have led. He tried to lose himself in the rush of blood. Sebastian knew the local people feared him, though his presence was little more than a bad story, a fairy tale, a superstition. That was the beauty of his kind—people found the horror of his reality so terrifying it could not possibly be the truth.

The young vampire shrugged. "Don't all creatures of God? What about those who kill for pleasure? Humans do, as do their companion, the common pussy-cat. Are you saying because the cat exists, God cannot?"

Sebastian's eyes narrowed. He didn't want to be here debating philosophical issues. Very young, perhaps only a couple of decades, the other vampire clearly reveled in his new vampirism, like a teenager who hadn't yet experienced the hard reality of life. Sebastian didn't want to be the one to teach the young vampire these lessons.

He opened his mouth to ask the other vampire to leave, but the vampire interrupted.

"Anyway, I hear something much worse has been created—something abhorrent."

Sebastian stopped. He, too, had heard such rumors. The first time someone told him of the creature, he laughed—treated the tales as a human would treat the possibility of the vampire—but when the next vampire brought up the topic, Sebastian recognized an undercurrent of worry in the stranger's voice.

"Nothing more than hearsay," Sebastian said, deliberately dismissive. "Our own version of the bogeyman."

"No, it's real." The young vampire's yellow eyes shone with enthusiasm. "The creature is not a vampire, but is also a long way from being human. It walks the streets, taking lives without mercy."

"Where is the proof? Have we seen it?"

He leaned forward, his elbows resting on his knees. "No one has seen it. The creature appears in the light."

"My point exactly. How convenient."

The vampire shook his head. "Rumors are the thing is searching for something, for someone. Others say it used to be human, but now is a monster."

A sense of unease stirred within Sebastian. Something had always troubled him about the events of four years ago. He'd turned over the memory of his search for Serenity's necklace and of the empty grave he'd found the jewelry beside, again and again.

"So where is this thing supposed to be?" he asked.

Sebastian received the answer he didn't want to hear.

"America."

Instantly, his thoughts turned to Serenity. Was she safe?

The United States was a big place for a human; not so big for one of his kind. But then this thing was not one of them. He'd never heard of a vampire being out in the light, which told him whatever this thing was, it wasn't a vampire. Yet the thing killed and fed, and possessed a vampire's strength.

The thought sent chills through Sebastian's heart. In truth, this creature might be humanity's worst nightmare; possibly even a vampire's worst nightmare. Light was a vampire's main weakness. If something existed with all of a vampire's strengths, but none of its weaknesses, it might be an enemy to both species.

Sebastian could easily have ignored the rumors, staying saturated in his own well of self-pity, but he experienced a kind of uneasy recognition at the vampire's story. He had always wondered why Madeline moved Serenity's husband's body. Had his maker taken Jackson's body to turn him but, because Serenity had fought back, Madeline had been unable to complete the process?

The idea was horrific. Sebastian didn't know if giving life to a recently dead body was even possible, but Madeline had been much older and she possessed knowledge he did not. It sounded like the sort of twisted, sick thing she would attempt.

If there was any chance of the thing having once been Serenity's husband, he couldn't ignore it. Sebastian had to go back and make sure she was safe.

"I must leave," he said, abruptly, marching from the cave.

The other vampire leapt to his feet, close on Sebastian's heels. "Wait! I thought we could go hunting."

"Do I look like I want a bit of male bonding?" Sebastian snarled.

The younger vampire reared back. He wasn't stupid enough to push Sebastian. At six feet two, with a shock of dark hair, Sebastian made a striking figure and his years of underground living had left him ravaged.

The other vampire slunk off into the night. Sebastian didn't give him another thought, his mind already elsewhere.

By Sebastian's calculations, he had about six hours of night left.

He could move fast and was strong, but laughed at the myths of vampire's being able to teleport or change into a bat and fly. Vampires still had to abide by physical laws. He would have to get to America the old fashioned way—by boat. Flying posed too much of a risk. Though he owned fake passports and other documentation, allowing him to travel as a human, he couldn't guarantee not being exposed to the light. Even if he caught a night flight, he risked the flight being delayed or rerouted, exposing him. The threat was too great.

Sebastian set off on foot.

He didn't need to take anything with him. Nothing he owned meant anything; he cared about no part of his existence. He was as transitory as the wind.

Sebastian planned to stow away on a ship heading to the States, hide beneath deck until the ship docked and night fell. His speed made it easy for him to sneak on board. He moved too quickly for the human eye to register.

Once aboard ship, he'd find the time of passage frustrating, though things had sped up over the last hundred years. Previously, months on board passed before they covered any great distance. Sebastian appreciated the improvement. Months on a vessel meant he'd need to hunt and this created fear and chaos. Now it took only ten days to make the same journey. Sebastian survived without feeding and in far more comfortable surroundings. Cinemas and swimming pools graced the deck, a far cry from the smelly and uncomfortable trips he'd made in the past.

He hoped Serenity stayed safe until he reached her. He might be wrong about the whole thing, inflating the stories in his mind so he had an excuse to see her again. Had he been waiting for a convenient excuse this whole time?

I won't speak to her, he promised himself, remembering the number of times he made exactly the same promise four years ago and how quickly he'd broken them.

Sebastian's heart contracted at the thought of seeing Serenity again. She'd been in his thoughts constantly since the moment he left.

The memory of Serenity made him increase his speed. He flew through the night, across the strange, arid landscape. He could take a car if he so desired, but he'd always been uncomfortable in any kind of machinery and when he needed to move fast, he traveled faster and safer by foot.

Sebastian headed to Istanbul.

He reached the busy city frighteningly close to day break, but he was in luck. The bulks of several ships loomed in dock. Ahead, the night sky faded from black to blue. He needed to act fast in order to sneak on board and find himself a secure hiding place before morning.

The early hour meant the port was all but deserted. Sebastian headed for an American ship named, 'The Ocean Voyager'. He hoped the boat was on a direct route and didn't stop in every country along the way.

Boarding the ship, he approached a reception desk, much like one found in an expensive hotel. A woman in her early twenties sat behind the counter, stifling a yawn with the back of her hand.

Sebastian scanned a framed poster of the ship's layout hung on the wall beside the desk. At the bottom of the ship were rooms with neither a porthole nor a balcony. In truth, these were the rooms no one wanted, the cheapest rooms on the ship. For Sebastian, they were perfect.

He slipped past the woman at reception and headed down to his chosen deck. He paused outside each room, listening. The shallow breathing and snoring of the room's inhabitants as they slept met his sensitive ears and Sebastian by-passed each one. Finally, he happened upon a room where no sound came from behind the door.

Sebastian made his way back up to the reception desk. He wished he could go back to the days when actual keys were used; life had been easier when he only needed to steal a key. Moving quickly, he snuck behind the desk and took one of the cards used to open the bedroom doors. The receptionist sensed something happening around her. She frowned and rubbed at her arms, but didn't glance up.

Sebastian went back to the doorway and walked through as though coming up from below deck. He hoped he didn't appear too disheveled.

The woman still sat in her chair; head tilted back, eyes closed. Sebastian walked too quietly for her to hear him— something he hadn't intended—and he cleared his throat.

She jumped and looked up to find Sebastian standing in front of her desk. Her cheeks flushed with color and she pulled herself upright, smoothing her hair back from her face.

"I'm so sorry," she said. "It's been a long shift."

Sebastian gave her what he hoped was a winning smile. A long time had passed since he'd been in any human company and he was out of practice.

"Don't worry. Actually, I should be the one who is embarrassed. I've only just got back to the ship and discovered my key card won't work."

He held the card out over the desk and she reached out, taking the slip of plastic. Sebastian held her gaze for a moment too long and she glanced back down, flustered.

"Oh, it happens all the time," she said with a dismissive shake of her head. "What room number are you?"

"Three-four-six."

The woman ran the card beneath a scanner and typed the number into a computer. A line of red light ran across the card and something beeped. She handed the card back to him.

"There you go. You shouldn't have any more problems."

He smiled again, "Thank you so much."

Down in the hull of the ship, Sebastian entered the tiny room. A narrow bunk was attached to the wall and a second bunk pulled down directly above. When lying down, Sebastian's feet would hang over the end. The bathroom was little more than a closet, one inconvenience he wouldn't be forced to use.

Sebastian hung the 'do not disturb' sign on the outside of the door and locked it from the inside as an extra precaution. He didn't expect to be disturbed but, even if someone did try to come into the room, Sebastian could open the door without any fear of being caught in the light. Like the cabin, the corridor contained no windows.

He flung himself down on the narrow bunk, the back of his arm covering his eyes. As expected, his feet hung over the end and he felt like a giant sleeping in a child's bed.

Vampires didn't sleep—at least not human sleep. Instead, they entered a type of meditation so time passed faster. Their kind needing to sleep in a coffin was no more than a myth.

Within an hour, the ship's engines thrummed beneath him and shortly after, the ship began to move, slowly edging its way out of the harbor and out to the open sea.

What am I doing?

Serenity was probably fine. She had almost certainly gone on with her life by now and thought of him only as a monster, if at all. Why was he torturing himself, probing an open wound, by going back to see her?

Sebastian sighed and rolled over to his side as best he could in the confined space.

He wanted to be like other vampires. In the years since Serenity, he'd tried to embrace his nature. To kill was his only pleasure but it didn't bring him peace. He wished he was like the younger vampire, to whom the torture and fear of the humans he killed was all part of the fun, but Sebastian couldn't detach himself. Not all humans deserved to live, he believed as much, but he didn't want to be the one who chose.

Part of him wished he'd never laid eyes on Serenity, but the other part couldn't stand the thought. He'd fought against the need to see her every moment of the last four years, like an alcoholic fighting the need to drink. She was the reason he'd killed so many; the only way he'd been able to block out the pain, with the euphoric rush of blood.

As hours passed and the ship ate away oceanic miles, Sebastian stayed hidden in his cabin, lost in the wave of memories he'd worked so hard at blocking out.

He'd last been in Serenity's presence after he'd pulled her out of the pipe at the pier. He'd said goodbye to her then, but hadn't left before seeing her with the police officer. The way the other man looked at her, the obvious affection in his eyes, hadn't gone unnoticed. If she were ever to have a normal life, Sebastian couldn't be around her. The type of life the officer would be able to offer Serenity was what Sebastian wanted for her, even if it caused him pain.

So he'd left, certain she would forget him in time and move on with her life.

The ship stopped only once, in Crete, before crossing the Atlantic to New York.

Once they docked, Sebastian would travel across America. He had many miles to cover and hoped in the time it took him to make the journey, Serenity would stay safe.

Chapter Two

In the four years since Serenity Hathaway murdered her husband, she'd learned a lot about fear.

Where she once thought of fear as being external, created by something she was afraid of, she now understood to be internal. Like her eye color or the way her second toe was slightly longer than the others, fear had become part of her.

Serenity was a haunted woman.

She was haunted by the things she'd seen and done. She was haunted by the ghost of her dead husband. But most of all, she was haunted by a man who had turned out to be so much more than just a man.

Serenity ran down the steps of the night school, clutching a folder of notes to her chest. Her eyes picked out the police car, parked a couple of vehicles away on the other side of the street, and raised her hand in greeting, as yet unsure if he had seen her.

In response, the driver's door opened and James Bently climbed out. He scanned the street, one arm resting on the roof of the car. Upon spotting Serenity, he smiled, raising his own hand in greeting.

She checked to ensure the street was clear and ran across the road toward him.

"I hope you're not going to charge me for jay-waking," she said, grinning.

James leaned down and kissed her on the cheek. "I'll let you off with a caution. You got time for a coffee?"

Serenity looked at her watch; a little after eight. Early fall, it was only just starting to get dark and the late evening air still held the warmth of the day.

"Are you sure Amy won't mind?" she asked, glancing at the ring binding the finger on James's left hand.

"No. She called to say both kids are asleep and not to rush back."

"Your wife is an angel," she said.

"I know. She must have been insane to marry me."

Serenity had been relieved when James met Amy. The two of them fell in love almost instantly. The match left Serenity not only pleased for her friend; she had her own reasons for wanting to see him with someone.

Despite James's insistence at being happy with them as friends, after he met Amy the pressure had been taken off Serenity. She'd been able to relax into the friendship without worrying about a second agenda.

Of course, Amy had been a little harder to convince at first. Naturally, she'd thought something was going on between Serenity and James, but once Serenity's condition became obvious and Amy had been assured James had absolutely nothing to do with it, Amy soon relaxed.

In the end, Amy quickly became a friend as well.

A year after they met, James and Amy were married and not long after, Amy announced her pregnancy. Their son had recently turned one and the little family couldn't be happier.

Serenity and James walked down the street until they reached a small coffee shop. Tables and chairs were set out on the sidewalk.

"You didn't need to come pick me up," Serenity said, pulling out a wrought iron chair at the nearest table and sitting down.

James sat opposite. "I don't mind. Amy said we never get the chance to see each other anymore, what with these new shift patterns I'm doing, so it seemed like a good opportunity to catch up. Besides, until you get yourself a car, I'll feel bad heading back to the same part of the city without offering a lift."

Serenity grinned. "I'm doing my bit to save the planet," she said. "This city has too many cars already without me adding to the problem."

The waitress appeared beside their table, catching their attention, and James ordered two lattes.

"So how is the new job going?" Serenity asked after the waitress moved away with their order. James Bently had taken the job of Police Sergeant a little over a month ago.

"Good," he said, nodding. "I miss some parts of the old job and there's even more paper work, but it has its good points. I'm enjoying the extra responsibility and at least I'm not picking drunk kids up off the street anymore."

"That's great, James. I'm so pleased everything is working out for you."

"Yeah, well things are kind of hectic at the moment. I'm sure you've heard about what's been happening in Angeles Forest..."

Serenity nodded. A spate of murders had occurred in the area. No, 'murder' implied the killings were planned or methodical in some way. These were frenzied attacks.

At first, the police thought dogs may have been used as the flesh had been ripped from the victim's bodies like an animal attack but, after forensic analysis had been conducted, they discovered the few bite marks clear enough to get imprints from were those of a human. The thought chilled her to the soul. She found the possibility of one person doing such a thing to another unthinkable.

Now the police thought more than one person might be involved. In the cases of more than one victim being attacked at once, both victims had been easily overpowered with no signs of a struggle. This suggested someone else must have been present, restraining the other victim while the killer did his worst. To inflict so much damage would take time and the police found no signs of rope burn or any other restraints being used, and no drugs were found in the system of any of the victims.

The first victims, a young newlywed couple, had been out hiking for a few days in Los Angeles National Forest. They weren't reported missing until a week after they'd left—they were on vacation and no one thought it strange that they hadn't been heard from. By the time their bodies turned up, most of the evidence had been corrupted.

The police had no idea who was committing these heinous crimes. The perpetrator seemed to disappear into thin air.

The body of a young man was the first of the victims to be found. Initially, the cops thought his murder to be a horrific, isolated case, but then the bodies of the first victims were discovered, happened upon by a park ranger. By the time the bodies were found animals had gotten to them, making the forensic work nearly impossible. Even so, they were obviously dealing with the same killer, or killers.

Several weeks passed before another two walkers were reported missing. By this time word was getting round. Patrol officers had been assigned to the Angeles National Forest, but the area covered a thousand miles of forest, impossible to cover. The most worrying thing was that the killings were getting steadily closer and closer to the city. Where the first had been in the depth of the forest, where only very experienced hikers would go, the latest had been a dog walker.

The area drew millions of visitors every year and, while the police warned people to stay on designated trails and to camp only in the provided sites, not everyone listened.

Visitor numbers had dropped off, but still people thought, 'it couldn't happen to me'. Even worse, groups of young men went out, looking for trouble.

No one knew if the killer, or killers, were moving closer to the city because of the absence of people from the centre of the forest, or if they moved closer with intention?

Whatever the motive, whoever was committing the murders left no traces for the police to follow.

Serenity pulled her thought from the murders; James wouldn't want to discuss them again. He dealt with all this horror at his job. He wouldn't want to come for coffee with a friend and have work brought up again.

"So you made the right choice by taking the job?" she asked. "No regrets?"

James shrugged. "It wasn't a difficult decision. With Amy not working we needed the money, so no regrets."

They fell silent as the coffee arrived. Around them the street lights flickered to life and the café's outside lamps came on. The cars streaming past all started to put their headlamps on.

Night had fallen.

"What about you?" he asked. "How's life treating you?"

She mimicked his shrug. "Busy, but that's good. Helps keep my mind off other things."

She trailed off, not needing to mention what consisted of the 'other things'. James had been with her through everything and knew most of what she'd experienced, though he didn't know the whole truth. Some things, she would never tell him. She wouldn't put him through the dilemma of knowing one of his friends had killed.

"You know Amy and I will help out wherever we can," he said. "All you have to do is ask…"

"You guys help enough," she said, shaking her head. "I couldn't ask for any more."

He held his hands up in mock defense. "The offer is open. Especially if you needed, say, an evening off for a date…"

She faked a scowl. "I don't have time for dates, and anyway, I'm fine on my own. I don't need the complication."

"You can't be on your own forever, Serenity."

Serenity raised her eyebrows, lips pressed together, but remained silent.

"Okay, okay. I'll drop it," he said reluctantly.

Serenity picked up her coffee and took a sip. She wished James hadn't brought up her total lack of a social life; the topic only brought painful memories. Easy for him to be flippant; he had found his soul mate. She'd found that person and lost him again. How was she ever supposed to settle for someone else?

As though the thought of Sebastian conjured up his presence, she sensed him near, like fingers lightly touching the nape of her neck or the sensation of someone standing right behind her.

Serenity spun around in her chair, her heart beating out of her chest. The street looked normal. A young couple strolled by holding hands, the girl laughing at something her boyfriend had said. An older woman walked a small dog, dragging the animal along as it tried to stop and sniff at the legs of a newspaper stand. The owner of an antiques shop across the street pulled shutters down over the shop windows with a pole, the sound clattering across the street.

She shook the thought from her head. This was no different than the thousands of times she'd believed him close. Yet if that were true, then why did her heart race? Why were the hairs on the back of her neck standing up as though a cold wind had kissed her?

"Are you okay?" James asked, reaching across the table to lightly touch the back of her hand with his fingertips. The contact brought her out of her reverie and she shook her head slightly and frowned.

"Yeah, of course."

"Someone walked over your grave, huh?" he asked, grinning. He must have seen the look on her face and remembered how close she had come to death, as the smile faded. "I'm sorry, I shouldn't tease you about finding a date. I'm sure someone will come along when the time is right."

Though the events of four years ago remained a secret between them, they rarely discussed the time. James had only experienced a brief encounter with Madeline, but it had been long enough to leave him shocked and questioning his new reality. His world had been opened up. All of the things he'd never thought possible—ghosts, demons, vampires—had suddenly become a reality. Of course, Serenity had been more deeply affected. Her life had been completely and irrevocably changed by the events of four years ago, and though she'd been left scarred and with her own demons, she would not change a thing.

After all, she'd been left with a constant reminder of Sebastian.

Serenity didn't want to be sitting here anymore. All the warmth of the night had disappeared, every muscle in her body tense. She felt as though she was waiting for someone to reach out of the dark and grab her.

"Can we go?" she asked, taking another gulp of her coffee.

"Of course," James said, his brow creasing in concern. "Do you want me to ask if we can get these to go?" He nodded to the still full coffees.

She shook her head. "No, I'm fine." Then she remembered her manners. "You get your one though. I'm fine, honestly."

James wedged a ten dollar bill under the sugar canister, leaving his un-drunk coffee where it was. "A little less caffeine will do me good," he said, offering her a smile.

From the other side of the street, Sebastian snarled. He wanted to leap at the man and tear out his throat. His back bristled in fury. It killed him to witness her with someone else. Even though he'd told her to get on with her life, seeing her with another man wasn't easy.

He wanted to reach into his own chest and rip out his heart. Maybe that was his issue? His heart had broken, turned into something black and damaged. He wasn't the same person as when he'd met Serenity. Now he was different, and not for the better. Before Serenity, he'd been dead. Now he was dying every minute—every second—of the day.

Rage fired from within, burning through every muscle. He wanted desperately to kill, take his rage out on whoever was closest and lose himself in the rush of blood he knew would follow. Every male human suddenly became the enemy.

His legs crumpled beneath him and he curled into a ball, trying to fight the instinct threatening to overwhelm him. His long coat hung down either side of his body, his arms clutched over his head. He felt his body changing and he hunched around himself, fighting the struggle within.

People continued to walk by on the busy street, unaware of the darkness and danger they passed.

"Hey, man," a man's concerned voice asked from above. "Are you…"

"Don't!" Sebastian put out one hand, stopping the man in his tracks, the other still clutched over the top of his head. Sebastian struggled to get the words out. "Don't come near me."

The young man was little more than a boy. Sebastian knew if he raised his head, the boy would never be the same again.

His fangs jutted from his mouth, visible over his lips. The fangs did not grow, but instead the musculature of his jaw changed so they became more prominent when he needed to feed. No longer were they tucked away in the corners of his mouth, hidden beneath his lips. His eyes would be glowing yellow in the dark.

Sebastian didn't need to worry. The young man heard the growl in Sebastian's voice and quickly hurried away

Sebastian forced himself to bite back his anger and control his emotions. Slowly, the need to kill ebbed away and he regained his humanity once more.

Allowing himself to unfurl, he stood straight. He wasn't here to get Serenity back, he reminded himself. He wanted to find out what the monster was and learn if his fears were real. Once done, he would go back to Europe and leave her to her life.

Sebastian peered around the corner. Across the street, Serenity stood from her chair and picked up her belongings.

She looked well. Over four years had passed since he'd last lain eyes on her. He worked out her age; she would be thirty-two now, the same age he'd been when Madeline stole him from his family. She'd cut her hair slightly shorter, so the locks brushed her shoulders, framing her big dark eyes.

The extra years on her fascinated him—he found the whole aging process mesmerizing. He wished he could touch her face, trace the fine lines apparent around her eyes.

The police officer placed his hand on Serenity's lower back, gently guiding her around the table.

Sebastian gritted his teeth and forced himself to turn away. He would let them go for the moment. He didn't trust himself to follow them home tonight; didn't think he could handle the pain of watching them play happy family.

Had she forgotten him so easily? As soon as he'd left, had the police officer taken his place?

Sebastian was angry at himself for ever thinking what had been between them was real. Maybe she'd only seen him as a means to an end—a way of getting rid of her husband. Sebastian tried to tell himself as much, but it didn't ring true. He knew what she'd been through and how she'd begged him to take her with him. It didn't make sense that she'd gone through so much for no real reason.

Yet the presence of this man in her life made him question; had she ever really loved him?

Chapter Three

Serenity stood behind James as he opened the front door to his house. The home—a large three bedroom, with a generous front yard and on a good street—put Serenity's small, two bed apartment to shame. She didn't hold their success against the couple. She was proud of what she'd achieved over the last few years. She'd built a life by herself, without relying on anyone else.

However, she would be lying to herself if she didn't admit she experienced a little pang of jealously toward the couple sometimes, but not for their material possessions. When she saw them together, with their son, she envisaged a family. Perhaps the family would have been hers if she'd accepted James early on, but the relationship wouldn't have been real. She couldn't love James when she was always going to be so utterly in love with someone else.

Amy appeared to greet them before they even made it through the front door.

"Hey, you two," she said, a warm smile on her face. "You didn't stay out long."

James smiled and bent to kiss his wife on the mouth. "You talk like we're teenagers coming home."

She shrugged. "I just thought you might take some advantage of being childless for once." She peeped around James's broad frame. "Hey, Serenity."

"Hi," she grinned. "How're you doing?"

At only five-feet-two, the other woman was shorter than Serenity by five inches. With shoulder length blonde hair and cheeks that always had healthy glow to them, Amy was all curves and smiles. Serenity couldn't help but love her.

"Fine, thanks. They're asleep." She motioned her head to the front room. "Come and take a look."

Serenity followed Amy into the living room. Curled up on the couch, thumb in his mouth, was their son Noah. The boy had Amy's fine blonde hair and rosy cheeks, especially as he slept. Beside him lay a little girl, a couple of years older, also asleep.

Serenity crouched down beside the girl. A fan of dark eyelashes rested on her pale cheeks. Clutched loosely in one hand was a piece of muslin cloth; her comfort blanket. Serenity reached out and pushed a strand of dark, wavy hair away from her face.

"Elizabeth," she spoke gently. "Hey honey, it's time to go home."

The girl stirred, and pulled her muslin blanket closer to her face, but didn't wake up.

"She exhausted herself running around after Noah." Amy's voice came from behind Serenity.

Serenity stroked her daughter's cheek. It was cool to touch. "She does love Noah."

"Yeah. I love watching her fuss over him. She always seems to know exactly what he wants, like she's talking for him. 'Amy, Noah wants some juice', or 'Noah's feet are cold'." Amy laughed. "I guess that's kids for you—always a bit more perceptive than adults."

Serenity smiled to herself. Elizabeth wasn't just perceptive with Noah, she did it to everyone. "As long as she's not in your way."

"Of course she's not. She's a pleasure to have."

"Elizabeth?" Serenity said again, a little louder. "You need to wake up now."

Elizabeth's eyes fluttered open. She rubbed at her eyes with the back of her hand and pulled herself to sitting.

"Hello, Mommy."

"Hi, sweetheart. It's getting late. We need to get home now."

"I helped Amy bath Noah, and we had spaghetti for dinner."

"That's great, honey," she said, gathering her daughter in her arms.

"Let me drive you home," James offered.

Serenity's apartment wasn't far but night had long since fallen and the memory of someone watching her still clung to her. She wanted to turn down the offer out of politeness, but she didn't want to take her sleepy daughter out in the dark.

"Thanks," she said, reluctantly. "You guys are too good to me."

What she said was true. They didn't need to provide her with the free child care so she could take her night course in Contemporary Architecture. Serenity didn't have any other real friends—only acquaintances—and she wouldn't manage without them.

James drove the ten blocks to her apartment. Elizabeth had fallen asleep in the back again and Serenity climbed out of the car and lifted her daughter from the back seat.

"Do you need a hand?" James offered.

"No, no. I'm fine."

Serenity fished her keys out of her purse with one hand, supporting her daughter on her knee with the other. She gripped the keys between her teeth as she shifted Elizabeth's weight, and dropped them into her palm.

She was grateful for her apartment's ground floor position. The location offered a small yard coming off the kitchen and also meant she didn't have to struggle with stairs.

Stepping in the front door, she smiled at James still sitting behind the wheel, watching her get safely inside. Serenity gave him a half-wave with her spare hand. He lifted his in return and then pulled the car out into the road.

Serenity shut the door behind her. She dropped her bag on the floor and, her heart sinking, realized she'd left her folder of paperwork in James's car. He wouldn't notice in the dark and she'd shoved the folder down by her feet. The thought of the work she needed to complete before her next lesson flicked across her mind. She would have to get hold of James and pick up the folder.

With Elizabeth still in her arms, she carried her daughter to her bedroom. Serenity had done her best to make the small room as girly as possible—a flower fairies bedspread covered the bed and a pink rug softened the floor. An assortment of stuffed animals and dolls were piled down one end of the bed. Serenity didn't have much spare cash, but whatever she had was spent on her daughter.

Carefully, she laid the child down on the bed. Elizabeth gave a small moan and tried to roll to her side, but Serenity pulled off her daughter's sweater and got her nightdress on over her head before she got the chance. Next Serenity tugged off Elizabeth's shoes and leggings, and pulled the bedspread up over the child's body, tucking it around her shoulders.

She reached down and smoothed Elizabeth's hair away from her face. In her sleep, her daughter reached out, searching for her security blanket. Serenity found the comforter on the floor and handed it to her child. Elizabeth tucked the material close to her face and settled into a deep sleep.

Serenity stood, watching her daughter. This was her favorite moment of the day, being able to watch her sleeping child. Elizabeth was her miracle baby—the child she never thought she'd have—and she was thankful every day for Elizabeth being in her life.

How did something so perfect come from me, she wondered?

In her sleep, Elizabeth's small rose-bud lips parted and her impossibly long eyelashes rested on her pink cheek. With her smooth, clear skin, she was beautiful.

Serenity wished the secret she kept from her daughter didn't mar the happiness the child brought. The secret hung over her every minute of every day. Though Elizabeth didn't look like her father, Serenity saw him in her constantly.

Serenity sighed and bent down, kissing Elizabeth's soft cheek.

"Goodnight sweetheart," she whispered.

Though barely ten o'clock, Serenity was exhausted. Being a single parent was hard, and she also worked and studied. Sometimes the day seemed never ending. Now she only wanted to crawl into bed, sink her head into her pillow and close her eyes.

Serenity went to her front door and flicked the dead-lock. She repeated the motion with the door leading onto her small backyard. Yawning, she made her way to her own bedroom and pulled off her clothes, throwing them on the occasional chair in the corner. She needed to go to the bathroom, wash her face and brush her teeth, but her bed drew her.

I'll just lie down for a minute, she thought.

The sheets were smooth, her pillow cool against her cheek.

Her thoughts drifted to her experience at the café. After so many years, to sense Sebastian's presence so strongly was crazy. He was part of her now and she couldn't find a way to drive him from her mind. The memory of the nights they spent together haunted her. How his touch left her faint, his fingers tracing their way down her stomach, leaving her breathless in anticipation. Serenity remembered his cool fingers slipping inside her, the dramatic contrast of hot against cold. She thought of his hard body pressed against her own. Back then, she wanted to be consumed by him, to somehow find a way to meld their bodies together.

No one would ever make her feel like that again.

Serenity bit down on the memory, clamping her thighs together, trying to stem the fire racing up between them. Her eyes burned with hot tears. How could his absence still hurt after so long? Why hadn't the pain dulled?

She wiped her damp face against her pillow. It was stupid to be so caught up in someone. Serenity was angry at herself for her weakness, for not being able to stop her emotions. She had everything she'd ever wanted; independence, and the child she had always longed for. Yet she couldn't escape the emptiness inside, the feeling of something missing.

Serenity wasn't stupid; she knew what that something—or someone—was. But she'd long since given up hope of him coming back.

Sighing, she hugged her pillow closer, like a teenage girl mooning over her first love. She needed to get up and wash her face.

I'll get up in a moment. Maybe I'll just rest my eyes first...

A high-pitched scream wrenched Serenity from sleep.

In an instant, Serenity leapt out of bed, her feet pounding on the hall rug as she ran toward Elizabeth's room, her heart thumping.

Elizabeth was crouched on her bed, her knees up to her chest, her small arms wrapped around her knees.

"Honey?" Serenity rushed to her daughter's bedside and pulled her into her arms. Elizabeth trembled. "Hey, honey," she said again, her mouth pressed against the top of the child's head. "What's the matter? What's wrong?"

Elizabeth cried into her arms and said something Serenity didn't understand.

"What?" she asked, trying to pull Elizabeth away to catch her daughter's words, but Elizabeth clutched to Serenity, her thin body shaking.

"Oh, sweetheart," she said, gently rocking Elizabeth back and forth. "Did you have a bad dream?" She'd never heard her daughter scream like that.

"Men in my room," the little girl managed.

"There was a man in your room?" Serenity said, relief washing through her. Elizabeth had been dreaming.

Elizabeth sobbed again. "Two men. I saw two men."

Serenity frowned, suddenly worried about the security of their little home. Might someone have broken in? Two kids trying to rob the place? She was certain she'd locked both doors before going to bed, but being so tired, mistakes were easily made.

Serenity's ears pricked for any sounds she might have missed. Their apartment only consisted of a few rooms. The kitchen also served as their living room and the only other room, other than the bedrooms, was the bathroom.

Again, the distinctive memory of someone watching her crossed her mind and she shivered.

"Wait here, honey."

She crept out of Elizabeth's room and made her way to the kitchen, her feet padding silently. Pausing outside of the door, her ears strained but no sounds came from inside. With her heart in her throat, she peered around the corner.

The room was empty.

Serenity breathed a sigh of relief. Even so, she checked the bathroom to be sure. The bathroom was tiny, windowless and also empty. No one could have made it out without her seeing.

Elizabeth had been dreaming.

Serenity went back to her daughter's room. Elizabeth had snuggled back under her blanket, but was still awake.

Serenity sat on the edge of the bed. "You had a bad dream," she said. "It's nothing to worry about."

"It wasn't a dream, Mommy." Her voice was thick with sleep and Serenity knew oblivion would claim her again soon. "I saw two men. One of them wanted to hurt you and the other one tried to stop him."

"Shush, no one is trying to hurt me," she said, but the words chilled her. Not so much time had passed since she'd lived under Jackson's tyrannical rule and the memories of the beatings she'd suffered at his hands were fresh in her mind. Her back still troubled her from the number of times he'd hit her.

Serenity bent down and kissed her daughter on the forehead. Elizabeth was already asleep.

She made her way back to her bedroom and slid into the warmth of her bed. Elizabeth's words echoed around her head;

Trying to hurt you.

Elizabeth had always been hugely perceptive around other people. Serenity didn't think her daughter had experienced some sort of prophetic dream—though her experiences four years ago had certainly opened her mind to those sorts of things. But the bad dream combined with the intense feeling of Sebastian being near left her spooked.

Had he come back to find her?

She had to stop thinking in such a way; she was only torturing herself. The same thought had passed through her mind hundreds of times over the past four years; this time was no different.

To learn about the murders, Sebastian only needed to pick up the local paper. The story was plastered all over the front page. As soon as he read the words, 'Angeles National Forest', his heart sank.

Sebastian walked at human pace, enjoying being alone in the night. An animal moved somewhere close by, twigs cracking beneath foot. The wind rustled leaves above his head. A bat swooped down, emitting a high-pitched squeak. The forest smelled different. Though the end of summer, the ground still emitted a damp, earthy smell, such a contrast to the dry heat of Turkey

How strange to be back in these forests again. He'd not set foot here since the night he returned to reclaim Serenity's necklace—the same night he'd almost lost her for good.

Though seeing Serenity with another man bruised his soul, he was relieved to find her safe, happy and settled. He told himself he'd made the ultimate sacrifice of love, to give up someone he so desperately wanted—her happiness at the sake of his own. Even so, knowing she'd found love with someone else, hurt.

Sebastian picked his way through the forest, moving with grace. He knew by instinct which direction to head in. He had no idea what he expected to find when he reached Jackson's un-marked grave. The body hadn't been there when he last visited the site but, should Madeleine have done something to him, Jackson may have needed to return to the place he'd been originally laid to rest.

Of course, the whole thing might be a fantasy of his own making. The murders might have been committed by a human, high on some kind of illegal drugs, or even a vampire driven crazy by his immortal life. The chances of the monster being Jackson were slight enough to be laughable. Yet he couldn't shake the thought which rode on his back like an evil monkey.

Finally, Sebastian reached his destination. Slightly sunken ground marked out where the make-shift grave had been. Over the years, nature had started to reclaim the area, the grass encroaching on the fresh soil, a sapling sprouting up from the ground, yet the earth appeared new compared to the rest of the area.

Sebastian knelt beside the empty grave and ran his fingers through the soil.

A strange sense of déjà vu washed over him, such a strong connection to Serenity by being at this place. He felt as though he'd been transported back four years and only a matter of hours had passed since he last held her in his arms and tasted her mouth.

His heart clenched with pain. The memory took his breath away and he clamped his teeth together, every muscle in his body tightening as though dealing with a physical pain.

He was no closer to learning anything about who had committed the murders. The person—or thing—responsible hadn't been here or disturbed this area.

Sebastian needed to get back. He needed to find shelter before day broke and it made sense to go back to his house in the hills. The house was the safest place for him, though the property was locked up and an agent held the keys. He'd not thought to organize for the place to be opened and at this hour he couldn't arrange something with the agent. Even so, he wasn't worried. Scaling the tall wall surrounding the grounds wouldn't prove a problem and he'd find a way to get inside the house.

Dried twigs cracked beneath his feet as he started the long walk back. He didn't tire physically but his soul was weary.

Had he come on a fool's mission?

Sebastian sighed and pulled his woolen overcoat tighter around his body. The cold didn't affect him either, but he struggled to forget the small habits of humanity.

Four hours remained until dawn; plenty of time to get back, especially if he picked up his speed.

How long he would stay at the house, he didn't know. Part of him thought he should head straight back to Turkey, bury himself beneath the ground again.

Was that what the rest of eternity held for him, hiding away? Perhaps once Serenity's time on this earth passed, then he could rejoin 'normal' society, but until then he would always be haunting her. He'd seen how she sensed his eyes upon her, how anxious she seemed and how she made the policeman leave. He was nothing but a bad dream to her—something she must have wanted to forget—and he would do her no good by being near her again.

He didn't want to go back to the house; the place never felt like home to him.

Had anywhere?

Perhaps for those few hours he spent in Serenity's arms, returning to a place with the knowledge she was waiting for him. Was that what home felt like?

Ahead of him the night sky lightened, though Sebastian knew the change was caused by the millions of fluorescent lights that lit the city rather than the sun. The low thrum of traffic filtered through to his ears. In the far distance, a siren wailed through the night like a banshee, drowning out the more favorable sounds of nature.

Sebastian stopped suddenly, his nostrils flaring. Like a tidal wave, the scent of blood rushed over him, knocking him back like a physical force. For a moment, the smell of blood acted like sensory deprivation, blocking all other thoughts from his mind. It was the scent of blood, but not only that, blood strengthened by fear, anguish and torture.

Blood had been spilled—a lot of it—and not that of an animal.

Sebastian started to run.

His feet barely touched the ground as he ran, momentum carrying him forward. He followed the trail of blood on the night, the air rushing past his ears.

The scent of blood drew him out of the forest, back toward the city.

Abruptly, he drew to a halt.

Right on the edge of the forest the mound of a body lay beneath a tree, as though they'd stopped for a rest and fallen asleep.

As he drew closer, he recognized the body as that of a young woman.

Congealed blood thickened the woman's long, wavy hair, plastering strands to the side of what was left of her face. One large, dark eye stared up at him, blank and lifeless. The other side of her face and throat had been torn away, exposing the flesh beneath. The remaining eye socket was dark with blood. Blood soaked the ground beneath her.

Another vampire hadn't done this. A vampire would never spill precious blood on the ground in such a way—blood was their life-force, their religion. A vampire had too much respect for blood.

From the wounds, he suspected an animal was responsible for attacking this poor woman but in his heart he knew different.

It wasn't the ferocity of the attack that struck fear through Sebastian's heart. Even with all the gore, the woman was the spitting-image of Serenity.

The similarity was uncanny.

Sebastian's fears had stemmed from a rumor, but all rumors started somewhere. All fables, legends and myths came from something. However stretched the story, some element of truth was found in their beginnings.

He knew an animal hadn't done this, the wounds were too methodical, nothing apart from the throat and face had been touched. No bite or scratch marks blemished the woman's arms or hands where she would have tried to ward an attacking animal away.

Sebastian feared his worst nightmare had come true.

Chapter Four

Another girl had been killed.

Serenity spread the newspaper out on the breakfast bar in front of her, staring at the front page as she absently chewed on a piece of toast.

The young woman, Bethany Phillips, had been found just before dawn by a man walking his dog. She'd only been twenty-seven. A picture of the girl beamed at Serenity from the front page, smiling at whoever had been behind the camera.

She looks like me...

Serenity didn't know where the thought came from, but it sent a shiver down her spine. She quickly folded the paper back over, hiding the girl's face from view.

"Mommy? What's wrong?"

Serenity twisted around on her seat to find Elizabeth standing in the kitchen doorway. Her dark hair was tousled from sleep and an imprint of her blanket marked one cheek.

"Nothing, sweetheart. Nothing for you to worry about."

A wave of fierce, protective love washed over her. How awful for the murdered girl's parents; to have loved and nurtured her all those years, only for some lunatic to take everything away in a moment. She couldn't imagine how she would cope should something ever happen to Elizabeth.

Serenity pushed the thoughts away and forced a bright smile for the sake of her daughter.

"What do you want for breakfast? Juice? Cereal?"

"Mmm, yes, please!" Elizabeth said, clambering up on the stool beside her.

Serenity stood and started to prepare Elizabeth's usual breakfast of Cheerios. She splashed milk on top of the dry cereal and filled a plastic cup with orange juice. Serenity placed them both in front of Elizabeth and the little girl picked up a spoon and tucked in with enthusiasm.

"Come on you," she said when Elizabeth started picking Cheerios out of her bowl and lining them up on the counter. "If you're all finished, we need to get you ready for preschool."

Elizabeth picked up a large spoonful of cereal and shoved it in her mouth. She reached across the counter and touched the folded newspaper with her free hand.

"That man hurt someone else, didn't he, Mommy?" she said, her mouth still full.

Serenity's blood ran cold. "What do you mean? What man?"

"The bad man I dreamed about last night—he hurt a lady."

"Don't say things like that!" Serenity snapped. Elizabeth's face crumpled and Serenity tried to backtrack.

"I'm sorry, sweetheart. But you scare Mommy when you say things like that. You just had a bad dream last night. The man in your dream wasn't real."

"I'm sorry, Mommy."

Guilt swamped her. She'd never want to make Elizabeth feel bad for telling her what she knew.

"Don't be sorry, honey. You haven't got anything to be sorry about. Mommy's just tired. I didn't mean to shout."

Again, Serenity forced a bright smile; trying to shatter the uncomfortable tension in the room. She couldn't stand to see that expression on Elizabeth's face, the one that said 'what's wrong with me?' It broke Serenity's heart.

"Come on!" she said again. "We need to get ready or we're going to be late."

She went behind Elizabeth's stool and tickled her under the ribs. Elizabeth squealed with delight, squirming under Serenity's hands.

"Hey!" The girl exclaimed in pretend protest. But within a moment Elizabeth laughed at her mother, her normal, happy self. For Serenity, things weren't so easily forgotten. A sense of doom hung over her, smothering her heart like a thick, acrid fog.

Elizabeth ran off to her room to pull on the clothes Serenity laid out for her first thing that morning.

"Do you want me to help?" Serenity called.

"I can do it myself," the little voice answered and Serenity smiled properly for the first time that morning. Elizabeth wanted to do everything by herself, even if it meant putting both legs in one pant hole and her sweater on back to front.

A few minutes later, as Serenity cleared away the breakfast dishes, Elizabeth reappeared with, miraculously, all her clothes on the right way round.

"Ta-da!" Elizabeth said, spinning in a circle, her arms outstretched. "I did it.

Serenity clapped her hands. "And you look beautiful. When did you get so grown-up?"

As Elizabeth beamed with pride, Serenity wondered if it was possible to love another person more than she loved her daughter.

Elizabeth's preschool was only a few blocks away, easily within walking distance. The little girl ran ahead of Serenity, her small backpack bouncing on her back.

"Don't run too far," Serenity called out to her.

They reached the gates of the preschool. Elizabeth ran into the classroom, barely giving her mother a backward glance.

Serenity jumped on a bus to the city, to the office building where she now worked. The office wasn't far from her old job, but even passing the place made her feel physically sick. She found the memories overwhelming and tried to avoid the area as much as possible.

Heading into work, she sat down at her desk and settled down for what would be a busy day. She'd started working at the firm as a temp, but the boss liked her work so much, he'd kept her permanently. It had been a big step for Serenity; leaving Elizabeth and integrating back into the work place. But she had surprised herself. She discovered how much she could get done without the distraction of wondering if her husband intended on keeping his threat of 'showing her his fist' when she got home, or without the constant pain she'd been in back then. Within a year, she'd been promoted to the boss's personal assistant and now he depended on her to run his day. It wasn't the job dreams were made of, but the position paid surprisingly well and her boss understood enough to let her work flexible hours should Elizabeth get sick or her childcare let her down. Serenity couldn't ask for much more.

Serenity tried to settle down at her desk for the day. Despite the numerous telephone calls she needed to make and the reports she still had to write, she struggled to concentrate.

How had Elizabeth known about that poor girl being murdered? Had she snuck into the kitchen and seen the front page of the paper? But Elizabeth didn't have the ability to read the words—her reading standards didn't reach much beyond recognizing her own name. Perhaps Elizabeth switched on the small portable television on the kitchen counter and had seen the report on the news.

She wanted to believe either explanation; but Elizabeth had been sound asleep when she got up herself, and she'd only left the kitchen to grab the paper off the front step.

She could pretend all she liked—Elizabeth wasn't a normal child.

Serenity only ever tried to give her daughter a normal, stable life; desperately hoping to enforce normality upon her. But she couldn't change Elizabeth's genes.

During her daughter's birth, Serenity had been absolutely terrified. She hadn't known what was going to happen to her baby. Thank God, Elizabeth turned out to be perfectly normal and healthy, and Serenity allowed herself to relax into motherhood.

But she'd never been able to completely relax. Constantly alert for things differentiating Elizabeth from other children, she worried every single day her daughter would change.

Elizabeth.

Her daughter's name filled her heart with love.

Serenity hated her own name—her drunken mother's permanent reminder of her past. An ironic memento—nothing about Serenity's life had been serene. From the antics of her drug-addled, hippie mother, to her abusive stepfather, to her even more abusive husband.

When the time came to name her own daughter, she chose what she always wanted for herself: something traditional, solid and steadfast. Serenity wanted Elizabeth to have everything she never had. She wanted her to always feel loved, wanted, and like she was the most important person in the world. She never wanted her daughter to grow up as she did: always the outsider, the odd-one out, filled with the certainty that there was something wrong with her.

Her own past made keeping such a huge secret from Elizabeth—the secret of her father's identity—hard. Serenity had never known her own father and she worried about the cycle of this part of her childhood.

Every day, she thought today would be the day she'd tell her daughter. But she never seemed to find the words. The secret played on her mind and sat on the tip of her tongue, yet she never forced the words out.

Could she really tell her daughter the truth? Elizabeth would never understand. Serenity barely understood herself; how could she ask the same from a four year old?

The day Elizabeth asked her who her daddy was would be when Serenity told her the truth. Serenity made this promise to herself eighteen months ago and still held the secret tight inside, eating away at her. Every day she waited with baited breath, expecting Elizabeth to say something, but she didn't.

The strangeness of her daughter's silence didn't go unnoticed by Serenity. Elizabeth understood James was Noah's daddy, yet she never asked about her own. Serenity put it down to her age—still so young—yet part of her wondered if Elizabeth picked up on Serenity's reluctance to talk.

Serenity only wanted her daughter to lead a normal, happy life; yet she had something woven so deep into who she was and it threatened the chance of 'normal' ever happening.

That thought broke Serenity's heart.

Elizabeth was strong, a fighter. Serenity suffered five miscarriages before having Elizabeth and thought she would never be a mother. Elizabeth had been her little miracle.

She wondered how much of Elizabeth surviving, where her other babies had died, was down to her genetic make-up. Yet to think about Elizabeth's lineage terrified Serenity.

How could you love someone so utterly, so completely, and yet fear a part of them so intrinsic to making them who they were?

Though this was not the first time Serenity felt this way about someone. Of course it was different with your own child—she couldn't even contemplate not loving Elizabeth—but hadn't she also felt the same way about Elizabeth's father?

Chapter Five

The lights and sounds of the city drew the creature like a magnet. The city was exciting and enticing, but those weren't the only reasons it wanted to get out of the forest. The more it fed, the more the pieces of its broken mind mended. The fog of confusion no longer surrounded it. The initial painful, jarring flashes of memory now took on fluidity. The constant agony burning through its flesh finally subsided, though if it went too long without feeding the pain returned with renewed force.

Of course, it did not only kill to help the pain or to feed. The creature rejoiced in its new strength, taking pleasure in the terror and pain it created. Human matters no longer concerned it and it had no worries about reprisal. Strong and fearless, it could do whatever it wanted.

Over time it edged closer and closer to the city. Waiting and preparing for the time that would come soon—for the time to head back into the city.

The creature was searching for something.

It remembered things now about its past life—it used to be human, a man—and it searched for a certain woman. It longed to be near her again, but no love lingered in its still heart. Memories of her brought only fury, pain and anger. It wanted to curl up its fists and pound them into the woman's soft flesh. Draw its lips back from its monstrous teeth and bite… and bite… and bite.

The time to find her had arrived.

The creature moved with long, lolloping strides; an uneasy grace to anyone who may be unlucky enough to catch sight of it. To a human, the thing appeared to be an unfortunate specimen of their own kind. With its ravaged face and mangled clothing, it passed for a down-and-out bum or, possibly, an escapee from a lunatic asylum. The expression on the thing's face made people give it a wide berth, but should they get close enough, they noticed the smell. After years beneath the ground, the creature had taken on the scent of the dead.

It stepped from the forest onto a road. The tarmac felt strange beneath its bare feet, rough and hard, but it would get used to the new sensations. This journey would be an excess of new experiences; at first it would take things slowly in order not to damage its fragile mind.

The thing followed the road, heading toward those ever tempting city lights. The metropolis held the promise of so much death. No longer would it need to wait for an unfortunate victim to stumble across its path—humans were everywhere. It would have its pick of humanity—a living, breathing buffet.

A car blared past and it cringed at the sudden noise and speed.

Anger toward itself rose within. The creature did not allow itself the emotion of fear; fear was for the weak.

Fear was for the hunted.

It had periods of speed, moving faster than its human counterparts, followed by episodes of walking, its head tucked between its shoulders. People it encountered either crossed the street before they reached him or shot him looks of disgust and revulsion.

The creature laughed inside. If only they realized what it imagined doing to them? If it showed them what it was capable of, they would run in terror. It had lived beyond them, returning from a place they couldn't even comprehend. They would scream in horror as it fed upon them, still unable to believe what was happening to them.

It believed it had been blessed for a reason; brought back for a purpose it intended on fulfilling.

The city grew busier—the traffic heavier around the creature, their headlights blinding.

Though night, people still walked the streets. It could go out in the light if it wanted, the sun did not cause any harm, but its natural intuition was to stay in darkness.

Following its instincts, it traveled across the city, not checking street signs or road maps. It knew where it was heading.

Not knowing how much time had passed since last being here—it had no real concept of time—it found itself standing outside of a small duplex building. A small yard was out front, a window box in each window.

Home.

With the warm night, a bedroom window had been left open. Luck or perhaps simply fate? It lowered to a crouch and leapt, springing to the second floor with no more effort than a cat leaping to a windowsill. The creature wanted to turn around and roar at the world, make them feast upon its power, the sheer beauty and majesty of what it had become. But it restrained itself. To kill her quickly would be too easy. No, it planned to watch and learn before making her suffer.

The place smelled different.

Narrowing its eyes, it deftly stepped off the windowsill and into the room.

In the dark, two figures lay beneath the sheets, still and sleeping. The steady rise and fall of their deep breathing and the slow *thu-thump* of their heartbeats filled the room. One male, the other female.

So the bitch had found herself a mate.

The thing bristled with anticipation, with longing. It needed all of its resolve not to kill her here and now.

It walked slowly to the side of the bed where she lay sleeping. A thin drool of saliva ran from its mouth and down the side of its face. It wiped the dribble away with one filthy hand, its nails black and encrusted with dirt.

Something wasn't right.

The thing narrowed its eyes again and bent closer. The woman sensed something was wrong and moaned in her sleep, twisting her head against her pillow. Dark hair fell back from her face, caught beneath her cheek.

This woman wasn't her.

A low moan of anger started deep in its chest. Much older, the woman looked nothing like the one he sought.

The moan turned into a growl and the noise woke the humans. The male bolted up in bed, fumbling for the bedside light. The woman groaned and put her arm across her face, trying to block out the horrific smell she had woken to.

"What the fuck…" It heard the male's voice.

The man's fingers finally flicked the switch, flooding the room with light.

Horror filled their faces as they both took in what stood above them. The woman screamed; a high-pitched shriek loud enough to alert the whole neighborhood.

The creature just smiled, revealing the teeth responsible for killing so many before them.

Then it spoke for the first time since returning.

"Where... is... the... woman... who... lived... here?" Its tone rasped from lack of use, like the voice of a tracheotomy patient.

Hope dawned in their eyes; hope that their cooperation would result in them being spared. They had no idea that where the creature was concerned, hope did not exist.

The man spoke. "An elderly couple used to live here," he stumbled over his words, stuttering from nerves. "Do you mean that woman? She left two years ago."

Time meant nothing. It didn't know how long it had been gone.

For the first time doubt crept in. Had it been buried for so long? Was it possible the woman it sought was the elderly woman? Had it been gone so long she may even have died?

No, not so much had changed. She was still alive. It sensed it.

"She... is... young... dark... hair. Her... name..." It searched the pits of its mind. "Serenity."

The woman shot her husband a look of confusion and fear.

"Serenity?" she managed, obviously recognizing the name. "She owns this place. Why do you want...?"

It needed nothing more.

A hand shot out, grabbing the woman by the throat, strangling her words.

"Hey! Hey!" the man shouted, rearing back, his hands held up as though in surrender. "You leave her alone!"

The woman's eyes bulged with fear and she made a strange clucking sound at the back of her throat. Her hands scraped at the ones holding her with no avail. Her tongue protruded from between her lips like a slab of meat.

The man leaped on the creature's back, trying to pull it off, only to discover the muscles beneath its skin were as cold and hard as stone, and just as immovable.

It reared around with a snarl, drawing its foul lips back from its teeth. Staring the man in the eye, it gave a vicious smirk of satisfaction before twisting back around and leaning down, tearing a huge chunk out of the woman's throat.

Shock flashed in her eyes.

Blood flooded from her, spilling down her chest, soaking into the bedclothes beneath.

The man squealed and fell away. He landed on the floor and scrambled to the corner of the room. His eyes were locked on his butchered wife, watching as the light dimmed from her eyes and the monster, with the body of a man, crouched over her. The sounds of an animal feeding filled the room; sucking, tearing, chewing.

The man leaned to one side and wretched.

The creature turned to face the man, momentarily forgotten during the kill. Fresh blood coated the lower half of its face and, as it walked slowly toward the man, its next victim screamed in the same exact pitch as his wife's.

Standing amongst the small crowd gathering on the opposite side of the street, Sebastian watched as two paramedics carried out a body on a stretcher. The people flanking him gossiped, their tone a hushed mixture of fear and horrified excitement. The crowd took a strange pleasure in what they witnessed, as though this terrible thing happening to someone else meant it less likely to happen to them.

Street lamps lit the street, casting an eerie light over the faces of the paramedics and those watching. A small group of police officers stood in front of the crowd, warning them to keep back.

Sebastian knew the stretcher didn't carry Serenity's body. The body remaining inside the house wasn't hers either. He'd recognize the scent of her blood anywhere.

When he first arrived and saw the flashing blue lights of the emergency vehicles, dread seized him. He thought he'd been too late. After taking a moment to calm himself, he realized the blood on the air didn't belong to Serenity.

Sebastian stuffed his hands in his pockets, tucked his head in and ducked away from the crowd.

His worst fears had come true. He needed no more convincing that the thing had once been Jackson and it was trying to find Serenity. Well, that made two of them now. Sebastian just needed to get to her first.

Jackson had become vicious and merciless; he hadn't been much better human. Sebastian had seen the state of the poor woman in the forest and now another innocent couple had been slaughtered. If Serenity still lived here, she would be dead now. Only by luck was she still alive.

He needed to find Serenity and he needed to do it fast.

With only rumors and the violence of the killings he'd witnessed to go on, Sebastian had no idea what he was up against.

The rumor of the monster appearing in the light worried him most. Strength and brutality, Sebastian could beat, but when it came to the light there was no contest. Sunlight would kill him in minutes.

A vampire's one weakness filled him with frustration. He was helpless in the hours of daylight. If the thing that used to be Jackson walked among humans in the daytime, Sebastian was at a huge disadvantage. The thought of the monster killing Serenity while he lay helpless in the dark made him furious.

He needed to warn Serenity.

Already the early hours of the morning, the huge city of Los Angeles stretched out around him. She lived somewhere in the city, but where? He wished he'd followed her before, but his anger had been too great. When she climbed into the other man's car, Sebastian forced himself to walk in the other direction, not trusting himself.

He would have to scour the city, keeping his senses alert for her. The memory of Serenity was ingrained upon him— her taste, her scent. He could pick up on her trail if he crossed it, but he couldn't follow from anywhere. He'd automatically gone back to her local area but finding her the first time had been no more than chance. To assume she would be living in the same place—just as Jackson assumed the same—was naïve.

One person knew Serenity's location; the police officer he'd seen her with. The man had been wearing plain clothes when Sebastian saw him with Serenity, but he remembered him from the last time with Serenity on the pier. That night the man had been in uniform. Sebastian flicked through his memory, going back to that fateful night. Had he learned the police officer's name?

Yes, Serenity had told him: Bently.

Sebastian didn't know where the man lived but he knew where he worked.

Los Angeles Police Department.

Harnessing his speed, Sebastian flew across the city to the downtown station. He had expected the place to be empty so late at night, but the building seethed with people. A couple of prostitutes stood chatting at the front desk while a uniformed officer booked them, every bit at ease as if they were hanging out at a favorite bar. A skinny Caucasian man sat on one of the plastic chairs in front of the desk, the rows of chairs bolted to the floor to stop anyone picking them up and using them as weapons. Tattoos ran down both of his arms in sleeves and he hooked them over his knees, his head hung.

None of these people interested Sebastian. He needed to find the police officer, or, if not the man himself, something that would tell Sebastian the location of his house.

Moving quickly, he whisked past the people. A couple of the more perceptive ones glanced up, sensing movement nearby. Most ignored the change in the air pressure around them, too high or jaded to care.

He passed the front desk and down the hallways, past the interrogation rooms, leaving the hubbub of the people behind.

Most of the offices were closed and locked. It was the middle of the night and the majority of normal office staff had gone home. Sebastian kept all his senses alert for any sign of the police officer. A name on a door caught his attention; Sergeant James Bently. Sebastian stopped short. This must be the man, he doubted numerous 'Bentlys' were running around the place.

Like the rest of the offices, the room was locked and in darkness. Sebastian grasped the door handle and, with a swift twist of his wrist, yanked open the door. He hoped no one would notice the broken lock, at least until morning.

Sebastian crossed the small, orderly office to the desk. He pulled open the drawers and rifled through the paperwork, searching for something with not only Bently's name, but also his address. His fingers closed around a credit card statement.

Jackpot!

He didn't want to be in the presence of the two of them together again, the experience was too painful, but he needed to make Serenity and the cop aware of the danger threatening her. How something terrible sought its revenge. They could get away, far from Los Angeles, and Sebastian would spend the rest of his days tracking down the creature that had once been Jackson and killing him. *Again.*

Sebastian left the police station and once again set off across the city.

Daybreak approached, although the sky was still dark and no houses were lit, their inhabitants sound asleep. In this part of the city, the vehicles in the driveways were all expensive, top range. Bently's house stood out because of this. A modest car—a Ford—was parked out front, not a top of the line SUV like the rest of the houses.

Sebastian stood in the street, looking up at the property. Two stories, the house would be at least three bedrooms. The white wooden cladding gave the home the appearance of a Los Angeles beach house.

This was exactly the sort of property he'd hoped Serenity would make her home. Sebastian pushed away the stab of jealously threatening to rot his heart.

Slipping around the side of the building, he entered the backyard. A white balustrade porch ran along the length of the building. A wicker couch and table sat beneath the awning, a cozy area for alfresco eating.

Sebastian leapt silently up to the roof of the porch. Two windows looked out on the backyard. Stilling his nerves at seeing her once more, he peered into the bedrooms. The first was empty, a double room neatly made up for guests. The second held two sleeping figures, lumped under the covers.

Sebastian frowned. Something wasn't right. The sense of Serenity should be washing over him right now, but he felt nothing.

He had no problem seeing in the dark and as he looked closer he recognized the sleeping face of the policeman. Serenity must be the figure asleep on the other side.

The frown deepened. He didn't want to go into the house, invading her privacy. His presence would frighten and upset her, something he hated; though what he needed to tell her would do both.

A baby's cry came from somewhere inside the house, startling him. He'd never considered the possibility of her having a family, yet now it seemed so obvious—the perfect life with the perfect man, of course she would have a child to complete the bond. The bitterness overwhelmed him, coursing through his system like bitter salt in his blood stream. The knowledge of the child made everything so final. She would never be his.

She sat up and Sebastian jolted back in surprise.

The woman was small and blonde, everyway Serenity's opposite. He could never mistake this woman for Serenity.

His head reeled in confusion. He'd watched this man and Serenity together; witnessed the affection between them. Serenity had gotten into his car and they drove off together. Yet here was the man with another woman and apparently a family. Were he and Serenity having an affair? That didn't ring true. He didn't believe Serenity capable of such a thing, especially not with someone with a young family.

Whatever the truth, Serenity wasn't here.

Sebastian hoped wherever she was, she was safe.

He leapt from the porch roof and down to the yard. He could get Bently out of the house and demand to know where Serenity lived. A vampire had ways of making people talk, but he didn't want the man to tell Serenity he was looking for her and scare her before he reached her.

Also, part of him simply didn't want to frighten the young family. Now Sebastian knew the other man wasn't married to Serenity, his hostility toward Bently melted away.

Sebastian walked back around to the front of the house.

A security light on the side of the house flicked to life the moment it sensed his presence, flooding the driveway. Cupping his hand to the side of the passenger window, Sebastian peered inside.

At first nothing caught his attention, but then he noticed a folder of paperwork lying in the foot well of the passenger seat. In his mind, he saw Serenity running down the steps of the tall white building, clutching the folder to her chest.

With his immense strength, he wrapped his fingers inside the edge of the passenger door and swiftly pulled, wrenching metal, bending steel.

He smiled at the irony of the cop not having an alarm system fitted in his car. Not that alarms bothered Sebastian. He would be long gone before anyone approached him; being questioned by a human was not of his concern.

Sebastian pulled the door open and reached down and picked up the folder.

Chapter Six

James Bently went into work that morning to discover the place in chaos.

The murderer—or murderers—had moved into the city.

A specialist team was already working the case, but the detective heading the team wanted to use a few of his men to cover more ground; asking questions in the surrounding area, trying to find witnesses. Glendale was a built up area; for two people to be murdered so viciously in their beds without anyone seeing anything bordered on impossible. A couple of the closest neighbors reported hearing screams and called the police, but no one reported actually seeing something suspicious.

Already in a bad mood, this new development did nothing to help his frame of mind. Someone had vandalized his car during the night, breaking in without bothering to even steal the CDs out of the glove box or rip out the radio. The only damage was some kind of wrench used to jimmy the passenger door open. He suspected kids to be the culprits, practicing their skills or messing around, knowing the vehicle belonged to the neighborhood cop.

James picked up the report requesting the extra men and started to read. The name of the neighborhood brought back memories. He'd spent time in the area himself, four years earlier, when he first met Serenity. She still owned the house and rented the property out to tenants since the whereabouts of her husband had yet to be determined.

He frowned. *23 North Louis Street.* The address struck a chord of uneasy recognition. Surely the crime hadn't occurred on the same street as Serenity's house? If so, perhaps her tenants saw or heard something.

James tapped his pen against his desk, the curious part of his brain sparked.

He glanced at the pile of paperwork lined up to do that day.

It can wait, he decided. *Maybe they could do with another person at the crime scene...*

James drove down Serenity's old street toward a marked police car parked further down the street.

Craning his neck as he drove, he peered up at the houses. Many years had gone by since he was last here, but he thought Serenity's house must be close by. Being back churned up so many memories; a lifetime's worth since first meeting Serenity.

Their relationship had come a long way since then, surprising even him. Serenity meant a lot to him, but he quickly discovered he couldn't love someone so obviously in love with someone else. Of that person's identity—her husband, or someone else—James had never been sure.

Serenity found out about the pregnancy during the early days of their friendship; he'd never questioned his desire to support her as a friend. Even though they weren't involved as a couple, she'd been through a lot and had no one else. He couldn't just abandon her to deal with her pregnancy alone.

Then he met Amy.

Meeting his wife put his feelings for Serenity into perspective. Serenity wasn't the type of woman he could ever be in a relationship with. After the things he saw at work, he needed to come home to laughter and fun. He needed someone like Amy. Serenity contained too much of a dark side—no surprise after the life she'd led. Soon, James found his feelings towards her morphed into those of protective father more than anything else.

He pulled his own unmarked vehicle up behind a Crown Victoria. A police officer stood outside the door of the closest house. Yellow tape sealed the front door. The officer glanced up as James pulled in.

James's heart tripped a beat as he recognized the front door. Serenity's old house was taped up. He was certain. His stomach sank. Did this mean her tenants were the victims? No one had told Serenity yet; he'd have been the first person she'd call.

He opened the car door and climbed out. The young officer spotted him but no recognition lit his eyes. James held out his badge as he approached. The officer gave him a nod and removed the tape, like a bouncer at a club. James walked into the house and the officer sealed the door back up behind him.

Waves of déjà-vu swept over him. To his left was the small sitting room where he'd first interviewed Serenity. At the end of the hallway was the kitchen.

The place had been ransacked. The contents of the dresser drawers had been emptied all over the floor, paper lay scattered everywhere. Someone must have been searching for something, but it was impossible to tell if they found what they were looking for. The television and stereo-system were still in place and an expensive i-Phone sat on the hall table. Whatever this was, it wasn't a burglary gone wrong.

James climbed the stairs.

Ahead, the doorway to the bedroom where the murders took place loomed. To the left was the bathroom and a small spare bedroom Serenity's husband had used as an office.

Even from the end of the hall, James saw the blood splattered against the doorframe.

He took a deep breath and walked down the hallway toward the bedroom.

Blood coated every surface, soaked the bed and the carpet, and splattered up the walls.

"Jesus," he muttered, his hand over his mouth.

The bodies had been removed early that morning, taken to the morgue for autopsy, though from the amount of blood, James wondered how much of the bodies would be left to analyze. Forensics had also been in and swept the place for fingerprints and samples.

James frowned. The neighbor called the police as soon as she heard the screams—just after eleven. From the records, only twelve minutes passed between the call and the first patrol car arriving at the scene. The victims, a Steve and Jocelyn Bainbridge, were alive when the screams had been heard—or at least one of them was. The murderer didn't ransack the house first; the noise would have woken the victims. They would have either come down to investigate, or else called the police themselves. Both the victims had been murdered in the bedroom, the woman still in bed. The killings must have been fast—only minutes—yet the volume of blood implied the deaths had been anything but quick.

Also, whoever committed the murders would have been covered in blood. How could someone not notice them leaving the house? The area had properties on all sides and it hadn't been the middle of the night.

The perpetrator must have been fast, really fast.

James pushed away memories threatening to resurface.

How the hell was he going to tell Serenity? He wished he could stop her from finding out. He wanted to protect her from this. She'd been through so much already and had just started to get her life back together. The last thing she needed was this sort of horror linked to her old home, on top of the bad memories of her abusive husband.

But she had to know what had happened and James had to be the one to tell her.

Serenity was at work when James called.

She answered on the first ring, "Mr. Berry's office. This is Serenity."

"Serenity? It's me."

She recognized his voice immediately and smiled. She'd been planning on calling him later. She still needed her notes back.

"James. How are you? I was going to call you."

"Serenity, there's something I need to talk to you about," he said, his tone level and serious.

Bile rose to the back of her throat, sudden nerves churning her stomach. Part of her wanted to slam the phone back down, not wanting to hear what he had to say.

Sometimes in life things turned on a dial. One moment everything was fine, besides all the usual worries and stresses life, carrying on as normal; the next something happened that turned everything else on its head, all those worries became meaningless and trivial by comparison.

She feared this to be one of those moments.

"What's wrong, James? What's happened?"

"It's the tenants at your house. They've been murdered."

"What?" Disbelief and shock knocked her breath from her. "When? By who?"

"Last night. As of yet, we don't know the culprit. We think it's the same person who committed the other killings. But, this is the first time he's been in someone's house."

"Jesus Christ." Her hand clamped against her mouth.

"Can you come down to the station for me? Even if you didn't know them well, the murder still happened on your property. The detective in charge wants to ask you a few questions."

"Yes, yes, of course," she said. "Just let me talk to my boss and I'll come down as fast as I can."

"Okay, see you soon."

About to hang up, she heard his voice filter down the line. "And don't worry. I'm sure none of this has anything to do with you."

She frowned. "No, of course not." That possibility hadn't occurred to her.

Her head was reeling. Why would someone want to hurt the Bainbridges? They had seemed like such a nice couple; it was impossible to imagine why anyone would want to do such a horrific thing to them.

She had no idea what the police thought she could tell them. She had hardly known the couple; they paid their rent on time and their references all checked out. Other than the occasional phone call, they pretty much kept to themselves.

Serenity put her head in her hands and took a deep breath. That more violence had occurred in that house shocked her. The situation brought back such horrific memories, rocking her to the core. She pictured the blood all too easily.

Nausea roiled in her belly and her hands trembled, but she needed to pull herself together. She had to get down to the station before she was due to pick Elizabeth up from preschool.

Pushing her chair back, she stood and made her way to her boss's office.

Serenity faced the closed door and took another deep breath, steadying her nerves. She knocked gently before opening the door.

Mr. Berry glanced up from beneath big, gray bushy eyebrows, a slight frown etched in lines between his eyes. His eyes narrowed slightly behind the small wire-framed reading glasses he always wore.

"I'm sorry to disturb you," she said. "But I wondered if I might have a word?"

He straightened, putting down the pen he was holding. "That's okay, Serenity," he said, gesturing to the chair on the other side of his desk. "What can I do for you?"

She opened her mouth to speak but found tears were perilously close. She bit her lower lip and swallowed hard.

Concern filled her boss's face. "What is it? What's happened?"

She tried again. "The police just contacted me. The couple I rent my house to were murdered last night."

"My God!" he said, shocked.

"They want me to go down to the station and tell them what I know—which really isn't anything. I wondered if I might leave early so I can finish there before I need to pick my daughter up."

"Yes, of course." He thought for a moment. "I'm just about to head out to a meeting with some clients. I've got a couple of phone calls to make first, but if you want to go down to the parking garage and bring my car around to the front, I'll drop you off."

The small act of kindness touched a smile upon her lips. "Thank you, Mr. Berry. I appreciate it."

He reached into his desk drawer, pulled out the car keys and passed them across the desk. She'd been trusted to move his car before; if he had to get across town quickly she would be called upon to bring the car around to the front door of the building, saving him precious minutes.

Although Serenity didn't own her own car, she'd passed her test as a teenager. Wanting to use her as his personal taxi driver, her stepfather had encouraged her to learn so he could drink as much as he liked without worrying about the repercussions.

Fourteen flights led down to the underground garage that served as private parking for the whole building. Only the top dogs got a space—the executives and high-flyers—the rest of the staff mostly relied on public transport.

Serenity walked into the corridor and pressed the button to call the elevator. Four elevators served the whole building. She glanced up at the lit arrows above the doors, indicating which direction the elevators headed. The one directly in front of her was going down and, within moments, the doors slid open, revealing an empty space.

With the car keys dangling from one finger, Serenity stepped inside and pushed the button for the garage.

Mirrors surrounded her and she couldn't help but stare at her own reflection. Serenity reached up and tucked her hair behind her ear. She still hadn't got used to her shorter style. She'd had long hair her whole life but demonstrated her independence by cutting it to her shoulders. Jackson would never have allowed her to cut her hair.

She glanced at herself again. The memory of the murdered woman's face flashed in her mind. A much brighter, younger version of her, but even so the likeness couldn't be missed. Now she had the Bainbridges to think about as well.

Death surrounded her.

Serenity shivered.

The elevator doors opened with a 'ping'. Now mid-morning, everyone had been at work for hours, so she found herself alone.

She headed across the tarmac to her boss's allocated space. Diesel fumes caught the back of her throat. The cars she passed were all top range; BMW, Audi, Mercedes. She remembered a comment she had made to James about not having a car because she was trying to save the planet. She smiled to herself; in truth, she would love to own her own car; life would be so much easier without relying on public transport to get everywhere. But she couldn't afford one by a long stretch—not that she would admit as much to James. She still had her pride.

From out of nowhere, a horrendous stench washed over her, drowning out the scent of fuel.

"Oh, God!" Serenity put her hand over her face and pulled up the sleeve of her sweater, trying to use the material to stifle the smell. The stink was like trashcans after a few days in the sun, or like road kill that had crawled under a bush to die. The stench seemed so thick she struggled hard to breathe. Like tendrils of smoke, it crept up her nostrils and down the back of her throat, as though it were a living thing and intended on smothering her.

Serenity tucked her chin down into her chest and walked faster.

What the hell was the cause? Had something actually died down here? She couldn't believe no one else had noticed and a team of people weren't fumigating the garage. The people she worked with were normally such a fussy bunch—

they complained if their coffee had been stirred the wrong way.

She glanced around, trying to pinpoint the source of the stench. The stink made her eyes water; she would report it as soon as she got back in the building. Yet everything looked much as it always did and the place was empty.

Her footsteps echoed as she walked across the garage, her low heels clicking on the ground. She hurried toward Mr. Berry's car—a jet-black Audi A6—parked over the other side of the garage. Desperate to escape the smell, she felt as though she was suffering a slow suffocation.

The sound of heavy footsteps came from behind. Serenity glanced back but the garage was empty.

Serenity picked up her pace to a trot; her heart thumping hard enough in her chest to hurt. Adrenaline raced through her veins.

The footsteps came again, slow and steady, like boot heels clicking on the sidewalk.

Scared now, she looked back around, but still no person made themselves visible. Was someone following her, someone hiding from her now?

She wanted to call out, but scenes from a dozen horror movies flashed through her mind and her sensible part knew if someone were hiding, they certainly wouldn't answer to her calling out, 'hello'.

Serenity gripped the keys in her fist, holding them so the car key stuck out between her clenched fingers, like a dagger. Though only a makeshift weapon, it was better than nothing. She focused her sights on the Audi, now only thirty feet away.

Suddenly, a heavy breath rasped in her ear, the putrid smell strong enough to knock her sideways.

Serenity screamed and spun around, lashing out with the key, certain she would be faced with an attacker, but the key only swiped thin air.

Tears of fear flooded her eyes. She hadn't imagined the footsteps or the cold breath against her cheek.

She turned and ran for the car, unlocking the door with a push of the button on the key-fob. She wrenched open the driver door and threw herself behind the wheel, pulling the door closed behind her and slamming down the lock.

The smell was gone.

Her hand still shaking, Serenity started the engine. Though fluorescent lighting shone overhead, she flicked the switch for the headlights anyway, needing the extra light.

What was wrong with her? She hadn't experienced a panic attack like that for years. She was sure she had gotten over the worst of her problems, (or maybe not gotten over—after all, murdering your abusive husband and falling in love with a vampire was hardly something you just forgot about), but she certainly thought she'd dealt with her issues. Only now a wormhole into the past had opened and she was plummeting, freefall.

The paranoia, grief and horror; all those memories flooded back as fresh as the day they happened. Had the murders brought the recollections back? Or perhaps Elizabeth's strange premonition had caused the relapse?

She must have imagined the whole thing. She had experienced similar things many times four years ago, but she hadn't felt an attack of such total paranoia for a long time.

That feeling of being watched, of constantly looking over her shoulder.

Serenity didn't want to go back to the dark place of her past, trapped in her house, too scared to leave. She'd come a long way since then; built her life back up from scratch and dealt with the trauma for the sake of her daughter. She'd been so tempted back then to let everything consume her. So many times, it would have been easier to simply give up.

The loneliness—missing Sebastian every moment of every day—almost pushed her over the edge. If not for Elizabeth's arrival, she wouldn't have made it. She'd never been on her own before and Sebastian's abandonment hurt all the more because of it.

It's the murders, she told herself.

Any sane person would be shaken after hearing people they'd known had been murdered in their own house—in the same house where she murdered her husband.

She needed to get a move on. Mr. Berry would be waiting for her and she didn't want him to think he had an unstable employee on his hands.

With one hand clutching the wheel, she pushed the car into first.

Chapter Seven

Serenity turned up the ramp too fast and the Audi's tires screeched against the tarmac, making her wince. The car mounted the top of the ramp and pulled up on the road. Serenity squinted against the sudden sunlight. The parking garage exited onto the adjacent street to their office so she had to drive around the block, to the front entrance.

Serenity pulled up in front of the office building, her heart still pounding. There was no sign of Mr. Berry. Relieved she had a few moments to compose herself, she let her forehead fall against the steering wheel and exhaled slowly. She glanced down at her hands, still clutching the wheel, and willed them to stop shaking. Here in bright daylight, her panic seemed stupid.

Had she actually felt someone breathing against her cheek? Had the stench really been so bad or had her already stressed imagination over reacted?

She raised her head in time to see her boss trotting down the steps toward the car. He raised his hand to her. With legs trembling, she opened the car door and slid out. She made her way round to the passenger side and got back in. Mr. Berry climbed into the driver's seat and looked at her curiously.

"Are you okay, Serenity? You look pale."

She forced a smile. Her cheeks scrunched up but the smile expression never touching her eyes. "It's all been a shock."

"Of course, how stupid of me. If you need tomorrow off just call and let me know."

"Thanks, Mr. Berry."

His kindness brought her close to tears again and she turned to face the passenger window, hiding her emotions.

Her boss indicated and pulled out into the traffic.

Serenity watched the city flow past her window as they headed deeper into the city, towards the station.

She hoped he took her silence as her being upset and didn't think she was rude. She certainly didn't want to make small talk. So many thoughts filled her head, she didn't know where one ended and the next started. Her brain was trying to process everything at once.

For once, the traffic in the city wasn't too heavy and within fifteen minutes they pulled up outside the LAPD.

"Thank you," she said, climbing out of the car. "I'll call if I need tomorrow off."

"No problem," he said with a smile, his eyes creasing behind the wire-frame glasses. "Let me know if I can help in anyway."

The world contained so much violence and pain, yet people like James, Amy and even Mr. Berry, still surprised her with their kindness. How strange to think one species varied so much. One person might live their lives filled with anger, violence and hatred, while another went out of their way to help others. When Jackson had been alive, Serenity struggled to envision the good in anyone. His cruel way of viewing the world somehow blinded her to its pleasures as well. Like a glacier-hiker, Jackson had been the hard ice, transforming the warmth of the sun into something harmful. Her proximity to his glare blocked out her view of everything else.

Walking into the station, Serenity was relieved to find James waiting for her behind the front desk. He chatted with one of the uniformed officers, but must have been keeping an eye out for her as he broke off his conversation as soon as she walked in.

At six feet, with his light brown hair cut close to his head, flecks of white now crowning his temples, James was still an attractive man. Crow's feet had deepened around his eyes, giving him an air of maturity. He was one of those men who commanded a quiet authority over others. People paid attention when he walked into a room; people listened to him. His fortieth birthday was next year and Serenity knew Amy had already made plans, hoping to surprise him with a couple of nights in Vegas. She told Serenity, with a mischievous look on her face, she intended to treat her husband to a bit of 'illicit behavior for once'. Naturally, Serenity offered to take Noah while they were away, trying to repay the hundreds of times they'd sat Elizabeth.

"Hey," James said, his face grim. "Thanks for coming down so quickly."

"No problem. My boss was more than understanding."

"So he should be, given the circumstances."

James guided her past the reception desk and they headed down a corridor lined with doors. A small sign hung above each door indicated the room number.

"We're in room three," he told her.

James opened the door and she walked through. The room was set out exactly as she had expected. A table stood in the middle of the room, two chairs either side. Recording equipment sat in the middle and a reflective film made up one wall; a one way mirror.

A tall, skinny man wearing a dark gray suit leaned against the table. He stood straight as they walked in.

"This is Detective Gingham," James said, introducing her.

Detective Gingham held out his hand. His pale blue eyes, large in his thin face, searched hers. He looked like he didn't miss a thing. Serenity shook the offered hand, keeping her grip firm.

"Thank you for coming down, Mrs. Hathaway," he said. Deep and velvety, his voice surprised her, nothing like the one she'd expected to come from him. "Please have a seat."

Still shaky, she pulled out the chair and sat down. She wondered where James would sit: with her or opposite, on the side of the police department?

You're not on trial here, she had to remind herself. *They just want to ask a few questions. You haven't done anything wrong.*

James didn't choose a side. Instead, he pulled a spare chair to the end of the table.

"Do you mind?" Detective Gingham asked, nodding toward the recording equipment.

"Oh," she said, surprised. "No, I guess not."

"This is the interview with Mrs. Serenity Hathaway, on September third. The time is two fifteen p.m." He cleared his throat and leaned toward her. Serenity smiled back, nerves jarring through her. "Mrs. Hathaway, this is going to seem like an obvious question, but do you know of anyone who might have something against Mr. and Mrs. Bainbridge?"

"No, not at all," she said. "But I hardly knew them. They just rented my house."

"Did they have any debts you were aware of?"

Serenity shook her head, baffled at why they thought she would know any of this, but Detective Gingham nodded toward the recording equipment.

"Sorry," she said, realizing she hadn't spoken aloud. "No, not that I know of."

"We need to figure out why the killer chose that house out of all the ones on the street. These things are rarely random."

"How did they die?" she asked, turning her attention to James. He didn't answer her, but his eyes flicked to the detective.

"Were they shot?" she persisted. "Did they use a knife? Did someone strangle them?"

A look passed between Detective Gingham and James.

"Oh God. Was it bad?" Her hand was back at her mouth, her mind turning over a hundred possibilities.

"We're trying to keep the exact details under wraps at the moment," James said.

Detective Gingham cleared his throat again and she wondered if he had a nervous tick. He ran a hand through his hair. It was thinning on top and had a too-black sheen, which made Serenity wonder if he used a cheap dye.

"We wanted to ask you one other question."

"Sure. Go ahead."

"It's about your ex-husband—"

"Husband," she corrected. Technically, she and Jackson were still married. Because he had 'disappeared,' she was forced to wait seven years before he'd be certified as 'Death in absentia', making the property hers. Of course she could tell them she knew Jackson's death to be fact, but considering the repercussions of that knowledge, she'd decided to wait.

She hated his name even being mentioned, the guilt coursed through her like blood, but he was also the owner of the house, so she couldn't be surprised.

"Have you heard anything from Mr. Hathaway?" Detective Gingham asked.

"The guy disappeared years ago," James interrupted, leaning forward in his chair. "He was a scum-bag. She hasn't seen or heard anything from him."

The detective glared at James and he sat back in his chair.

Serenity frowned and shook her head. "No, nothing. Why?"

"Is it possible he came back to the city without your knowledge?"

She wanted to tell the truth but it stayed buried deep inside. "I guess."

"Would he be angry to find someone else in his home? Did he know you were no longer living at the property?"

Her frown deepened. "What are you getting at, Detective?"

"A number of prints were pulled from the crime scene. Several of them matched one's we have on file for your husband." He glanced down at his notes. "Mr. Hathaway was cautioned for battery seven years ago, and then a possible assault four years ago…"

Serenity's cheeks flamed red and she stared down at her hands. The accusation of assault had come from Madeline, trying to cause trouble for Serenity after she murdered Jackson. She remembered the battery charge. Jackson had hit her in their backyard. He'd been taking out the trash and lifted the bag over his head when it had split and trash emptied all over him. Serenity had made the mistake of laughing, which bought her a slap in the face so hard it knocked her to the ground. He rounded off the slap by kicking her in the stomach. The neighbors saw and called the police but Serenity had been too scared to press charges. She had nowhere else to go and didn't think she had any choice.

That occasion was the one and only time Jackson made the mistake of letting anyone else know about how he treated her. He'd learned his lesson. After that he made sure he only ever hit her inside their home and only in places no one would spot the marks—the lower back, in the kidneys. He'd even branded her with the metal on a lighter, on the inside of her thighs. She still carried the scars.

The memories made her cringe. She was still so ashamed. How could he do all those things to her—things *he* did to *her*—yet *she* was left ashamed and embarrassed, dirty even?

"The prints must be old," she said, going for the only rational explanation, wondering why the police hadn't picked up on the obvious.

He shook his head. "They were definitely new. The prints were partials but unmistakable."

Dread settled on her shoulders like death itself stood behind her, hands weighing her down. "They must be old," she said again, her voice barely a whisper.

"The prints were in the blood of the victims, Mrs. Hathaway. There's no possibility of them being made any time other than either during or shortly after the murders."

Her nostrils flared, her eyes burning with tears. Her hands tightened on the edges of the table, her knuckles turning white. The interview room swam away for a moment.

It was impossible, but she could never tell the detective as much. Someone had made a mistake.

"You can't think Jackson killed them?"

"We're not sure what we think right now. Given that he owns the property, there's a good chance he came back and contaminated the scene. After all, no one saw anything and this is the first time any prints have been found near the victims."

"So you think you're dealing with the same murderer as the one who's been killing all those people in Angeles Forest. The same one who killed that girl the other day?"

The detective nodded. "The profiles match the same killer."

"Jesus."

Yet the news brought her some relief. Jackson committing all of those murders was impossible. Someone hadn't been doing their job properly and had made a mistake.

She sighed. "I don't know what more I can tell you. The Bainbridges were good tenants and I have no idea why someone would do something so terrible to them. As for Jackson, I doubt he's back in the city. Even if he was, I don't think he'd be capable of murdering total strangers. The man was a horrible bully, but he was also a coward."

Detective Gingham studied her face for a moment and she forced herself to stare back.

"All right," he said. "That's everything for the moment. If you see or hear anything from your husband, you'll be sure to let us know."

"Of course."

Serenity pushed back her chair and stood. She felt numb from the waist down, as though her body didn't quite belong to her. Still, she forced herself to move, her face a mask of stability. She didn't want them to realize how much the accusations against Jackson affected her. Though it was only natural for her to be shaken up after being told her abusive husband was back in town and had possibly murdered two people in cold blood, she only felt guilty and was terrified they'd read that exact emotion on her face.

James also stood up and reached across to open the door for her. Pleased to escape, she hurried from the room. James turned and said a few words to Detective Gingham, before following her out.

"You need a lift?" he asked as they walked down the corridor, toward the front doors.

Serenity glanced at her watch, almost two-thirty in the afternoon. The day had disappeared. She was due to pick Elizabeth up from preschool in a half hour.

"That's okay," she said. "I can catch the bus. I should make it on time."

"Let me drive you. You came down here on police business, the least I can do is give you a ride."

"Well, since you insist."

Serenity followed him out of the door and around the back of the building to James's car.

As they drove across the city, James sat silent beside her.

"Is something wrong?" she asked, turning to take in his profile as he concentrated on the road.

"I just don't understand," he said, shaking his head. "Jackson made your life a living hell for years and yet you still stand up for him."

Serenity's mouth dropped open. "I didn't stand up for him!"

"Then why are you so insistent he didn't commit those murders? The man has a history of abuse and violence, and his fingerprints were found in the victim's blood. You don't know what he's been doing these past four years—he might have completely lost the plot—but you seem absolutely certain he didn't hurt the Bainbridges."

Serenity glanced away, her cheeks burning. She could never admit the reason for her certainty, but she didn't want the police to race off on a wild-goose chase, literally chasing ghosts, when the real killer was still at large.

"Is there such a thing as a wife's intuition?"

James raised his eyebrows.

"Okay, okay," she said, giving in. "Maybe Jackson did murder all these people, but I'm allowed to have my opinion, aren't I? I knew him better than anyone else. Yes, the man was a bullying bastard, but do I think him capable of attacking and murdering two strangers? No, I don't. He was a coward. He beat me because he liked the control. Simply murdering two complete strangers for no reason doesn't seem like his style."

James fell silent for a moment and then spoke. "It's hard not to believe evidence when it's right in front of your face."

"People make mistakes," she said, no longer sure if she meant the police forensic work or herself.

Chapter Eight

The tension simmered between them even as they picked up Elizabeth.

The little girl couldn't believe her luck as she scrambled into the back of the police car.

"Can we put on the siren?" she asked excitedly.

"Sorry, kiddo," said James. "Not allowed to unless it's an emergency. Police rules."

Serenity tried to ignore the curious stares of the other parents. Something of an enigma among them, she rarely got involved with the gossip that occurred outside the gates, though she remained friendly and polite for Elizabeth's sake. She'd never want Elizabeth to be excluded from birthday parties and play-dates purely because her mother was unsociable. Even so, the hole left by Elizabeth's father felt like a black mark above her name.

She was grateful Elizabeth was too young to find out what had happened to her tenants. Elizabeth had met the Bainbridges a couple of times and they'd always been kind to her. Mrs. Bainbridge had always managed to find a cookie for her.

They didn't need for James to drive them up the road, but neither of the adults could deny Elizabeth the excitement of getting to ride in the back of the police car.

Within minutes, they pulled up outside Serenity's small apartment.

"You'll be okay, won't you?" James asked her. "If he's back…"

Serenity widened her eyes in the direction of her daughter.

"Okay, but if you need me, you know where I am."

"Yes, thank you. I'm sure we'll be fine."

Serenity went through her evening routine; dinner, bath time, trying her hardest to hide her emotions from her daughter. Despite her best efforts, Elizabeth clung to Serenity's side, quiet and withdrawn. Serenity knew her daughter had picked up on something.

"Come on sweetheart," she said, dropping a kiss on top of her daughter's head. "Time for bed."

"Five more minutes," Elizabeth whined, though she had no concept of how long a minute was, never mind five.

"No, you've already staying up past your bedtime."

Elizabeth, tired from the previous night's broken sleep, put up no more of an argument. Clutching her cloth to her narrow chest, the little girl shuffled to her bedroom.

Serenity struggled to keep her mind on the bedtime story—a tale about a tortoise—as she read to Elizabeth. The possibility of Elizabeth dreaming about what had happened to the Bainbridges played on Serenity's mind. Add to that the impossible, but still terrifying, assumptions the police made about Jackson being back and the face of the murdered girl appearing on the back of her eyelids every time she closed her eyes, she wondered if she'd get any sleep that night herself.

Going through the motions, Serenity finished the story and tucked her daughter in.

"'Night, sweetheart," she said.

"'Night, Mommy."

"Love you," she told her.

"Love you," Elizabeth echoed back.

Gently, Serenity pulled the door shut and headed to the kitchen. She wanted to collapse on the couch and forget about everything with a couple of hours of mindless television, but the dirty dishes from dinner still sat in the sink, calling her and she knew she wouldn't be able to relax until she'd cleared up.

The trash teetered from the top of the can. Serenity sighed, a hand on her hip. It needed to be emptied and there was no point in leaving more chores to the morning. She struggled to get out of the house on time already.

Serenity pulled the full bag out of the can and walked out of her front door, carrying the bag in one hand.

She stopped at the edge of the sidewalk and pulled the lid off the large can serving the whole block. Dumping the bag, she turned to head back inside.

"Serenity?"

Serenity froze, her eyes pricked with tears. She'd heard his voice in her dreams. Surely she was dreaming now. She turned her head in the direction of the voice and saw the terrifyingly familiar figure standing, concealed by the night.

He stepped out of the darkness, into the streetlight.

Sebastian!

She put one hand out in front of her, warding him off, the other at her chest, protecting her heart.

"You can't be here," she gasped. "You're not supposed to be here."

"I'm sorry, Serenity," he took a step toward her, but she shrank away. "I needed to see you."

The shock of his presence left her dizzy. He'd appeared in her dreams every night for the past four years and now here he was, standing in front of her. But he wasn't the same as she remembered—he looked like a different person. His eyes were dark and haunted, bruised and hollow. His cheeks were sunken beneath sharp cheekbones, and his skin seemed even paler than before.

When she'd dreamed of being with him again, she never imagined she'd be so frightened.

Sebastian reached for her, his movements too fast, quicker than her eye could follow. It resulted in an unnerving, jerking action and she jolted away.

His face crumpled in hurt. "I'm sorry," he said. "It's been so long since I've been in the company of humans. I've forgotten how to act around them."

"You frightened me," she said, breathless.

"I didn't want to scare you. When I left you, Serenity, I promised I would leave you alone, that I wouldn't haunt you, and I meant it. But something has happened and I needed you to know."

She stared at him, not believing her own eyes. Perhaps she was in the presence of a ghost?

"You can't be here," she said again, as though repeating the phrase over and over would make it true.

Suddenly she remembered the little girl, tucked up in bed in the apartment behind them. Did he know about Elizabeth?

Her heart rate notched up and her cheeks flushed. Her whole body tightened with panic. She didn't want Elizabeth to wake up and come out to find her. She didn't want to have to explain the identity of this man.

"Please, Serenity. I understand this must be a shock, but I need to speak with you. I wouldn't be here if it wasn't important."

She stepped away, backing toward the house.

He moved suddenly, cutting through the air, reappearing between her and the front door. She spun around to face him.

"Don't do that!" she said. "I always hated when you did that!"

He stared at her in earnest, his green eyes so much darker than she remembered.

"He's back, Serenity. I think Jackson is back."

"What?" Her eyes widened in disbelief, but a tremor of unease quivered through her. "Jackson is dead. *I should know!*"

"He's still dead, but he's become something else. I believe Madeline took him from where I buried his body and began his transformation, perhaps hoping to use him against us. You stopped her before she could complete the process and, with no guidance, he's become what he is today."

She barely dared to ask the question, but she forced the words. "What is he?"

"A monster."

Tears sprung to her eyes, she shook her head frantically. "I don't believe you."

"You must," he grabbed her wrists and the memory of his cold touch flooded her, as though she'd been dragged back in time.

She felt as though she had been punched in the stomach, stealing her breath. She found herself in the middle of a nightmare and couldn't wake up. How was she supposed to believe him? She struggled to believe Sebastian, himself, stood before her.

Despite the terribleness of his news, only one thing sat at the forefront of her mind—their daughter. Had Sebastian already seen Elizabeth? Just because he'd seen her didn't mean he'd figured out she was his. Or would he be able to sense their bond?

"Please," she said, pulling out of his grip. "Go away. Leave me alone."

Sebastian stared at her. "Why aren't you listening to me? You know these things exist. Do you think the couple at your old house being murdered was a coincidence? It wasn't, Serenity. Jackson killed them and he is probably looking for you."

"Oh, God!" She put her face in her hands. "The police were right."

"What do you mean?"

"They found Jackson's fingerprints in the blood at the house. They told me he was a suspect, but I told them I didn't think him capable of murder. Of course I did! He's supposed to be dead, but now you're here telling me he's not."

"He's still dead, Serenity. At least in the normal sense of the word."

"No! Dead means gone, and gone forever."

He raised both of his hands, gesturing to himself. "Then what am I?"

She'd spent years desperate to be near him again; yet here stood the dream and he brought with it a nightmare. She always thought she would be overjoyed for him to step back into her life, but she never imagined he would be accompanied by such horror.

The phrase 'be careful what you wish for' mocked her.

She didn't want to believe Jackson's return possible. Her mind didn't want to accept it, pushing the possibility away. Jackson had been a monster when he'd been alive, and the thought of him transformed into something even worse was terrifying.

After Serenity killed Jackson and orchestrated Madeline's death, she'd been tormented by nightmares and paranoia of repercussions. She'd been terrified that Madeline hadn't died down the pipe; that she'd somehow escaped and now waited to take her revenge. Serenity never imagined it wouldn't be Madeline who came back from the dead, but Jackson. Madeline, she thought she could cope with, however terrifying the female vampire had been. Jackson coming back was unthinkable.

Suddenly, Serenity realized something worse might happen than Sebastian finding out about Elizabeth—and that was Jackson finding out about Elizabeth.

Her heart filled with fear.

"I can't do this again," she whispered. "I'm not strong enough. I can't do this again."

As a tear ran down her cheek, Sebastian reached up and stroked it away.

"You can. I'm here now," he said softly.

Serenity's heart had hardened over the years and she used its callus to sharpen her tongue.

"You left me alone," she said. "You can't just come back here and expect me to fall into your arms."

"I don't expect that. I only want to protect you."

"Like you protected me four years ago?"

Sebastian pressed his lips together. "I know about you and the police officer. The one from that night." Bitterness tainted his voice.

Serenity's eyes widened in surprise; he had been watching her?

"James is my friend!" she snapped. "He's been here for me over the past four years. He was here to pick up the pieces."

"I bet."

Serenity physically flinched and she shook her head in amazement. "Not that it's any of your business, but James is married now to a wonderful woman and they have a baby together. Nothing ever happened between us. You have no need—or right—to be jealous."

Sebastian gave a slight shake of his head, his gaze flicking to the ground. "I saw you together and it hurt. The last few years have been so hard…"

"Hard?" she interrupted; amazed disbelief still in her voice. "On you? You have no idea what I've been through, no idea at all. Remember, you left me! You were the one who chose to go."

They stood opposite each other, their faces cast in shadows beneath the street lamp. The rest of the world had fallen silent around them. No cars drove down the street, no one came out of their homes, not even a dog barked. Sebastian's presence had stilled them all.

"What am I supposed to do, Sebastian?" she said, finally. "If Jackson is back like you say, what am I supposed to do? Do I just go into my apartment and wait for him to track me down and kill me?"

"Don't talk like that!" he said, and she was reminded of her saying the same thing to her daughter that morning.

The thought of Elizabeth brought a wrench of pain. The thought of anything happening to her beautiful little girl was too much for her to stand. She would do anything to protect her. She didn't want Elizabeth to grow up without her, but she would sacrifice herself if she had to.

Serenity hadn't been expecting the anger that filled her heart. She'd worked so hard to piece her life back together. She'd been through so much. Now Jackson was back again, trying to control her life once more. She thought she'd taken the ultimate step to stop him from ever hurting her again, yet here she was, four years later, discovering he was out to hurt her all over again. All because of some bitch vampire who had been jealous of what she and Sebastian had shared.

Serenity couldn't help her resentment toward Sebastian. If he hadn't come into her life, neither would Madeline. But if they'd never met, she wouldn't have her daughter. In Serenity's eyes that wasn't a life worth living.

"I can take you away from here," Sebastian said. "Somewhere safe, somewhere he won't find you."

She shook her head. "I can't just up and leave. I have a life now, a job…"

The memory of being in the underground car lot flooded back; the horrendous stench, the sound of footsteps behind her and the rancid breath on her cheek.

The color drained from her face. Suddenly she felt the urgent need to be by her daughter's side, to make sure she was safe.

"What's wrong?" Sebastian said.

"I think he's already found me. Someone was following me at work today. I didn't see anyone but I was sure someone was there. The smell was terrible."

"You need to come with me, Serenity. We need to leave, now, tonight."

Again, her thoughts went back to Elizabeth. "You don't understand. I can't leave."

"Jackson can walk in the light," Sebastian said. "I can't protect you all of the time."

"So he's not like you or Madeline? He's not a vampire?" She held onto the tiny thread of hope, her heart hitching. She'd dealt with Jackson once before, however horrific the event. She could do it again.

Sebastian shook his head. "No. He's something much, much worse."

Serenity couldn't breathe. Here was the man she'd once loved more than anything else in the world and he just told her that her worst nightmare had come true. She couldn't handle this – it was all too much.

She stared at the ground, shaking her head. Being so close to him hurt. Every fiber of her body wanted to throw herself against him, rest in the safety of his arms, but now she had more than her own desires to consider.

"I'm sorry, but I can't do this again," she said, her voice breaking. "You can't just come back into my life bringing all your bullshit with you."

"No, you don't—"

"I don't need you to save me anymore, Sebastian," she said, louder now. She looked up, staring into the eyes she'd once fallen in love with. "I saved myself."

Before he could say another word, she turned and fled back inside the house.

This time he let her go.

Serenity slammed the door shut and leaned back against the wood. Her legs gave way and she slid down the door. Every muscle in her body shook and she hugged her knees into herself, trying to stop her body trembling. Emotion welled up inside, her mind a blur.

She couldn't go back to this; back to living in constant fear, terrified something unspeakable was going to hurt her. Only now the situation was so much worse. Her nightmares had been confirmed, actually spoken out loud, and now she didn't only fear for her own life but that of her child's. The terror of losing her baby-girl was so, so much worse.

Filled with panic, she leapt to her feet and raced around the small apartment, checked every room, made sure every window was deadlocked, the door double bolted. She caught sight of the street outside her window. No figure stood on the sidewalk. Sebastian had gone.

Knowing at least the house was secure, she allowed herself to fold. Her knees gave way and she ended up on the floor, doubled over. Tears barreled over her, consuming her.

"Mommy?"

Serenity glanced up to find Elizabeth standing in the doorway. She held her arms out to her daughter. Obediently, Elizabeth allowed herself to be pulled into Serenity's embrace and Serenity crushed the child against her. She cried into her soft dark hair, knowing she was probably frightening her daughter, but was unable to stop.

Chapter Nine

Distraught at her rejection, Sebastian fled back into the night.

Revealing himself to Serenity had been the most terrifying experience of his existence. He'd stood, waiting in the shadows, trying to build up the courage to speak to her. When she came out of the house, he forced himself to call out her name.

Sebastian only wanted to help, to make sure she stayed safe, but she no longer wanted him around. The strength and independence shown by her rebuke made him proud of her in some perverse way. The fragile, frightened woman he'd met four years ago no longer existed.

He hadn't expected her to be pleased to see him, but for her to look at him in such as way—as though he were no better than Jackson—cut him to the bone. His sudden reappearance was always going to be hard on her, especially considering the news he brought, but he'd hoped she would at least want to see him again.

No, he was lying to himself; deep down he hoped she would fling herself into his arms, tell him how she missed him and beg him to never leave again.

Sebastian hadn't prepared himself for the total rejection, for the pain and resentment trembling in her eyes. Clearly, she still blamed him for leaving.

Now the need for blood surged over him, as strong as an addiction. Like any other addict, during times of extreme emotion, he sought the one thing that would numb the pain.

Sebastian ran through the night, away from the woman he loved. He needed a victim, someone whose blood would fill the chasm inside his chest.

Things hadn't worked out for Serenity the way he'd hoped. Despite his pain at believing her to be with another man, if she'd been living the happy life she deserved perhaps she would have understood his leaving was best for her in the long run. But that had not happened. Serenity lived alone in a crappy apartment. She didn't have the life Sebastian wanted for her and she held him responsible.

Had he done the right thing, leaving her all those years ago? Or had they both been living in pain all this time, pining for the person who would stop the loneliness?

The faintest flutter of hope beat deep inside his heart. He'd done what he thought was right at the time. Had she simply proved him wrong?

Whatever he thought, two things existed that he couldn't escape; firstly, Serenity hated him, and the second was Jackson.

Jackson's presence somewhere in the city terrified Sebastian. If Serenity wouldn't trust him to help, he would do things his own way. He couldn't just accept her demands to be left alone and allow Jackson to slaughter her.

He had to find Jackson before Jackson could find Serenity.

Sebastian hardly knew where to start. Los Angeles was a big city and Jackson could be anywhere, searching for Serenity. Jackson obviously hadn't learned where she lived yet or he would have been there already.

Sebastian needed to pick up on some kind of scent or trail. The only other option was to stake out Serenity's apartment and wait for Jackson to come to her, but that felt like hanging Serenity out like bait.

The forest held the most promise. Jackson must have been buried somewhere while his resurrection took place.

The monster may be forced to return.

The rumor of vampires sleeping with a handful of dirt from the place they were created did, like most other myths, stem from the truth. A very young vampire had to go back to the ground where they completed their transformation until strong enough to survive above ground.

From what Sebastian discerned, Jackson wasn't a vampire, but the way he'd been created must have initially begun the same way. If the creature needed to go back to the forest, perhaps it was his weakness. Maybe Sebastian could pin him down and kill him, without letting him get anywhere near Serenity.

Sebastian hated leaving Serenity alone and defenseless. But then he gave himself a mental shake. Perhaps he didn't give her enough credit, underestimating her once again. After all, she'd dealt with Jackson the first time and tricked Madeline.

He needed to feed. If he found Jackson, he needed to be strong and several weeks had passed since he last fed.

Not yet midnight, Sebastian headed out of the city. Los Angeles Forest called to him, but he needed to feed before reaching his destination.

The vampire was a predator, every part built to hunt down and kill prey; from his strength, to his speed, to his ability to heal quickly.

And his prey was human.

Though he only ever killed men and tried to only hunt those who wouldn't be missed, for him to never cause pain verged on impossible. Even the worst of men normally had people who loved them and would miss them.

In many ways, he was no better than Jackson.

Since Serenity, Sebastian had killed for pleasure. It had been the one thing he'd been able to lose himself in, if only for a moment or two. It had been the only way he'd been able to forget her. He hadn't been proud of his actions, but whatever humanity he tried to retain, at heart he was always a vampire.

He walked through the streets, keeping every sense alert for a suitable victim. He would know the right person when he came across them.

Within minutes, he approached a park. A homeless man sat on one of the benches, a brown paper bag containing a bottle clutched between his hands.

At once, Sebastian's nerves went on high alert.

He wanted the kill to be fast. Though the victim needed to be alive during the feeding, Sebastian had no wish for the man to die in terror.

In an instant, he stood in front of the man. "Excuse me, Sir," he said, "Do you have the time?"

The man—a skinny, worn-down guy in his fifties—lifted his head and Sebastian struck.

His jaw realigned, the muscles and bones distorting. The top of his jaw protruded forward, extending the fangs normally hidden further back in his mouth. His now yellow glowing eyes narrowed, his mouth opened wide—like a baby latching onto a nipple—and his teeth sank into the man's jugular.

The man batted at him weakly, his defenses no more than butterfly kisses to Sebastian.

Sebastian drank, thick warm blood flooding down his throat.

He caught glimpses of the brain waves of the person he fed from. A glimpse of a child, now grown, but not seen for many, many years, but the man's last thought was of a bottle.

The man's struggles grew weaker and eventually stopped altogether.

Fresh blood coursed through Sebastian's veins, flooding his body with warmth. The man's pulse still beat inside Sebastian's head; *thu-thump, thu-thump, thu-thump*. The sensation of a beating heart would not last but he enjoyed the rhythm while it did.

The guilt Sebastian thought he should feel did not come. Maybe he'd made his own peace with his identity, or perhaps, with all his emotions tied up in Serenity, there was simply no room for anything else.

Emotions warred within him. He fed on humans, murdered countless men to survive. Yet he was in love with one of them.

Perhaps that he used to be human explained the reason for his connection with Serenity. Others of his kind would ridicule him, but he didn't care what they thought. It wouldn't be the first time a vampire brought over a human for companionship. After all, that was exactly what happened to him.

The memory of what Madeline did bit down on his heart like shock paddles. He didn't want his thoughts to follow this route. The other vampire had taken him unwillingly. If he ever turned Serenity, it would be because she wanted to become like him.

He struggled to comprehend how he and Serenity were even compatible. He had lived for over two hundred years, seen and experienced things she would never have even given thought to. He'd experienced numerous wars, watched while plagues stole thousands of lives. He'd born witness to the world growing from single story homes to huge skyscrapers. The speed of the growth of technology over the past few decades left his brain whirling.

He shouldn't even think of them being together, yet the last few years without her had been the worst of his existence. The idea of spending hundreds more was unbearable.

Had her life not panned out the way he'd hoped because of his involvement, or had she already experienced too much pain to allow her to live a normal, happy life?

Could he change her? Did he dare to even think it?

Sebastian couldn't help the frisson of hope sparking through him. He'd been lonely throughout his vampire existence. The possibility of that loneliness ending overwhelmed him.

Could he change her? Would she even let him?

Four years ago Serenity begged him to turn her. She'd told him she wanted to be with him, no matter the consequences. He hadn't been able to bring himself to make her a vampire because he wanted her to have a normal life, but what if her life wasn't happy? What if, because of him and everything else she'd been through, she would never have that life? Surely then it would be better for them to be together. Serenity had killed before—both human and vampire—so he knew she contained what was necessary to be one of his kind.

Sebastian carried the body of the man with him. The weight was no greater challenge than carrying a bag of laundry. He wasn't going to just leave the body in the street.

The dead needed to be dealt with properly—buried. Sometimes they came back and the result wasn't pretty—a zombie-like creatures that didn't last long.

The strength from the live blood coursed through his veins like PCP: brute vigor and vitality. His skin flushed with warmth, his muscles loosened and flexed. To have fresh blood after weeks of a drought beat any other feeling imaginable.

He would need all of his strength, though he doubted Jackson's ability to defeat him—Jackson was newly turned. What Jackson was made him nervous. When, years ago, Sebastian brought Jackson's body to the forest, Jackson had been dead. Could there have been some small spark of life still left in Jackson when Sebastian buried his body?

Madeline had been much older than him. Had she detected the faintest beat of Jackson's heart or even the firing of brain cells? It was the only explanation, unless she had brought Jackson back from the dead? Had Madeline known some kind of evil making her able to raise the dead?

Although technically the vampire was dead—the physical body needed to die—it did so with vampire blood coursing through its veins. He'd never heard of someone who'd already died being turned.

So if Jackson wasn't a vampire, what was he? A devil? A demon? A fiend?

What sort of black magic had Madeline used to bring him back?

Sebastian headed back into the forest, drinking in the night. Picking his way easily through the undergrowth, he made his way back to the place he'd found the body of the girl who looked so like Serenity. Previously, the sight and scent of the murdered girl blocked out all other senses but now, with his body full of fresh blood, he realigned his mind, searching for something else.

Without the girl's blood saturating the ground, Sebastian picked up on a smell jarring his whole body. Acrid and dank; the stench of decomposition and decay.

Jackson's trail.

Sebastian took off at a run, bounding through the bush, following the scent of death.

He reached the patch of ground he took to be Jackson's place of metamorphism—a hole several feet deep, clods of earth scattered either side. The scent was stronger here, but not strong enough. Wherever Jackson was, he'd not been back to ground—not here at least—in a good day or two.

"God damn it," Sebastian swore, kicking at one of the clods, sending it smacking against a tree trunk. The clod shattered into fine earth at the impact.

The monster must be in the city somewhere, hot on Serenity's trail.

Chapter Ten

Sitting, distraught, on her hallway floor, holding her daughter in her arms, Serenity lost track of time. She eventually calmed down, when the immediate flood of adrenaline subsided, and regained her senses. Serenity glanced down to discover Elizabeth had fallen asleep. Her daughter looked so peaceful; a gentle flush of pink in her cheeks, those thick dark lashes sheltering her eyes. Serenity barely believed someone so perfect came from her.

Guilt at letting her daughter down spiked through her heart. Despite all her efforts, she'd put Elizabeth in even more danger than Serenity had been exposed to during her own horrendous childhood.

Self-doubt swamped Serenity, uncertainty in her ability as a mother. She'd spent the last few years trying to re-build her own shattered self-confidence, but her new found independence and strength had been nothing more than a fragile façade. In the end, it had only taken a few words to break down everything she'd rebuilt.

Carefully, Serenity got to her knees, still cradling her daughter in her arms. She used the wall for balance as she got to her feet. Her legs were stiff from the time she'd spent on the floor and her hips groaned and clicked in protest.

As she walked toward the little girl's bedroom, Elizabeth shifted in her arms. Serenity held her closer.

Please don't let anything hurt her, she prayed, her throat constricting at the thought.

She put her daughter back to bed and Elizabeth rolled to her side, sighing gently. Serenity pulled the flower-fairies cover up over her shoulders and smoothed her hair away from her forehead.

Serenity felt as though she'd been run over and left for dead. Emotional exhaustion dragged down on her limbs and every time she blinked, she struggled to reopen her eyes. Her mind flicked between Sebastian and Jackson, not sure which to focus on, each topic seemed too big for her to grasp onto for long. She struggled believe Sebastian was back, that he'd been standing in front of her, that he'd touched her face.

Serenity lifted her own hand and touched her cheek, mirroring the position of Sebastian's cold palm.

Why did he have to come back now? Why did he have to tell her such a terrible thing as Jackson coming back to get her?

She didn't know what to believe. How did he even know the murderer was Jackson? Had he actually seen him?

Serenity desperately wanted to believe Sebastian was wrong, of course she did, but what did that leave? If she didn't believe Jackson was back, it meant someone murdered the Bainbridges for no reason, or at least for a reason the police couldn't figure out. It also meant the feeling of being chased in the garage had just been her imagination. Then there was the big one—the fact the police found Jackson's fingerprints in the Bainbridge's blood. How was she supposed to explain the fingerprints away, except to say someone made a mistake with the forensics?

No, too much evidence pointed toward Sebastian telling her the truth.

A deep shiver wracked Serenity's whole body and her eyes flooded with tears once again. To think such a possibility might be true made her want to reach inside her chest and rip out her own heart.

Leaving her daughter sleeping, Serenity went back into the kitchen and peered out on the empty street. There was no sign of Sebastian.

Where had he gone?

Was he still out there somewhere, watching the house, but staying out of sight? She desperately hoped he was. At least knowing Sebastian might be close brought her some kind of comfort. If what Sebastian said was the truth—and what reason would he have to lie to her—then her worst nightmare lurked in the dark somewhere, tracking her down. She'd never felt so vulnerable, so exposed. Her locked windows and doors were such feeble protection against the horror hunting her.

Serenity reached out to the window and pulled down the blind. The wooden slats came down with a rattle, shutting out the world.

Only one other person existed in this world that she trusted. Picking up the phone, she dialed James's number. As the phone started to ring she glanced up at the kitchen clock hanging above the sink and realized it was past midnight. She went to press the button to hang up the phone when a sleepy male voice answered.

"Hello?"

"James?" She choked back a sob as she said his name.

"Serenity?" He immediately sounded awake. "What's the matter? What's happened?"

"He's back, James. Elizabeth's father is back."

"Who?" he said, startled. "Jackson?"

"No," she said, and hesitated as she reconsidered. "Well, yes, Jackson is back but I don't mean him. Jackson isn't Elizabeth's father." She took a deep breath. She'd never spoken those words out loud and doing so made her dizzy. She and James never discussed what happened to them more than four years ago. After the final conversation on the pier, they never again talked about what Madeline had been.

"You remember that night on the pier?"

He paused, and said, "Yes, of course."

"You remember what I told you about the woman, the one you shot at, the one who attacked you?"

"Yes," he said again, this time more caution in his tone.

"Elizabeth's father was the same as her, James."

Silence echoed down the end of the phone. She was asking him to believe a lot, asking him to recall painful memories, memories he'd probably blocked out by now.

"The man they said you stayed with at the hotel," he said, finally, remembering.

"Yes. He was trying to protect me from her."

"He didn't do a very good job," James snapped.

Now Serenity fell silent. Despite everything, she still couldn't help but want to defend Sebastian. James shouldn't judge him. Yet here she was, in trouble once more, and the first person she thought to call was James. He had a right to be angry; she'd made this his problem.

"I'm sorry, James. I shouldn't have called you."

Serenity had overstepped the line. James wasn't her husband. He had his own family and her presence in their lives might be putting them in danger. She never wanted to put them in harm's way. The thought of the cherubic Noah and Amy being hurt because of her was unthinkable.

"Serenity, wait. I didn't mean anything."

"I understand. It's a lot to take in."

"I don't know what you want me to do?"

She sighed. "That's just it, you can't do anything. I don't expect you to do anything."

Loneliness pressed down around her. Had she been lying to herself this whole time, reveling in her independence yet relying on the support of James and his family? She'd taken him for granted and his solid, stable presence in her life gave her what she needed without demanding anything in return. Now it was her turn to help him. She needed to set him free from their friendship, from whatever misguided responsibility he thought he owed her.

She couldn't tell James about Jackson, about what Sebastian said he'd become. This wasn't James's fight. She'd gotten him involved the last time and it had almost cost him his life. She refused to make the same mistake again.

Serenity had two options; get away from the city without telling Sebastian where she'd gone and keep Elizabeth a secret, or tell him everything and accept his help.

In spite of the anger and fear, she couldn't help the hope in her heart at the thought of Sebastian being near. Would he hurt her again? Probably. With the exception of Elizabeth, nothing had changed. They were still the same people they had been four years ago, but she couldn't help how she felt. Maybe her emotions made her weak, but she wanted him to protect her, wanted to be safe and secure again.

Her love for Sebastian still existed. She'd spent so many nights dreaming of him and now he was back, wanting to help her. She only needed to let him.

Serenity didn't want to live her life in fear again.

The night stretched ahead of her, the morning a distant point that seemed would never come. Yet, what had Sebastian said? Jackson could walk in the light. He wasn't like Sebastian or Madeline, but something different. She shouldn't be scared of the dark, she realized. At night, at least, Sebastian was out there somewhere; she wasn't alone. If Sebastian was right, she should be frightened of the day.

In the daylight, she was on her own.

Chapter Eleven

Finally, it had found her.

After months of growing, changing, re-building its shattered mind, the creature located the person it searched for: Serenity. It had gotten so close, close enough to sneak out its rancid tongue and lick her face. Oh, how it enjoyed the scent of fear seeping from her skin. The smell brought back so many memories. It had not lost the skills of the man it once was—those of manipulation, confusion, torture.

The creature would not feed on this one. Even a slow and agonizing death would be too good for Serenity. No, it would break her. It would take everything she held dear and rip everything away. It would take her sanity and finally, when she had nothing left, it would consume her.

After spending almost two nights in the city, the creature returned back to its hole in the forest, muscles screaming in pain. The need to go back to ground was nearly as strong as the hunger plaguing it's every moment. The scent of earthy darkness, the dirt encasing every side, gave it comfort. Even the memory of the grainy earth on its tongue made it yearn with longing, like a child craving the comfort of a much loved blanket or well-worn toy. Only in the total darkness beneath ground did it truly feel at peace. Without taking the time to rest, the pain grew and grew, threatening to crowd out its recently acquired thoughts and memories. It didn't want to go back to the agonizing nothingness of when it had first emerged.

The creature needed to stay focused on the man it had once been and the revenge it sought, the sole purpose to its existence.

Yet something gave it cause to pause upon its return, a strange scent around its resting place. The odor was not that of a human nor an animal, but something different, something unrecognizable. However, the pain surrounding the creature did not allow it the time to ponder the reason for the change.

Relieved to be back, the creature settled back in the hole and pulled the dirt in over itself. Nestled within the earthen womb, it slept, repairing its tortured body and broken mind.

The thing still needed to feed; always, an all-consuming hunger. An incredible amount of strength had been needed not to reach out and clamp its teeth into Serenity's sweet, pale throat. It had always prided itself on restraint, on dragging out her torture so she never knew where the next blow was coming from. Her abuse had always been about the pleasure of her pain, seeing the fear in her eyes, making her cower. It never forgot the satisfaction of having the power to make her react in such a way.

It swiped its fat, bloated tongue across razor sharp teeth.

How it relished in its new found strength. Its muscles burned with pent-up energy. It wanted to use its power—run and jump, rip and tear. It wanted to tear stone apart with its bare hands and run across continents. Though animalistic in its strength and instincts, its mind grew sharper. It still contained all of the cunning and brutality of the man it had once been; only now the bitterness of revenge encompassed every cell.

The thought occurred that perhaps it should thank Serenity. Its body was so much better before, but then it remembered Serenity had not done this, but the other one, the one with fiery hair. It only experienced brief flashes of memory of the redhead, explosions of agonizing pain. She'd brought him back from nothingness. She fed him, nurtured him, and then one day she had not returned and he started to decline, slipping back into the void.

Serenity took its life. The redhead gave it back again.

The creature knew where she worked now; the couple he'd murdered had given him the information. Frustrated they'd been unable to supply him with a home address, he'd torn through the house, searching for contracts that might contain Serenity's address. The hunt had been unsuccessful. Perhaps if given more time, he'd have found what he wanted, but the police sirens had cut through the night, forcing him to abandon his search.

Such a minor setback was of no concern. It enjoyed the chase and intended to continue to enjoy every minute of the torture it planned for her. Tasting Serenity's fear was the point of its existence, just as it had been as a man. There was no point in rushing the sweet pleasure of revenge.

Still, it needed to find out where she lived.

The creature wanted to think of itself as a person again—it deserved that. Though no longer a man, it at least deserved to be a real being. If anything, it was so much more than the man it had once been. It—he—was stronger, faster and crueler. He could take all of the pleasures of life without needing to think about any of the repercussions.

'He', yes, 'he'. The creature was no longer an 'it' but an actual being with feelings, however repugnant.

Jackson.

Dawn threatened to break through the night sky. Though he still lay below ground, he sensed the change.

He needed to go back to the city. To find out where Serenity lived he would go back to the place he'd found her yesterday. He had no intention of harming her yet, but finding out where she lived would give him another avenue with which to torture her.

He broke out of the ground and shook the earth from his body like a dog shaking water from its coat. He stretched out his muscles, rippling strength.

A powerful hunger coursed through him, threatening to block out his thoughts. Torn between finding where Serenity lived and finding someone to feed on, he hesitated. If he was in luck, perhaps he could combine the two.

The thought tugged a smile on his face, but to an observer the expression looked more like a snarl.

Jackson took off in a sprint. The speed exhilarated him, almost as though he flew, his feet barely touching the ground. The forest wildlife silenced as he passed, some primitive part sensing something unnatural was near. The only sound was that of branches whipping past his head. Even his feet were silent, touching too lightly and quickly to so much as snap a twig.

All too quickly, he reached the city.

He moved so fast now the humans did not even see him, though they registered his presence. They wrinkled their noses in disgust, or clamped a hand across their mouths. They glanced around, the fear and confusion clear on their faces, but their gaze never settled upon him.

Though early, people still traveled through the city. As Jackson approached Serenity's place of work he noticed lights on in the building. Cleaners, early shift workers, overly keen executives were all in the office first thing. As the sky grew brighter, the lights extinguished.

Jackson headed back underground, back to the parking lot where he'd encountered Serenity the day before. He felt better beneath ground, in the dark.

He would wait.

It turned out he wouldn't wait for long.

The black Audi swung into the lot and pulled up in the same space as the day before. Jackson recognized the vehicle as the same one Serenity had gotten into. His jaw clenched in anticipation.

Except Serenity wasn't in the car.

An older man, at least late fifties, wearing glasses framed by two thick, heavy eyebrows drove now.

The man switched off the car engine, but didn't get out. Instead, he lifted some paperwork off the passenger seat and began to flip through.

Jackson took his chance. Moving quickly, he opened the passenger door and slid into the seat beside him.

The man's head jerked up in shock, dropping the papers. They fell to his lap and floated into the foot well.

"Hello," Jackson rasped. "I think you have information important to me."

The man's eyes widened and Jackson watched him trying to figure out where Jackson had come from.

"Who the hell are you?"

Jackson laughed; the sound like gravel against glass.

"An old friend of Serenity's."

The man leaned back, breathing only through his mouth to try to escape the stench. "I highly doubt that."

Jackson tasted the fear seeping from the man's pores, but the man didn't try to run. Instead he sat, defiant. The man kept his professionalism despite the circumstances. Jackson admired him for his bravery, but it wouldn't stop him killing the older man.

"You have information for me. You will tell me about Serenity."

"I'm not going to tell you anything. Who the hell do you think you are?"

He reached over and took the man's hand like a lover, drawing it toward him. The man immediately tried to pull away, but Jackson's strength left no room for maneuvering. The man's mouth opened and closed in surprise and his eyes brightened with fear. All of a sudden, the knowledge dawned on him that the person, now holding his hand in an ice-cold vice, was not human.

Slowly Jackson lifted the man's hand, the fingers spread out as though about to make a handprint on the windscreen. Jackson held the palm in front of his face.

"This little piggy went to market…" Jackson growled. As he did so he reached out with his other hand and snapped the man's little finger at the middle knuckle.

The man screamed—the high-pitched shriek of a rabbit caught in the jaws of a fox. His finger stuck out at an awkward angle, forty-five degrees from the rest of his hand.

"This little piggy…"

"No! No!" the man screamed.

His pleas would never be enough. Jackson was enjoying himself too much.

"This little piggy stayed at home," he continued and moved to the next finger.

Snap!

The man screamed again, longer and louder. The blood drained from his face and his eyes rolled back in his head.

Jackson frowned. That wouldn't do. At the least, he needed the man conscious. The second finger now also jutted at an angle, pointing backward, away from the man's palm. Jackson longed to bite, to sink his teeth into the man's flesh, but he controlled himself.

"Tell me where Serenity lives."

His voice brought the man back to consciousness. He caught sight of his mangled hand and began to cry.

"Why are you doing this to me?" he sobbed.

"Tell me where Serenity lives?" Jackson demanded again.

The man's eyes darted from side to side, never quite resting on Jackson's face. Was his unwillingness to look at Jackson because the horror of his face was too much, or because he could tell Jackson should not be alive—an abomination of nature? Maybe he feared if he focused too long, his mental health would never survive? Of course the man would not live long enough to need to worry about his state of mind.

He was gibbering now. All professionalism had been forgotten in his fear. "I don't know! The computer... The office..."

Jackson growled again, a low, throaty sound. He hadn't wanted to go in the building. It was still early, but there were bound to be other people around. Jackson moved fast enough to prevent being seen, but he wouldn't be able to do so with this screaming, gibbering wreck tucked under his arm.

"Think," he commanded.

"Oh God..." the man whined. "Please don't hurt me anymore."

"Then tell me what I need to know."

Jackson saw the man's mind frantically leafing through the information, desperately searching for the one thing he thought might save his life. It was a shame; whatever the man told him would not be enough to let him live. Jackson was hungry and the scent of the man's fear just made the hunger worse.

A light went on in the man's eyes.

"Burbank! She lives in Burbank!"

That was enough. He would stalk the district until he happened upon her scent. He would find her.

"Good," he said, slowly. "Very good."

He raised the injured hand as though about to kiss it, lifted the man's wrist to his nose and inhaled deeply, like scenting a perfume sprayed for a lover.

The man watched him in horror. His entire body shook. The motion made his huge eyebrows vibrate, Jackson noted with amusement.

Then he bit.

His sharp teeth sliced through flesh and tendons, crunched through the delicate bones of the wrist. He left a great, gaping hole; most of the man's inner-forearm now missing. Blood pumped out of the gash like an oil source recently tapped.

The man screamed, and screamed, and screamed.

Jackson put his mouth back down to the wound and slurped and licked, sating his hunger. The man finally fell silent.

When Jackson eventually glanced up, he saw the man had passed out. Within minutes he would be dead.

Chapter Twelve

Serenity didn't let Elizabeth go to preschool. Too afraid to even open the drapes, she checked every door and window, making sure they were locked, only to check them again ten minutes later, like a person suffering from obsessive compulsive disorder.

Elizabeth's wide, dark eyes followed Serenity around the room.

"Everything's okay, honey," Serenity said, trying to give her daughter the reassurance she longed for herself. "You and I are going to have a girl's day today, yeah? We'll watch movies and eat chocolate. I'll even paint your toe nails that pretty pink color you like?"

Despite her intuition, at only just four years old, Elizabeth was easily bribed. Her face lit up at the idea of having her toe-nails painted like Mommy's, something

Serenity never let her do for fear of making her baby grow up too fast.

"Yay!" Elizabeth exclaimed. Clapping her hands together, her whole face lit up.

She smiled back at her daughter but the expression was forced. Serenity barely slept the previous night. Every sound jolted her wide-awake and nightmares plagued her sleep. Now, as though suffering from a heavy night out on the town—something she never did anyway—exhaustion hung like a cloud around her and she struggled to string a thought together.

Going through the morning's normal routine, Serenity prepared breakfast for them both; toast, cereal, orange juice. Elizabeth tucked in with her usual gusto, though she didn't take her eyes off her mother, knowing something wasn't quite right. Serenity never let either of them take a day off for no reason.

Serenity stirred cereal around her bowl, sugar bleeding out into rapidly warming milk. The wheat had grown soggy and even more unappetizing. Adrenaline zapped her appetite, but she tried to pretend for Elizabeth's sake. She lifted a spoonful of the cereal to her mouth, but the wheat was just a mushy consistency against her tongue.

She forced herself to swallow.

Sebastian hadn't returned and there had been no sign of Jackson, much to her relief. Yet his presence pressed down upon her like an impending asteroid; knowing something huge, dark and life destroying hurtled toward her and she was powerless to do anything about it.

With breakfast finished and the dishes cleared away, Serenity set about trying to hide out and forget the terrifying things going on in her world. Tucked up on the small couch in the kitchen, Serenity cuddled Elizabeth under her arm. 'Finding Nemo' played on the television. Elizabeth stiffened and gasped as the two fish swam for their lives between the tentacles of hundreds of jellyfish. Serenity paid little attention to the movie. Instead, she remained lost in thought, her lips brushing the top of her daughter's head.

Serenity took comfort in her daughter's interaction with the film—the normality, how easily she could be transported into another world. Serenity couldn't escape her own thoughts so easily. Even the little fish on the screen would do anything to protect its offspring.

Suddenly her shoulders stiffened.

She must have heard something; her muscles tightened, her senses heightened. Her ears strained, trying to hear what had caught her attention, even if only on a subconscious level.

Her heart hammered inside her chest, so loud Elizabeth would surely hear the sound.

"I'll be back in a minute," she said, patting Elizabeth on the leg with a trembling hand.

Too engrossed in her movie, Elizabeth didn't even glance up.

Cautiously, Serenity got to her feet and crossed the small living area to the front hall. She checked the front door. Still locked. At least the house remained secure.

Had a noise outside caught her attention? Was someone out there?

Serenity made her way back into the kitchen. Elizabeth still sat, watching the movie, her blanket clutched close to her face. Serenity pulled the cord for the kitchen blind, raising the wooden slats by a few inches, enough to give her a view out on the street. A car drove past, but otherwise the road was quiet. Now mid-morning, most people were at work.

She frowned. Something had startled her, she was sure.

About to pull down the blind, shutting out the rest of the world again, something glinted off the windowsill, catching a flash of light in the mid-morning sunshine.

A gold ring sat on the windowsill, only inches from her face.

A wave of déjà-vu swept over her, accompanied by a sickness swirling deep in her gut. How could such a simple object hold such menace? She didn't want to touch the ring, yet she couldn't bring herself to leave it. She needed to know the ring was real.

Her heart pounded as she cracked open the window and snuck her hand out, grabbing the small band of metal. As though afraid something would reach up and grab her, she snatched back her hand and slammed the window shut, locking it again.

With shaking hands, she dropped the item into her other palm. The metal burned a ring of ice in her skin.

She knew the ring, she would recognize it anywhere, but to be certain she checked inside. Engraved was the date 19-09-97.

The date she married Jackson.

Her hand still trembling, she slipped the band on her ring finger. As she expected, the ring passed over her skin with too much space between her skin and the metal. The ring hung from her finger. It was a man's ring.

Jackson's ring.

A faint cry escaped her throat and she dropped the ring into the kitchen sink. The metal hit the porcelain with a 'clink'. The ring bounced a couple of times before coming to rest near the drain.

The doorbell rang, shrill and loud, and Serenity shrieked, her heart clambered into her throat once again.

"Mommy," Elizabeth said, her attention removed from the movie, staring at her mother with confusion and concern. "It's only the doorbell."

"I know, I know," she said, her hand at her chest, exhaling long and slow, trying to get a grip of herself. "It made me jump."

Elizabeth stared at her as though her mother had lost her mind. Serenity glanced down at the band of gold again. The ring instilled more fear and horror than any piece of metal ever should have the power to do. She wondered if her daughter's thoughts might be true.

The doorbell rang again.

"Mommy!" Elizabeth said again, irritation affecting her voice. The doorbell was interrupting her movie.

"Yes, Elizabeth," she snapped. "I'm not deaf."

He wouldn't ring the doorbell, she told herself. He wouldn't sneak around the place, leave his wedding ring as a calling card, and then sound the bell. What had Sebastian said: Jackson was no longer human? Whatever he was now, he wouldn't be hanging out on people's doorsteps waiting for an invitation to come in.

But he is dead! Her mind screamed, tears filling her eyes. She had killed him herself. Her mind didn't want to conjure up the horror of what Jackson might have become. In her head she envisioned him dead on the kitchen floor, his throat and chest coated in a slick of his own blood.

Despite her own reassurances, she didn't want to go to the door. She wondered if she should ignore it, but then the bell blasted again and Elizabeth shot her another glare.

Serenity took a deep breath, trying to quell the rising panic, and went to answer the door.

A small peephole had been put in the front door for security and she stood on tip-toes to look out. James stood on the step, looking impatient and worried, and she bit down on her lower lip, stopping herself bursting into fresh tears of relief.

Serenity cracked open the door.

"Christ, Serenity, what are you playing at?" he said. "You had me worried."

"How did you know I was home?" she asked, backing up, letting him through the front door.

"You weren't at work."

"Why were you—"

"Something's happened," he said, cutting her off. "I know you didn't go into work because I was just there. It's your boss, Serenity. Richard Berry was murdered in the parking garage first thing this morning."

"What?" The walls suddenly closed in around her and she put a hand out, steadying herself against James's shoulder.

Her head swam with shock.

"You heard me," he said, his voice harder than she thought it should be considering the news he'd just delivered. "Your boss has been murdered."

"My God…"

They stood together in the hallway for a moment while Serenity gulped back tears and waited for the color to return to her face and the room to stop spinning.

Taking a few deep breaths to compose herself, she opened the kitchen door. Elizabeth glanced up as they walked in.

"Elizabeth, honey, you need to go to your room for a minute. I need to talk to Uncle James."

Elizabeth opened her mouth to protest, but Serenity shot her a look.

"Now, please," she said.

Reluctantly, Elizabeth got off the couch and gave her movie a longing gaze.

James reached out and ruffled her hair as she passed.

"We won't be long, kiddo."

Serenity watched as Elizabeth went in her bedroom. She closed the kitchen door, hoping to stop her daughter from hearing anything else.

"Now are you going to tell me what's going on, Serenity?" James demanded, facing her. "No one at the station has made the connection between you and your boss yet. But as soon as they realize you work for him *and* own the house the Bainbridges lived in, they're going to be asking some serious questions."

Serenity's eyes filled with tears. Tears for the people who had been killed, but also tears of fear for the people she loved.

"You need to take Amy and Noah and get out of the city," she said. "It's not safe."

He started back, surprised. "What the hell has this got to do with Amy and Noah?" Real anger fired his voice.

"You're my friend, and so is your family. The person who killed the others could easily come after you guys and there is absolutely nothing I can do." Except that wasn't true. She could tell Sebastian she wanted his help. She had to now. If Jackson was killing the people around her, she owed it to James to do everything within her power to protect his family.

"So are you saying you know who did this now?"

She nodded. "I think so. I tried to tell you…"

"Are we back to what you were talking about on the phone last night?" James asked. The level of his voice dropped in horror and disbelief. "Surely the person killing these people isn't Elizabeth's father?"

The idea that such a sweet little girl came from someone capable of such horrific acts of violence was unthinkable.

"No! God, no!" she said. "Of course not."

Serenity had no idea how to even start to explain all of this to him. She barely believed it herself. She didn't want to tell James about murdering Jackson, never mind that he was now back for revenge. Whatever James thought of her, whatever he had seen and experienced himself, she would still sound like she should be locked up in a mental hospital.

"I think your detective was right. I think Jackson is committing the murders," she said, deciding to leave out the 'and he's dead' part. "He was here earlier. He left his wedding ring as a calling card."

"Jesus Christ, Serenity!" James's blue eyes widened. "Did you see him? Did he try to talk to you?"

She shook her head. "No, I found the ring on the kitchen sill."

He switched from friend to police mode. "At least we have something else to go on now. We can put out a full description. We'll pull up and circulate a photo from his driver's license. We're bound to pin him down in no time."

She stared at him, desperately wanting to believe him. But the lie was dangerous and thinking even for a moment that a police force could take Jackson down would get them all killed. They couldn't expect to put a pair of handcuffs on Jackson and haul him off to jail.

"Arresting Jackson won't be that easy, James. You're missing the point."

He stared at her blankly, and then realization dawned. "Please don't tell me Jackson is some sort of..." He couldn't bring himself to say the word. "Other creature, as well."

"I don't know exactly what he is, but I don't think he's human anymore."

James sank onto the small couch behind him and put his head in his hands. "I can't deal with this shit, Serenity. I don't believe in ghosts or fairies. I don't think I even believed in Santa Claus when I was a kid. Please don't ask me to start believing in this stuff."

She crouched in front of him and slipped her fingers through his, pulling his hand away from his face, forcing him to look up.

"I don't want to believe either and if I hadn't been exposed to this other world, I'm sure I wouldn't. But you know these things exist. You experienced it yourself, four years ago that night on the pier."

He stared at her. "You know I am doing everything in my power to convince myself you're crazy right now?"

"I honestly don't blame you. I've questioned my own sanity enough times, but I'm not crazy and I'm not lying. Jackson has become something else and he's killing people—people connected to me."

"And you think he might come after Amy and Noah?"

For the first time, fear replaced James's disbelief.

"I'm so sorry, James. The last thing I want is for you and your family to get involved."

"It's a bit late for empty wishes." His fear for his family sharpened his words. "You got me involved four years ago."

Her face colored with shame. What he said was true. Though some might argue his job had been to protect her, her telephone call was what brought him to the pier that night. If she'd never made the call, he wouldn't have been exposed to Madeline and everything she represented.

"I'm so sorry."

"You know I can't just leave?" he said. "Catching murderers is what my job is all about."

"Please, James. You'll never be able to catch him. You have to go home, get your family and get as far away from me as possible."

James stared at her. "What about you and Elizabeth? Amy's mother lives in Sacramento. If you really think all of our lives are in danger, I can send you all there."

Serenity hesitated for a moment. She couldn't go. Leaving would only give Jackson an excuse to follow them, but maybe she should send Elizabeth? Her heart clenched at the thought of being separated from her daughter. They'd never been apart before—not even for one night in the whole of Elizabeth's four years—and the idea of them not being together was heartbreaking.

She hated that she wouldn't know if Elizabeth was safe or not, but what choice did she have? Could she rely on Sebastian to protect them? Hell, Sebastian wasn't even aware of Elizabeth's existence.

"I couldn't go," she said. "I would only put them in danger again. But Elizabeth should."

James frowned. "Let's not jump ahead of ourselves. Amy's not going to take kindly to being sent off like a child refugee. She's going to want to be told what's going on and I have no idea what to tell her."

"Tell her about Jackson, but leave out what he's become. Tell her he's my sadistic husband out for revenge and wants to hurt anyone close to me. That should be enough."

"What about you?" he asked. "How are you going to stay safe?"

Her thoughts immediately turned to Sebastian. "Elizabeth's father will take care of me. And James, you need to let him be the one who goes after Jackson. If you or any of the other officers try, Jackson will kill them."

"So Elizabeth's father is back? Does she know?"

Serenity shook her head. "She's never asked about him so I never brought it up." Serenity wasn't sure if she wanted to tell James any more than she already had, but everything was coming to a head now. At some point in the next few hours, everyone would need to discover the truth.

"He doesn't know about her either," she admitted. Her chin wobbled as the sadness of it all swept over her. They'd already missed out on so much of each other's lives. Elizabeth deserved to have a father, however strange he might be, and Sebastian deserved the chance to get to know his daughter.

"Hang on a minute," James lowered his voice even further. "Are you telling me Elizabeth is not one hundred percent... human?"

Like Serenity, he was unable to bring himself to use the words: vampire, supernatural, immortal.

"I've never had any reason to think she's anything other than human. I was terrified at first, at what she might become, but she's as normal as you or I."

"Jesus Christ, Serenity." He was looking at her with different eyes; a mixture of fear and awe. The things he'd thought he knew about the world were shifting. Things he'd taken for granted about people he loved were wrong.

James retreated back to the one thing he could rely on— his work.

"Detective Gingham is going to make the connection between you, your boss and Jackson," he said. "He already thinks you might be protecting Jackson. Now your boss is dead, it's only going to reinforce his suspicions. You need to prepare yourself for him hauling you back down to the station. He may even get a search warrant to discover if you're concealing Jackson."

Serenity raised her hands, gesturing around her. "He can search all he likes."

A noise outside of the door silenced them both. The door handle wiggled a little and Serenity stepped forward and opened it. Elizabeth stood outside, a sheepish smile on her face.

"I want to watch Nemo," Elizabeth said.

Serenity and James shared a look.

"Sure honey. Your Uncle James is going to call me later."

"Sooner rather than later," he promised. "And lock your door after I leave."

"Of course," she said, but deep down she wondered if a locked door was any protection against something unnatural.

Chapter Thirteen

With James gone, Serenity found it impossible to settle. She paced her small apartment, periodically peeping out of the windows. Her ears strained for any sound that might signal Jackson's return. The thought of him so close made her sick with fear.

Poor Mr. Berry. Her soul welled with grief for the man who'd taken a chance on her and had always been there to help. What kind of torture had Jackson put him through before killing him? Though James had given her none of the details, she knew Jackson well enough to realize he wouldn't have murdered Mr. Berry without first having some fun. Her heart went out to her boss's family. How they must be grieving. They didn't deserve any of this—none of them did.

She prepared Elizabeth a sandwich but couldn't bring herself to eat. Hunger made her nausea worse, acid churning in her stomach, but the only thing she managed to chew were her cuticles. Though she went through the motions of being a parent, in truth she was barely present. Her body might have been in the room but she was disconnected, as though watching herself through a smoke screen.

Elizabeth ate sitting in front of the television. The little girl didn't understand the reason for this unprecedented access to the television, but she was going to make the most of it. Serenity didn't have the heart or the energy to tell her to switch the box off.

Jackson might attack them at any moment. What was stopping him? Serenity didn't think a few locked doors and windows would keep him out if he wanted to get to them. No, he hadn't killed her yet because he had other plans. When Jackson had been human, he'd always waited to make her pay after she'd done something to upset him. He enjoyed the buildup; watching her tip-toe around him, flinching at every movement, constantly questioning where the next blow would come from. Jackson had beaten and tortured her for such small things: being late, burning the dinner, asking the wrong question. She didn't want to think about what sort of punishment he had in mind considering her misdemeanor. After all, she'd done more than burn dinner this time.

She had murdered him.

Serenity glanced over to find Elizabeth asleep on the couch. Serenity pulled the throw off the back of the couch and covered her daughter. Elizabeth looked so peaceful. The little girl didn't even stir.

Serenity wondered when she would hear from James; she hoped he wouldn't be long. He'd probably fight with Amy about sending her away to Sacramento, but in the end Amy would listen. James was a Police Sergeant after all; she'd have to believe him if he told her their family was being threatened, and Amy would never put Noah in danger.

In the meantime she needed to be prepared. Elizabeth would need all of her things packed and be ready to go.

Serenity didn't own much in the way of suitcases. She hadn't taken a vacation since Jackson and got rid of anything she'd shared with her husband—including their luggage. She only owned a small canvas case but it would do for the minute. Elizabeth's clothes were small and didn't take up much room, though Serenity wanted to make sure Elizabeth had everything else she was used to at home.

She found the small case squashed beneath a pile of linen at the top of her bedroom closet. She pulled it down, having to use one hand to hold the linen in place, trying not to pull everything down on top of her. Pushing the closet door shut behind her, she took the bag to Elizabeth's room.

Serenity pulled open Elizabeth's drawers and selected a few different outfits and a couple of nightgowns. She picked up Elizabeth's pillow and the fleece blanket lying across the bottom of her bed. She hugged the pillow to her chest and lowered her head, inhaling her daughter's smell. With a shuddery sigh, she stuffed them into the bag on top of the clothes. She packed her daughter's favorite teddy and a couple of books Elizabeth liked to have read to her at bedtime.

Serenity's throat constricted and she paused, a Winnie-the-Pooh book held in one hand. Someone else reading Elizabeth her bedtime story felt so wrong.

The gravity of her actions swept over her.

Serenity sat down heavily on the narrow single bed. Her hands rested on top of her daughter's belongings, pressing them into her lap as though Elizabeth's things might join them.

Her eyes filled with tears. Was she really about to send her only child away? She wasn't going to be there to sing her to sleep that evening. What if Elizabeth woke in the night, scared and wondering where her mommy was?

Even worse, what if Jackson found out about Elizabeth and followed them to Sacramento?

She couldn't stand to think of Elizabeth terrified and hurt with Mommy not there to protect her. It hurt her in a way she couldn't even fathom.

How had her life turned upside down in such a short space of time? A part of her still couldn't believe all of this was happening? How could Jackson be back? How could he have become something even more terrifying than he was in life?

In her fear for her daughter's life, she'd barely given thought to Sebastian. The vampire had also returned and Serenity didn't think Jackson to be the sole reason. She thought she'd come to terms with what Sebastian was, but seeing him again brought back so many feelings.

Sebastian... Not human, yet the father of her child.

It shouldn't be possible but she couldn't change reality.

What would he do when he found out about Elizabeth? Would he be angry? Would he deny she was his?

Her emotions torn, she didn't know what to think. She couldn't get away from the anger; anger for him bringing Madeline into her life and resentment for him leaving. But if she'd never met Sebastian, she would probably still be living, terrified and miserable with Jackson, and Elizabeth would never have been born. She'd always lived with fear, but the fear she had for herself paled compared to the absolute, unremitted terror she felt when she thought about losing her daughter.

Serenity got to her feet. She wanted to be back with Elizabeth—who knew how much time they had left together?

She sniffed and wiped her eyes, hoping Elizabeth wouldn't notice her blotchy face and red eyes. The last thing she wanted to do was scare her.

Obviously she would need to talk to Elizabeth about going to Sacramento. Elizabeth had never been on a plane before. Would she be excited or scared? Whatever her reaction, the idea of bringing up the subject with Elizabeth made her nervous and she wanted to choose her moment. She didn't want Elizabeth to discover the packed bag first.

Serenity shoved the bag under Elizabeth's bed and made her way back to the kitchen.

Elizabeth had swung her legs off the couch; the throw was in a puddle on the floor at her feet. She sat with her head hung and her narrow shoulders slumped. Her arms rested on her knees.

"Everything okay, sweetie?" Serenity asked, but Elizabeth didn't answer. Slowly Serenity crossed the room until she stood in front of her daughter and then crouched in front of her.

Elizabeth's eyes stared wide open but they didn't focus on Serenity; they seemed not to focus on anything at all.

"Elizabeth?" A stab of fear jolted through her. What was wrong with her child?

"No, Mommy." Serenity jumped at the sound of her daughter's thin and distant voice. "Please… please don't make me."

"What's wrong?" Serenity asked. Panic rushed through her, adrenaline spurting through her veins. "What's happened?"

Was Elizabeth sleepwalking? She seemed to still be asleep even though her eyes were open. Serenity thought she'd heard somewhere that waking a sleepwalking child was dangerous and could give them a heart attack or something? Maybe the result wouldn't be anything quite so dramatic, but it would certainly scare her.

"Don't make me go away," Elizabeth moaned. "The man… He'll hurt you, Mommy."

Prickles of fear made her skin rise in goose bumps, her hair standing on end. Had Elizabeth overheard her and James talking? Had she seen her packing?

"No... no, Mommy. Not a man... He's not a man... It smells so bad." Elizabeth turned her face away as though trying to escape whatever plagued her dream. Her head twisted from side to side, her blank eyes darting around the room, never landing on Serenity. Her hands gripped the side of the couch, knuckles white.

"He's coming!" Elizabeth suddenly screamed.

Serenity grabbed her shoulders, all worries about waking a sleepwalking child completely flown from her head. She only wanted Elizabeth to stop and wake up.

"No, Mommy... The smell... Please, no..." She shrieked again and again, loud and piercing. To see such emotion come from Elizabeth's mouth, when her eyes were wide open but still horrifyingly blank, was terrifying.

The little girl fought against Serenity, her small hands clawing at her mother.

"Elizabeth," Serenity spoke loudly and firmly. "Elizabeth, baby. It's okay. Everything is all right." She spoke with an assurance she didn't feel. She was working on autopilot, on sheer adrenaline. The cold chill of horror bore right down to her bones. She wanted to cry and scream herself, '*What's wrong with her? What's wrong with my little girl?*'

Somehow Elizabeth managed to slip out of her mother's hold. Serenity dodged her daughter's hands but Elizabeth lurched forward and her small fist caught Serenity on the chin. The blow shocked her, her chin and lower lip tingling. Elizabeth packed a punch for a four year old.

Serenity had seen enough.

"Elizabeth!" Her voiced turned to a scream. "Wake up!"

Her daughter fell still, her shoulders slumped. Then she blinked once and all of a sudden she was back, like watching someone brought out of hypnosis.

Elizabeth took one look at her mother and burst into tears.

"Oh, honey, everything's okay. Everything's okay." Serenity repeated the words, as though saying them over and over would make them true. She pulled Elizabeth into her arms, Elizabeth's small body trembling against her.

"Don't make me go away," Elizabeth cried. "We're never going to see each other again."

"What? Don't be silly, of course we will"

She should have been used to Elizabeth's precognitive behavior by now, yet the things her daughter said always took her back. Still she tried to justify it, explain her daughter's uncanny knowledge away with the obvious answer. Elizabeth had been outside of the door when she and James had been talking; she must have overheard them.

"It'll only be for a few days, sweetheart. You should be excited! You're going on vacation with Aunty Amy and Noah."

Elizabeth stared up at her, her big, dark eyes wobbly with tears. "I don't want to go." Elizabeth's lower lip trembled. "I don't want to," she said again, but now less conviction affected her voice. "You need me."

"Of course I need you, but I also need a few days by myself." She took a deep breath. She didn't think she had ever told an outright lie to her daughter. "Mommy's got work to do. Think how much fun you'll have with Amy and Noah."

Elizabeth just stared at her. For a moment, Serenity thought she'd gone back to the strange and distant place she'd occupied in her dreams. But then she said, "Okay, Mommy," in a small, disbelieving voice that should never have come from someone so young.

It dawned on Serenity that Elizabeth had just realized her mother wasn't perfect, that she couldn't trust her mother on every count.

Serenity reached out and touched Elizabeth's curls. They sprang beneath her fingertips.

"I love you so much and I'm so proud of you. It won't be for long, I promise."

She bit her lip. Another lie.

When had she become such a liar?

Chapter Fourteen

The phone rang, shrill and piercing, making them both jump.

James.

Serenity gave Elizabeth another fierce hug and stood to get the phone. She considered taking the call out of the room, but the guilt remained with her after lying to Elizabeth and she didn't want Elizabeth to feel any more shut out than she probably already did.

"Hello?" she answered.

James spoke without bothering to introduce himself. "Amy is surprisingly okay with going to Sacramento. She's been meaning to visit her mom for ages. She doesn't like the idea of me being here and she's worried to death about you, but she's happy to take Elizabeth."

Serenity breathed a sigh of relief. Of course Amy always did what was best, but Serenity had been worried she would fight James and they'd all still be here, right in Jackson's path.

"That's great, James. Thank you so much, and thank Amy for me as well."

"A flight leaves at eight-fifteen tonight," he continued. "I've got the three of you tickets. Amy has some stuff she needs to do first, so she'll meet you at departures."

"Sure, no problem. I'll get a cab."

"You sure? You'll be safe?"

"I'll be careful, I promise."

She heard him pause, and then he said, "Jesus, Serenity. I can't believe it's come to this." Anger still affected his voice.

"I don't know what you want me to say." She glanced over at Elizabeth sitting on the couch. She watched her mother and so Serenity turned her back, as if her position could affect Elizabeth's hearing. She spoke into the phone, her head bent, hair falling in her face. "This isn't my fault. I didn't ask for any of this."

"You're the one who got involved with a ..." Still he couldn't bring himself to say the word.

"I didn't know what he was when I met him."

"You should have run as soon as you found out."

"I did," she said, quietly. "He found me again."

James sighed heavily down the phone. "I guess we can't change what's already happened."

Serenity bristled in irritation. "If we changed things, a certain little girl wouldn't be here. Would that suit you better?"

"No, of course not."

"Please, James," she begged. "Let's not fight. We've got enough trouble going on."

"You're right, I'm sorry. Be at departures by seven. You need to check in an hour before the flight departs."

Serenity glanced at the clock; almost four in the afternoon. Once again the day had flown by, but she still had plenty of time before needing to be at the airport.

"Don't worry. We'll be there."

"And you are certain your... friend... will be able to protect you?"

Serenity's thoughts went to Sebastian. Would he come back for her? She'd been hard on him last night and he might have easily decided she wasn't worth the hassle. But she couldn't bother James with their domestics now; he'd done enough.

"Don't worry about me," she said. "I'll be the one worrying about you. Please, remember what I said. If you see Jackson, you won't be able to arrest him. Just get the hell out of there."

"Okay. If you need me, I'm on my cell."

They hung up and Serenity was left clutching the phone to her chest. She hated fighting with him, it just felt wrong. James was her best friend—her only real friend other than Amy, and she was a friend by proxy. Serenity hated him thinking badly of her.

Once again the façade of her independence hit her. James and Amy had become her family.

She had to wonder, if someone had no real family of their own, was it so wrong to come to depend on their friends?

Jackson slunk around the side of the building like a city fox.

Every muscle quivered, his nostrils flared.

You're strong now, he told himself. *You have control.*

Though breaking into Serenity's sad little apartment would have been easy, he held himself back. His restraint wasn't only because of his desire to drag out her torture for as long as possible.

Something was wrong.

Though the scent of Serenity's blood wafted out to him like onions frying on a hot dog van, he clamped down on his hunger. His sense of smell wasn't the only sense heightened since the change. Humans gave out a field of energy—a field of *life*—which he could focus on if he directed his thoughts in their direction. But in Serenity's case, a mental hole had appeared beside her. He tried to focus on the strange space but the sensation sent spears of pain stabbing through his head, his muscles screaming like they had when he'd first burst from the ground. She seemed to have a protective aura surrounding her like a blare of static.

With all the blinds drawn, Jackson couldn't just look through the window. The temptation to simply burst through her door, shatter the wood around him, was almost overwhelming.

He couldn't; not without understanding this change in Serenity. When she'd been in the parking garage, she'd been normal. He'd been able to revel in every last part of her.

Could this thing weaken him? Make him vulnerable? Jackson didn't know but it did make him angry.

He bit down on the emotion.

Control. It was all about control now.

Hell, it had always been about control. Even when he'd been human, controlling Serenity had been the one thing that made his life worth living; his sole pleasure.

Jackson would need to kill again and soon. The taste of blood was like a drug or really good sex; the more he had, the more he wanted. To stop himself killing Serenity straight away, he needed to take out his urges on someone else.

He might not be able to get to Serenity, but he could still frighten her. Her fear would only make her blood sweeter.

He'd been wrong about his previous existence being about control. His human life had been as much about fear as his inhuman one.

Serenity's fear.

The minutes dragged like hours and Serenity found her eyes drawn back to the kitchen clock time and time again, willing the hands to both move and stay still. While she didn't want to be separated from her daughter, she was terribly aware of their vulnerability and she only wanted Elizabeth to be somewhere safe.

A waft of rotten cans and decomposing road kill crept through every gap in the windows and beneath the doors. Serenity wrinkled her nose, her attention shifting to the bin. Had she forgotten to empty the trash last night? Then she realized the smell came from outside and her stomach dropped out of its self.

Oh God, please don't let it be him.

"Mommy," said Elizabeth, her shirt sleeve clamped over her face. "Something smells bad."

"I know, honey," she said, going to her daughter on the couch. "Don't worry; it'll go away in a minute."

She curled up beside her daughter, her eyes flicking around the small apartment, terrified Jackson would materialize in the middle of the room.

A loud banging on the front door thundered through the apartment, making Serenity jump. She stifled a scream. A second later the banging came again, only this time at the back door.

Bang. Bang. Bang.

"Mommy?" Elizabeth's voice was a thin whine of fear.

Whoever pounded on the door—and Serenity didn't have any doubts about their identity—moved from the front door to the back, so fast the transition was almost immediate.

In one moment, the banging came from the back, in the next, the front. And then back again.

Serenity clutched Elizabeth in her arms, spinning from one door to the next. Elizabeth started to cry.

"Go away!" Serenity screamed. "Just leave us alone!"

All fell silent.

The atmosphere around the apartment changed. The tension—the thickening of the atmosphere—lifted. The oppressive stench lingered in the air for a moment, but soon drifted away like smoke.

He was gone.

Serenity heaved a sigh of relief and slumped down into her daughter. Elizabeth sniffed through her tears.

"He's gone now, Mommy."

"I know, sweetheart. You were so brave. Mommy's so proud of you."

Elizabeth nodded against her and Serenity kissed the top of her head.

Why hadn't Jackson burst through the door? Serenity didn't think for a second he wasn't capable of doing exactly that. She had to get Elizabeth away from here. The fear of losing her daughter overwhelmed any fear she had for her own life. The idea of any harm coming to Elizabeth was too much to stand. Just seeing Elizabeth scared hurt Serenity and if this monster got hold of her and did things to her...

Serenity shook the thought from her head. She couldn't even bear to think about it.

She needed to focus on that one thing right now: getting Elizabeth away from there. Getting from the apartment, to the cab, to the airport, would be dangerous, but she had no choice. She only hoped whatever kept Jackson out of the apartment, would also keep him away as they traveled.

Serenity gathered their things together and placed a call to a local cab company.

They sat nervously waiting for the cab to show up. The case holding Elizabeth's things sat at their feet like a patient dog.

Still Serenity couldn't shake the feeling that sending her daughter away was wrong. They shouldn't be separated.

The blare of a car horn brought Serenity to her feet. She ran to the window and pushed the slats of the blind open with her fingers. A cab waited on the street.

"Mommy?" Elizabeth grabbed her hand and Serenity glanced down at her. Fresh fear was written into her young features.

"Everything's okay, sweetie. Time to go."

Serenity grabbed her purse and Elizabeth's case. Sick with nerves, she opened her front door and they stepped out on the street. They were horribly exposed. At any moment, Jackson might attack them both. Serenity held Elizabeth's hand, keeping the girl tight to her side, pausing only long enough to lock the door behind them before they ran to the car. Serenity pulled open the door and half-pushed Elizabeth in first before climbing in behind. Quickly, she found the button to lock the doors and hit it down.

The cab driver, a middle-aged Indian man, eyed her curiously in the rear view mirror and Serenity caught his eye.

"She likes to open car doors," Serenity said, hoping he would buy her explanation and instantaneously wondering why the hell she cared.

Elizabeth sat silent in the cab. Serenity chatted inanely, trying to keep both of their spirits up.

"I can't believe you get to go in an airplane. How exciting!" Her enthusiasm was as fake as saccharine, but she couldn't seem to help herself. "And you'll help Amy with Noah, won't you? You're such a big girl now. I know Amy loves when you help her."

Elizabeth didn't answer. Her small mouth was pressed tight, holding in her emotions. She stared out as the freeway rushed past, the cars moving in the opposite direction in a blur of color.

While Serenity climbed into the cab outside of her apartment, Jackson stood one block from Serenity's house.

His senses were acute now—those of a predator—growing more powerful by the day. Smell, sight, hearing; everything was so much stronger than when he'd been human. Through the buzz of noise around him, he distinguished the sound of a rat scurrying behind a trashcan, a woman tearing a waxing strip from her leg, her gasp of pain as the strip tore the hairs from the root. He heard the clang of metal on metal as someone replaced the lid of a trashcan, and the faint sliver of a knife slicing though a vegetable.

And then there was his other sense; the one he didn't believe he possessed as a human. Jackson was tuning in on another level. He sensed the presence of people. He felt their shapes in the atmosphere, as though they left some kind of psychic mark, a dent in the environment.

With his now supernatural hearing, he'd been able to differentiate Serenity's voice from the rush of other noise around him. He heard her telling the cab driver she wanted to go to the airport, the small grunt of acknowledgement from the driver, and the sound of the key turning in the ignition.

Jackson bristled with rage. Did she think she could run away from him? He would never allow it.

This time he didn't want Serenity to be aware of his presence. In the apartment he'd had her trapped, but he didn't want to give her any chance of doing something drastic to escape him. If she died before he got his hands on her, his whole existence lost purpose.

The strange hole beside her had him worried. Perhaps it signaled another of his kind or even the one who changed him? He didn't understand what the glaring gap meant, but he would have to take things more cautiously than he had intended.

He would run again—he loved to run now. The power and strength he experienced as his legs propelled him forward.

It felt like flying.

Chapter Fifteen

In the back of the cab, Serenity approached the huge terminal, Elizabeth cuddled into her side.

Cabs and free coaches transporting tourists from the big hotels pulled up in front of the terminal, passengers spilling out of the vehicles. People pushed trolleys piled high with luggage. A woman in stiletto heels, carrying a small dog in a carry-case, teetered along the sidewalk.

As the cab pulled up, another woman lost control of her trolley. The wheels caught on the curb and her cases spilled out into the drop-off bay. No one stopped to help her pick up her bags and the woman swore and kicked out at her luggage.

The last time Serenity had been at the airport had been against her own will. Another vampire had been involved then: Madeline—the one who turned Sebastian— abducted and held her in one of the disused hangers.

The sight of the place brought back a wave of emotions and memories; none of them good. Though she made sure both she and Elizabeth had passports, they'd barely been outside of the city. Serenity hadn't been able to afford a vacation but that hadn't stopped her making sure they'd be prepared should the opportunity arise.

Serenity paid the driver and added twenty percent on top. During the journey she'd sat with Elizabeth's case on her lap, so the driver didn't even bother getting out of the cab to open the door. Annoyed, Serenity felt like asking for her tip back.

Serenity helped Elizabeth jump out of the car and took her hand. People rushed on each side. Business travelers walked brisk and determined, knowing exactly where they were headed. Tourists stood in small groups, staring at information boards, trying to figure out which way to go.

Elizabeth stayed close to Serenity's side, staring around with big, frightened eyes.

Serenity stood with the tourists for a moment, looking for which check in desk they needed. She found the United Express to Sacramento desk number and they headed into the terminal.

It didn't take her long to spot Amy. The blonde stood beside the check-in desk, Noah in her arms. Noah's stroller and a roll-along suitcase sat on the floor beside her.

As Serenity raised her hand to catch the other woman's attention, Elizabeth flung herself in Serenity's path.

"Don't make me go!" Elizabeth wailed, on her knees now, her arms wrapped around Serenity's legs. "Don't make me go, Mommy. He'll hurt you if I go."

Her words weren't meant as a threat; Elizabeth simply said what she believed to be true.

Across the terminal, Serenity looked up at Amy with beseeching eyes. Amy shook her head and held up her wrist, the one with the watch. Serenity knew what she was saying. If they didn't check in soon, they would miss their flight.

"It's going to be okay, sweetheart. Everything is going to be okay. Amy will take care of you."

"No! He'll hurt you. You need me, Mommy."

Serenity glanced back up at Amy and held out her hands. Amy settled Noah back in his stroller and grabbed her own case. She struggled across the terminal toward them.

Amy flashed a smile of sympathy at Serenity. "Hi," she said. "Hey Elizabeth!"

Elizabeth ignored her and continued to cling to her mother's legs.

"Where's James?" Serenity asked, noticing his absence.

"He's still working."

"What? He let you guys come here on your own? What if something had happened to you on the way?"

"We were fine. We caught a cab just like you did. He's got to find this guy. You know James wouldn't let any of us come to any harm. He'll always do everything he can to stop this S.O.B."

Serenity's heart sank. "But I told him to stay away!"

"It's his job, Serenity! What else was he supposed to do? I'm frightened for him too, you know?"

"Of course you are."

Amy being angry with her made Serenity feel wretched. She didn't know how much James had told Amy about her past, but she read the other woman's thoughts on her face as clearly as if she had spoken them out loud;

Her ex-husband has murdered countless people. How could she be married to someone like that? What does that say about her?

Serenity didn't blame Amy for being mad at her. Amy was as frightened as Serenity, and it was easy for her to blame Serenity for dragging her family into this.

"I'm so sorry, Amy."

153

Amy didn't respond, instead she squatted in front of Elizabeth. "Come on honey, it's time to go." Elizabeth continued to sob and hug Serenity's leg. "I bet you'd like some chocolate on the plane."

Amy had settled for plain bribery to get Elizabeth to calm down. This would normally work, but Elizabeth didn't even acknowledge her. Switching tactics, Amy tried to pry Elizabeth from her mother's leg, but Elizabeth only clung tighter.

Noah started to wail in his stroller.

"Go on, sweetheart," said Serenity, rubbing her daughter's back. "You're going to have so much fun." But even saying the words make her sick to her stomach. How could she send her hysterical daughter away?

It's for her own good. There's too much danger here.

Serenity felt the eyes of strangers upon them. Two screaming, hysterical children always grabbed people's attention. Some people purposefully tried not to look at them, obviously embarrassed on their behalf, but others stared openly. Noah's wails built into a crescendo and Amy turned her attention back to her own child.

What was she supposed to do? She could hardly expect Amy to take Elizabeth like this? Serenity doubted the airport staff would even allow Amy to take a hysterical child she wasn't related to on the plane.

Amy glanced at her watch again.

"It's okay, just go," Serenity told her, her stomach sinking.

Her hopes of sending Elizabeth somewhere safe vanished before her eyes. Yet was part of her was relieved. She didn't want Elizabeth to go, but she was terrified of her staying.

"What about you and Elizabeth?" Amy asked, her blue eyes wide with confusion and worry. "I can't go and leave you both here." She lowered her voice as best she could amongst the screaming children. "After all, we're running away from your ex. It seems nuts that we're going and you're both staying here."

"I don't know what else to do," Serenity said in desperation.

"Come with us! Elizabeth will come if you do."

She shook her head. "I can't. My coming will defeat the whole purpose. It's me he's after. Being near you will only attract him to you."

"Oh, Serenity," Amy grasped Serenity's hand. "You'll be safe won't you? I'm so frightened for you." She glanced down at Elizabeth. "For both of you."

Serenity bit her lip, trying to hold back the tears. "We'll be safe," she said, hoping she spoke the truth.

From the other side of the terminal, Jackson watched the two women talk.

There she was, the bitch who stole his life.

Rage powered through him, but he bit down on the emotion once again. When he'd been human he'd always been able to contain the rage. He'd been able to hold his temper until the perfect time, dragging out his pent up fury until she quivered with fear, strung like a piece of elastic.

Seeing her now made him furious. Did she really think she would just be able to continue with her life? She had fucking *murdered* him! Did she think she would get away with it?

How dare she walk around as if nothing had happened? The thought that she believed she had beaten him made him livid.

A low growl emitted from somewhere deep in his chest.

A young man walking past jumped at the sound. He flung a glance Jackson's way and then quickly turned and hurried off.

Jackson needed to watch himself. He didn't want to attract even more attention than he already had.

Around him people shied away, grimacing. One woman even put her shirt sleeve over her mouth and nose, trying to stifle the smell.

He carried the stench of death with him. It was his one downfall; the thing that made him standout from the crowd, made him noticeable. The smell was part of who he was now—ingrained into his flesh like his DNA—and wasn't something he'd ever be able to wash off.

Jackson doubted anyone would approach him. His presence instilled emotions of both fright and embarrassment in the people around him. He might catch the attention of airport security, but he was fast and strong. He would do exactly what he wanted.

He focused his attention back to Serenity. Whatever had been protecting her in the apartment was still with her. Some kind of strange aura surrounded her, as though he needed glasses to see and couldn't focus on her properly. Staring too hard hurt his head.

It was easier to focus his thoughts on the other woman; a short, dumpy blonde with too many curves for his taste. Nevertheless, he still imagined sinking his teeth into her flesh. The rush of her blood would be sweet and warm. The thought made Jackson drool.

The two women obviously cared about each other. The hurt it would cause Serenity to witness her friend mauled and dismembered would be make him feel better.

Were the women getting on a flight together?

Their plans made no difference to him. If he attacked them here and now, what would be the worst that could happen? Could the thing seeming to be shielding Serenity harm him?

A frission of fear trembled through him and he growled again. Fear wasn't part of who he was now.

The two women embraced and Serenity turned and started to walk out of the terminal. Jackson was torn. He wanted to follow Serenity, but her time hadn't come yet. He would take everything from her before killing her, so instead he followed the person he intended to be next on the list.

The short blonde pushed a stroller towards the check-in desk.

Jackson waited and watched.

He would need to get to her before she boarded the plane. He didn't want to start ripping her to shreds in front of all of these people. The security staff would have guns. While Jackson suspected their bullets would not affect him, he wasn't prepared to take the risk.

The woman would be alone at some point. He only needed to bide his time.

At security, people removed belts and shoes, passing their possessions through huge metal detectors, pushing bags and laptops through scanners. Uniformed men and women patted the travelers down on the other side.

Using his speed, Jackson slipped quickly and silently behind one of the operators doing security checks. The man, middle-aged and overweight, glanced up from the monitor he was watching, his nose wrinkled in disgust, his eyes narrowing. He looked over his shoulder and suspiciously at the people queuing to pass through the detector.

At the gates, people shopped, picking up last minute souvenirs. Some sat in the chain-restaurants—Garfunkles and Starbucks—eating or drinking coffee, wasting time before getting their boarding calls.

Standing still, Jackson felt exposed. People shot him nervous glances and gave him a wide berth.

Jackson caught sight of his reflection in a mirrored window of one of the restaurants. His too long hair was lank and hung down by his jaw. His face was different and not just because he no longer wore—or needed to wear—the glasses that had adorned his face for most of his adult life. His complexion was white and pallid, every pore and acne scar magnified. Dark marks shadowed beneath even darker, haunted eyes.

Dead.

He looked like he was dead.

Jackson thought he should be shocked, but somehow his appearance felt right. His outside now matched his inside. When he'd been alive he'd been a lanky, geeky-type. No one ever suspected the cruelty, the evil that had resided within him. In many ways his mild appearance had been his blessing, but now he took pleasure in what he was.

Where was the blonde?

His eyes scoured the terminal, searching for her. He knew she would be here, after all, where else did she have to go.

Jackson spotted her, heading towards the ladies room. Moving quickly, he closed in on her, breathing in her scent. The skin of her throat and her bare shoulders was pale and smooth. A fat toddler cried in the pram and she stopped still and bent over, distracted by the child.

How would the baby taste? He wondered. *Fat, juicy and innocent.*

Jackson smiled—a horrific sight. The toddler was an unexpected bonus to his meal.

"Hey!" The shout made Jackson look up.

Security guards, two of them, ran at a jog toward him. Both of them had a hand on the pistol at their sides.

Were they suspicious of his behavior and the way he looked? Or was it something more? Perhaps they had been notified because of the other murders. Despite his change in appearance, Jackson still resembled his old self enough to be recognized from a photograph, if one had been issued for his arrest. Serenity might have told the police about him, though he had to question exactly what she would have said. After all, she was the one who had killed him. What exactly could she report to the cops?

Damn it.

Jackson hesitated on the balls of his feet, torn between making his escape and killing the woman. He roared. The sound echoed through the terminal in an inhuman howl. The blonde screamed in response and threw herself across the pram, protecting her child with her body as though Jackson were a bomb or a fast moving vehicle.

Jackson spun from one side to the next, indecisive.

Suddenly he decided what he wanted most and, as though she weighed no more than a child, he reached down and picked up the woman and flung her to the ground. The back of her head smacked against the hard floor, but terror and misery reflected in her eyes as she reached up toward him in a silent plea for the life of her child before she lost consciousness.

"Freeze!" The security guards yelled, drawing their weapons. They both pointed the black barrels toward Jackson's head.

The baby's wails were now screams of fury, its plump face red and screwed up in anger.

Quickly, his movements a blur, Jackson reached down to the chubby child, his vile hands touching the baby's soft white skin.

Bang! Bang!

The shots rang out. All around, people screamed and dived to the ground. Jackson jolted backward twice, both slugs hitting him in the upper torso; one in the shoulder, the other above his ribcage, piercing his lung.

The shots threw him away from the baby, but he experienced no pain from their impact. He stood, hunched over; amazed someone had actually had the nerve to shoot him.

"Hold it right there," the officer said again, his weapon still held.

Another two security officers ran down the concourse toward them, their hands on their own weapons.

Jackson roared again and leapt, like a huge wild animal, into the air. Another shot rang out, but this one missed, and he landed on the ground, several hundred feet away from the officers. Their mouths hung open, unable to believe what they'd seen. Jackson did not spare them another thought.

He turned on his heels and ran.

Chapter Sixteen

By the time the cab turned down Serenity's street, night had fallen.

As the vehicle approached her building, she frowned and leaned forward in her seat. A figure stood outside her front door. Her heart leapt in alarm, but then she reasoned with herself. Jackson wouldn't just be standing there.

So was it James waiting for her? They grew closer and she realized the tall, broad build was all-wrong. Her visitor leaned against her small porch with an uneasy grace, arms folded across their chest, one ankle hooked over the other.

Serenity's heart clambered into her throat and she swallowed hard.

Her hopes of the vampire showing up after dark had been correct.

Sebastian.

Serenity pulled Elizabeth closer. Though hugely relieved to see him, she also felt sick with nerves. There was no hiding Elizabeth from him now; father and daughter were about to meet each other for the first time. Of course she could lie about Elizabeth's identity, but what would be the point? Some part of her wondered if, on a sub-conscious level, they would recognize each other anyway. Perhaps part of their shared blood would connect them.

She'd put off telling Elizabeth about her father for such a long time, telling herself she was waiting for the perfect time.

Finally, after all these years, that time had arrived.

The cab pulled up outside the apartment and Elizabeth peered out of the window.

"Mommy? Who is that man?"

A small smile tugged at Serenity's lips. "He's a friend, sweetheart. An old friend."

She took money from her purse, leaned forward and paid the driver. Sebastian stepped off the threshold and took a couple of steps toward the car.

Serenity opened the cab door and started to climb out. Sebastian approached her, his face shadowed in the streetlight. Again, how much his appearance had changed in the past few years struck her. His eyes were deeper, darker, his cheeks hollowed beneath his cheekbones. He seemed so much more dangerous than before. Serenity hadn't thought it possible for a vampire to change, at least physically, but what did she know?

Elizabeth's small hand appeared on the car's doorframe and Sebastian stopped. Confusion flickered across his face. His head tilted to one side like a curious animal as he took in the sight of the child and what her presence meant.

Serenity turned and took Elizabeth's hand, and the little girl jumped down on the sidewalk.

Jackson might attack them at any moment, and, despite her overwhelming emotions, Serenity remained hyper-alert, taking in every detail of the street. As always when Sebastian was around, the normal world made themselves scarce. Lights illuminated her neighbor's homes, but the street itself remained quiet. Did people know to stay away? Subconsciously were people aware of something unnatural in their vicinity?

The deserted street felt haunted and did nothing to improve Serenity's nerves. Every dark corner contained the possibility of a threat, but Sebastian's presence reassured her. She doubted Jackson lurked nearby without Sebastian knowing.

Sebastian's green eyes moved between her and Elizabeth, drinking them both in.

Serenity clutched Elizabeth's hand.

"I'm glad you're here," she said.

"I couldn't stay away. Not anymore."

Hearing his words, her heart filled with hope. Maybe things would all turn out all right?

She glanced down at her daughter. Elizabeth stared up at Sebastian with open curiosity. They couldn't have this conversation standing out in the street.

"You should come inside," she said.

Sebastian's eyes never left Elizabeth. "Yes, you're right. Let's go in."

Still holding Elizabeth's hand, Serenity walked up the small pathway to her front door. Sebastian followed close behind. He was on edge. Serenity sensed tension vibrating from him like static electricity. She didn't know if his disposition was because of her, because of Elizabeth, or because Jackson might be near.

Sebastian quickly made the reason for his tension clear.

"He's been here," he said. "I can smell him."

Elizabeth spoke so quietly at first Serenity didn't hear her, but then her brain pieced together her daughter's words: "Me too."

Serenity glanced down at Elizabeth. She didn't seem to be scared. Instead, she looked determined, as much as a four-year-old could.

Serenity fished her keys from her purse and slotted the front door key in the lock. "He left his wedding ring on the window ledge for me to find." Her head was bent, concentrating on getting the door open. The door swung open and she glanced back up to find Sebastian's eyes glowing yellow in the darkness.

The vampire looked furious; his jaw set, his lips a thin line.

The sight shocked her. So many years had passed; she'd almost forgotten what he was. She realized in her memories she had almost made him human. It only took the momentary sight of those eyes for her to remember he was not.

Serenity didn't want Elizabeth to see him like that. Elizabeth's first memory of her father shouldn't be one of fear.

Serenity reached out and took Sebastian's hand. His large palm felt cool and smooth beneath her fingertips. The intense color of his eyes melted at her touch, fading back to green.

"Come inside," she said.

The invitation had nothing to do with any old myths about vampires not being able to cross a doorstep without being invited. As far as Serenity knew, vampires could enter any home they wished. The thought didn't bring her any comfort.

The three of them walked into the apartment and Serenity led him through to the kitchen-diner.

Sebastian seemed uncomfortable in the cramped surroundings and Serenity's cheeks colored as he took in her cheap possessions. Her small couch was sunken and shabby, the kitchen table worn and scarred. Sebastian had money and she was ashamed at her lack of it.

Then she realized Sebastian's awkwardness had nothing to do with her poverty. He didn't know what to say in front of the child.

Serenity took control of the situation and smiled down at her daughter. "Her name is Elizabeth."

One of Elizabeth's arms curled loosely around Serenity's leg. Big dark eyes studied Sebastian with seriousness beyond her years. Dark, spiral curls sprung down to her shoulders.

"She's yours, Sebastian." Serenity's eyes filled with tears.

He gaped at her, his square jaw dropping open, his green eyes wide. "What? How did that happen?"

"I don't know," she said, incredulous. "I guess it happened in exactly the same way it normally happens. You were there..."

He shook his head. "No, I mean... because of who I am." He chose his words carefully, aware of the little girl still standing beside them. "How is it possible?"

She stared at him, searching his face for his emotions. Reading a vampire was almost impossible; they simply didn't portray their emotions the same way humans did. They had too many years to learn to control them.

"I don't have the answer to that," she said.

"No, of course not." He glanced back down at Elizabeth. "And you're sure," he said. "There is no possibility that Jackson..."

"Don't even say it," she shot back. "Do you think I would put something like this upon my daughter if I wasn't one-hundred percent certain?"

Sebastian crouched to Elizabeth's level. The breadth of his shoulders beneath his overcoat made him seem more real, more solid than ever, despite the apparent weight loss. His presence felt too big for the relatively small room.

Serenity took hold of her daughter's hand and gently pulled her in front. "This is your daddy, Elizabeth. Do you want to say hello?"

The little girl slowly walked up to the big man and held out her hand. He took her hand, her small fingers appearing so fragile in his grip.

"Mommy cries about you at night," Elizabeth said.

Serenity couldn't look at him, her heart thumped and her cheeks flushed even deeper.

"I've cried over her too," he said, still not making eye contact with Serenity, both of them now communicating through their child.

"Why did you leave us?" Elizabeth's small, high-pitched voice spoke the words Serenity asked herself every night since he left.

He shook his head. "I thought I was doing the right thing."

Elizabeth smiled. "That's okay then."

Serenity reached down and ruffled her soft hair. She wished her own heart were so forgiving.

"Can I watch television?" Elizabeth asked, her small face turned up to her mother.

"Sure, honey," Serenity smiled back. "Just keep the sound down, okay?"

Serenity gave a slight shake of her head. Elizabeth's acceptance of the situation amazed her. After all she had been through; Elizabeth seemed the most relaxed she'd been all day.

Though the hour was late, almost ten o'clock, Serenity had no intention of sending Elizabeth off to bed. Even with Sebastian with them, Jackson knew where they lived. She wasn't going to allow Elizabeth out of her sight, not even to sleep in the next room.

As Elizabeth took up her position back on the couch, Serenity wrapped her fingers around Sebastian's wrist and pulled him into the small section of the kitchen. The distance wasn't much, but Elizabeth quickly became reabsorbed in the Disney movie, paying no attention to her parents.

"I'm so sorry I left you with this," Sebastian said, gesturing around. "I assumed you would be fine. You had the house, and of course I had no idea about Elizabeth."

"No," she pressed her lips together. The words, filled with the bitterness trapped in her heart since the day he left her on the pier, sprung from her mouth. "You didn't stick around long enough to find out."

His eyes opened wide but she didn't give him the chance to speak.

"As for the house," she continued. "I couldn't live there after what happened."

"You know why I left," Sebastian said. "I had no choice. But I wish I'd known. I never imagined your life would end up like this."

An old familiar pain and anger speared within her. He'd had a choice and he'd chosen to leave. She'd begged him to take her with him, to make her like him, but he refused. Her life might not be flash, but she had supported herself and raised their daughter on her own. She was proud of what she had achieved. She didn't need him coming back and making her feel her life wasn't good enough.

Serenity bit down on her anger. She didn't want to start a fight.

"I didn't want your money, Sebastian. We might not be well off, but we've managed."

"You should never have needed to manage. I'm sorry."

"It's too late for sorry."

She'd loved him once. Did that love still exist? At that moment she only felt anger and bitterness toward him. She didn't hate him but his abandonment still hurt. Yet she had to ask herself, if she didn't love him, wouldn't she be over him by now? Even before he turned up again, Sebastian filled her thoughts and dreams. Maybe her preoccupation was simply because of what he was? After all, not every day did a vampire, a creature supposed to only exist in horror stories, come into your life. Yet when she thought about Sebastian, she hadn't thought about him being a vampire. Instead, she remembered how he'd made her feel—as though she could be anyone she wanted. Somehow, he'd given her the strength to stand up for herself.

If she had never met him, she would still be with Jackson and Elizabeth would never have existed. That wouldn't even be a life worth living.

Serenity glanced over to find Elizabeth asleep on the couch.

"You don't have to stay here," Sebastian said. "I still own the house in the hills. You can both come with me now."

Once again Serenity felt like she was running away. She hated having to rely on Sebastian to help her, as though she was weak and useless. But what choice did she have? She wasn't going to stay here and put them at risk just because of her pride.

"Okay," she agreed. "But we need to come up with some kind of plan to end this. I won't let Jackson make me a victim again."

Her voice was fierce, her mouth set in a thin, determined line.

Sebastian studied her for a moment. "You've changed," he said, quietly. "You seem… harder."

She lifted her face to him. "I have to be."

Sebastian looked away.

Was it guilt she saw? Did he feel guilty about leaving them?

She couldn't imagine Sebastian ever admitting he was wrong—that his decision had been the wrong one—but the idea that he felt bad about what had happened made her soften toward him.

"We should go now," he said.

"I'll grab some things for myself and wake Elizabeth." The packed case still sat on the floor. "I guess she's already got everything she needs."

"Don't wake her," Sebastian said, lightly touching her arm. "I can carry her like that."

Elizabeth was fast asleep, her lips slightly parted, her curls crushed against her cheek.

"Okay. Just give me a minute."

Serenity went into her bedroom and grabbed a couple of changes of clothing. In the bathroom, she picked up her toiletries bag and threw in her toothbrush and a comb. She didn't know how long they would be gone, but she prayed this would all be over within a couple of days. Either Sebastian would find Jackson, or Jackson would find them.

One way or another, it would be over.

Sebastian scooped Elizabeth up in his arms and the sight melted Serenity's heart. The little girl looked tiny cradled against Sebastian's broad frame and she had to hold herself back from walking right up to him and wrapping her arms around them both.

Together they headed out. Serenity held open the front door for them, but the phone rang, making her jump.

"Damn it!" Serenity paused, indecisive. The phone continued to ring—insistent.

"Just leave it," said Sebastian.

"I can't. It might be important." She closed the door again and sighed, her head bent. Whoever was calling wasn't going to give up and Serenity had a horrible feeling the news wouldn't be good.

She went back to the kitchen. Sebastian lurked in the kitchen doorway, Elizabeth still cradled in his arms. The girl's head lolled to one side, her mouth open, clutched in the depths of sleep.

Serenity answered the phone and James spoke before she even had the chance to say 'hello'.

"He was at the airport. He hurt Amy and tried to take Noah."

"What?" Tears of fear pricked like hot needles at the back of her eyes.

"They shot him but he got away. The bullets didn't seem to affect him. Jesus, Serenity. It's madness down here. People are talking. They shot him twice, at close range, but then he jumped into the air like a fucking animal and ran away."

"Oh my God."

Sebastian was watching her, his face grim. Serenity understood that with his hearing he heard everything James said.

"What about Amy?" she asked. "Is she all right? He didn't hurt Noah, did he?" Her voice increased in pitch as she spoke, and she forced herself to calm down. She didn't want to wake Elizabeth and upset her.

"Amy's got a concussion," James's voice sounded thick with unshed tears. "They're keeping her in hospital overnight. Noah's fine, he's asleep."

"I'm so sorry. Can I do anything?"

"No, just get somewhere safe."

"We are."

James paused, "Is he with you?"

Serenity glanced at Sebastian and gripped the phone tighter. James wasn't talking about Jackson.

"Yes," she said. "He's going to take us somewhere Jackson can't find us. What about you? Are you going to go somewhere safe?"

"He hurt my family," James growled. "I'm not just going to let him get away with it."

"This isn't a 'him'!" she said, her panic running high. "This is an 'it'. He's not human any more—you can't fight him. Please don't try. If you try to go after him, he will kill you."

"The entire LAPD is after Jackson. I intend on being there when they get him."

She wanted to reach through the phone and shake him. His male bravado was taking over his common sense.

"Watch the security cameras footage," she said. "Make sure people see what they are dealing with. They need to know these things exist now. They need to understand the world is not as clear cut as we've grown up to believe."

James spoke, "They've watched the CCTV. They think he's on PCP or something. If I start spouting about vampires and zombies—or whatever the hell Jackson is—they'll lock me up in the loony bin."

"Maybe that would be the best place for you," she said, desperate now. "At least then you'd be safe." She took a deep breath. "Listen to me, James. He went after Amy because he saw me with her. Jackson attacking her wasn't a coincidence. He must have been at the airport, and we don't know where he's gone now."

James fell silent again as he considered her words. "Do you think he'll go to the hospital to finish what he started?" he asked.

"I don't know. You need to hide—all of you. The three of you need to go somewhere Jackson would never think of looking for you."

"If you're telling me the police won't be able to stop him, who will?"

Serenity glanced at Sebastian. He gave her a tiny, almost imperceptible nod.

"Elizabeth's father."

"I hope you're right, Serenity. But in the meantime it simply isn't within my power to stop the LAPD from going after him. I'll make sure Amy and Noah go somewhere safe, but I still have a job to do."

Her heart sank, knowing she would never convince him not to try to catch Jackson. Tears threatened once again and she put her hand against her eyes, as though she could physically hold back the tears. She couldn't stand the thought of losing him, of Amy losing her husband, and Noah growing up without a father. It would all be her fault. She had brought this monster into all of their lives. She was like a poison infecting everyone around her; she didn't deserve good people in her life.

Serenity caught sight of her sleeping daughter and forced herself to squash the destructive thought pattern. It was all too easy to fall back into the person she had once been, and she wouldn't allow that to happen. She had Elizabeth in her life and she needed to be strong for her sake.

"You still there?" James's voice startled her from her thoughts.

"Yeah, sorry."

"Is there a number I can reach you on?"

Sebastian shook his head.

"Not yet, no. But I'll get a disposable cell and call you with the number. In the meantime, I think you're all best keeping well away from me."

"Okay." James wasn't going to argue.

"Stay safe," she said.

"You too."

She hung up the phone, but the dread and desperation didn't leave her. She swallowed back tears again. Amy and Noah must have been so frightened. Thinking of Jackson touching the little boy hurt her deep inside.

"Oh, God, this is all such a mess," she cried.

Sebastian was beside her in an instant. With one arm he held Elizabeth, the other he wrapped around her, crushing their daughter between them. Serenity allowed herself to lean against him, her cheek pressed against his chest.

"He won't hurt you," Sebastian said. "I won't allow it."

Chapter Seventeen

Being back at Sebastian's house was much like being back at the airport. Serenity hadn't realized she'd avoided the places that would remind her of him.

The memories washed over her as though she'd stepped back in time. She remembered the staircase where Madeline told her about Sebastian's real identity, the gravel she'd run across, trying to escape, the bed where Sebastian held her while she slept.

The house remained as impressive as before. Embedded deep in the hills, the property was both private and imposing. A ten-foot stone wall ran around the property and electric gates barred the way to visitors. A huge double wooden door marked the entrance to the house. Inside, the kitchen and living room were an open plan layout and a huge curved staircase wound through the centre, leading up to the first floor.

Without asking, Sebastian carried Elizabeth up the staircase to one of the bedrooms. Serenity followed closely, not wanting to lose sight of her child.

Smooth cream walls rose on each side of the large bedroom, huge thick drapes covered the tall windows. Behind the four-poster bed, a textured paper of white and silver ferns papered the wall.

With tenderness, Sebastian crossed the room and laid Elizabeth down on the bed. Elizabeth appeared so tiny in the giant bed, so vulnerable. Instinctively, she curled up on her side, her hand beneath her head.

Sebastian stood over her for a moment. His broad frame only helped dwarf his daughter. He hesitated, his hand held above her forehead, and then reached down and gently brushed a curl of hair off her face.

Watching him, Serenity thought her heart may break. To think she had convinced herself it was best for Elizabeth to never meet her father.

How would she ever begin to explain what he was to Elizabeth? She wondered if they might be able to figure out a way for Elizabeth to never find out. But Elizabeth would realize something was wrong if her father never ate and she only ever saw him at night. How could she live a normal childhood with Sebastian in her life?

The future was fraught with questions. She would not allow Elizabeth to be hurt by Sebastian's identity, but she wanted Elizabeth to have Sebastian in her life. Bizarrely her mind went to other 'unusual' families—gay couples, broken homes—but this was hardly the same thing. Sebastian should not even exist.

Except he did exist and he wasn't the only one. One day all the things people believed to be fiction would be proved to be reality, and then they would all be forced to rethink the definition of fantasy. Maybe the human race needed to adapt?

Sebastian turned to Serenity, his finger at his lips.

She smiled. Elizabeth was sound asleep and for the first time in the past forty-eight hours, peace settled around Serenity's shoulders.

"What now?" she asked quietly as Sebastian ushered her out of the room.

"I think we have a lot to talk about." His eyes flicked toward Elizabeth.

Together they walked back down the staircase. At the bottom of the stairs, two plush couches in dark brown leather faced each other. A glass coffee table sat between them, a cream wool rug lay beneath.

Serenity slid onto the soft leather and Sebastian sat facing her.

"She doesn't look like me," he said. "She's you through and through." He paused and then glanced up at her. "I'm glad about that."

"I can see you in her. She has your confidence."

Sebastian smiled and shook his head. "I still can't believe this has happened."

"You can believe," she said. "There's nothing like having the proof sleeping in your bed."

"She is beautiful, but is she..?" Though he couldn't finish his sentence, Serenity knew what he was trying to say.

"Yes, she's normal. She's highly intelligent and has an unnerving way of knowing what other people are thinking, but otherwise she is as human as I am."

"I didn't know such a thing was possible," he said, shaking his head in disbelief. "Before I left, I wish I had known."

"There's no way you could have. I didn't find out myself until about four months after. I was so caught up in everything that happened; that I had missed my periods didn't even occur to me. Only when my clothes started to get tighter did the penny drop."

"My God, Serenity," he said in awe. His green eyes flashed yellow for the briefest of moments.

"I was so scared," she admitted, her head hung. "Scared she wouldn't survive, or something would be wrong with her, but after I gave birth I realized she was perfect."

"She is perfect," he said.

A question burned on her lips, something stupid that wouldn't achieve anything, but yet she couldn't help herself. Like having a sore inside her mouth—however much investigating with her tongue hurt, she couldn't quite bring herself to leave it well alone.

"If you'd have known about the pregnancy," she asked. "Would you have stayed?"

Sebastian studied her face for a moment. It didn't matter how he answered—yes or no—he would still be in the wrong.

"If I had of known about your situation," he said, carefully. "I would have come back."

"So you'd come back for Elizabeth, but not me?" Bitterness fired within her.

To be jealous of her daughter was so wrong. What type of woman would be jealous of her own flesh and blood?

"Elizabeth changes *everything*," he said, leaning forward, his elbows rested upon his knees. "I didn't stay with you because I believed you'd still be able to lead a happy life. I never thought my being in your past would affect your present. All I ever wanted was for you to have a normal life."

She stared at him, her face impassive.

"What more do you want me to say?" he said. "I would have come back, because with Elizabeth, you'd never be completely free."

Serenity closed her eyes and pressed the balls of her palms into her eye sockets.

"So you wanted to be involved in her life? But you didn't want to be involved in mine?"

"It's different, Serenity. Can't you see that?"

She could, but she couldn't bring herself to admit it. The pain sat in her chest like a tiny nugget of red-hot coal burning within her.

"I don't need you any more, Sebastian," she said. "Neither of us need you."

He stared at her, the hurt rippling across his face like wind on a lake. Then his features hardened, his eyes narrowed, his full mouth compressed into a tight line. The sharp, dangerous look he had acquired during his time away returned. He was a creature who killed, and he wasn't going to take any of her bullshit.

"You do need me, though," he snarled, his teeth flashing. "If I dumped you back at your house, Jackson would kill you both."

Serenity flinched, but she wouldn't allow herself to be intimidated. She had spent years living under the wrath of bullying men and had no intention of going back.

She leapt to her feet, her hands on her hips. "Do it then!"

In a dramatic flourish, she spun away and stormed up the staircase. As she climbed each step she expected—and hoped for—the stirring of air signifying him coming to stop her, for the blur of movement as he appeared in front of her. But none came and he left her to storm up the stairs alone.

Behind her, the room felt as empty as crypt.

Only as she cracked open the bedroom door and saw Elizabeth still sleeping so peacefully, did her heartbreak. She wanted to change the past, she wanted for him to turn around and tell her leaving her was the worst mistake he ever made, but that wasn't going to happen. He was single-minded and resolute, and he would never admit he'd been wrong, even if deep down he thought it. Sebastian might be a vampire, but he was still as stubborn and pig-headed as any man she had ever known.

She turned and stared at the door, giving him a few minutes, still hoping she would hear his gentle knock. When nothing happened she sighed and turned away. He wouldn't dump them back at the house, but now she felt awkward being in his home.

Serenity stood above Elizabeth for a moment, watching her daughter sleep. Angrily she choked back the tears, furious at herself for letting Sebastian get to her so easily. She had so much more to worry about than him.

She wanted to curl up on the bed beside Elizabeth, wrap her arm around her daughter's tiny waist and snuggle her face into her hair, but at least twenty-four hours had passed since she had last taken a shower, and she was hot and sticky and uncomfortable.

An en-suite bathroom adjoined the room.

Serenity headed toward the bathroom, peeling off her shirt as she walked. A free standing shower took up the corner, a huge curved screen of glass separating it from the rest of the room. A double-wash basin stood opposite, a large mirror covering the wall above. Small cream tiles covered both the floor and the walls. Like the rest of the house, the bathroom was decorated like a plush hotel.

Serenity wriggled out of her jeans and leaned into the cubicle, pulling the lever, turning the shower on. Water thundered into the tray.

Standing in her bra and panties, she stared at herself in the mirror. Dark bruises sat like shadows beneath her eyes. No color adorned her cheeks or lips; she appeared to be as much a vampire as Sebastian.

Scars marked her body, her reminder of her life with Jackson. The thin raised line across her ribs, where he'd cut her with a piece of glass after she smashed his whiskey tumbler. A circle where he'd burned her with a cigarette.

Though her deepest and most painful scars were internal, she hated the visible ones more. Jackson had branded her. The marks make sure that every time she looked at herself she would be reminded of him and the things he did to her.

Carrying a child had also left its mark; her breasts no longer as high or full, her hips a little bigger, her stomach more rounded. These changes had been caused by the thing she loved the most in the world and she would not change them for anything.

Hot steam rose from the shower, fogging the mirror, disguising her reflection.

Serenity sighed and turned away.

She slipped out of her underwear and stepped into the shower. The water was hot, almost on the side of scalding, but she did nothing to adjust the temperature. She deserved the pain.

Finally she gave into the tears. She turned her face up to the shower, allowing the water to stream down her face. Overwhelmed, her legs gave out beneath her and she cried, crouching down in the shower, the hot water pummeling her head, shoulders and back, flushing her skin red. She cried for the horror that Jackson had been, and the monster he had become. She cried for the terror she felt at the possibility of losing her daughter, and the turmoil she was in because of Sebastian being back in her life.

"Serenity?"

The deep voice startled her from her remorse. Serenity lifted her head to find Sebastian standing on the other side of the screen. Her embarrassment and self-consciousness made her forget her misery. In her crouched position, she used her arms to cover her modesty.

"What the hell are you doing?" she exclaimed.

He didn't answer. Instead, he opened the screen door and stepped in fully clothed. He bent down to her and she put out an arm to ward him off, but he ignored the gesture and lifted her to her feet.

Water soaked through his clothes, matting his hair to his forehead. He held her against him, but she fought, shoving him away, feeling humiliated and exposed.

"Get off me," she said, pushing against his chest. "Leave me alone. I don't need you anymore."

He was so much stronger and she couldn't budge him. He stared down at her, an intensity on his face, a fierceness in his green eyes. Knowing she couldn't fight him physically, she stared back up, challenging.

Sebastian bent his head to hers. His lips pressed soft and cool against hers, drawing in the heat of her skin. At first she resisted, but his mouth moved, firm yet tender. Their tongues touched and immediately the pace of the kiss changed, hungry, devouring. She reached up, her arms wrapping around his neck, her fingers lacing into the soft wet hair. She no longer cared about her nudity, her breasts pressing against his still-clothed chest.

His hands pressed against her lower back, just above the curve of her buttocks, molding her against him.

Their breathing came, hard and fast. A fire raged up inside her; she was desperate for him. With urgency, she pulled at his soaking clothing. He quickly and expertly removed them, dropping them on the floor outside the shower.

Serenity marveled at him standing naked before her. Had he always been so beautiful? He was like a sculpture carved out of marble by the most talented hands. It was impossible for her to not reach out and touch the smooth skin, her hand tracing down the hard ridges of his abs.

Sebastian caught her hand and tugged her close, lowering his face for another kiss.

"Elizabeth...?" She spoke into his mouth. She didn't want her daughter to come in and catch them.

"She's asleep," he whispered back. "I'll hear her if she wakes."

His fingers touched her cheek, tracing her jawbone, down to her throat. His cold touch was like an elixir to the scalding water. He worked his way down, the palms of his hands against her breasts, his fingers teasing her nipples to hard points. She clutched at him, her face buried in his neck, gasping. With tenderness, he reached down between her legs and gently pushed a finger inside her.

Serenity moaned and held him close, hiding her face against him. This was the first time anyone had touched her intimately for years and her reaction made her self-conscious.

Sebastian pulled her away from him and she lifted her face. "You don't need to hide from me," he said.

She kissed him again and he wrapped his arms around her thighs, lifting her up. Her back slammed against the tiles, the water still rushing around their ears. There had been tenderness before now, but when entered her it was with force and she returned the need. Sebastian was holding back; his strength meant he might easily hurt her without realizing it. For Serenity, this was the outlet she had been desperate for.

She took out all of her anger and disappointment in this single act. She scratched her nails down his back, her hips hard against his, her mouth crushing. She bit the skin of his neck and shoulders, hard enough to hurt and he gasped in surprise, pain and pleasure, all mixed into one. She wanted to hurt him.

She wanted to love him.

Afterward, he picked her up. With his free arm, he threw the soft towels on the floor and laid her down on top. He lay down beside her, propped up on one elbow, looking down at her.

Serenity glanced towards the closed door. "Is she all right? Do you think she heard us?"

Sebastian shook his head. "She's still asleep. I can hear her breathing." He kissed her mouth. "Don't worry."

His fingers traced her curves; her belly slightly more rounded than before, her hips with their faint silvery lines. They were signs of her humanity, of her fragility.

He put his head on her chest, and she reached up and touched his damp hair.

"Am I ugly to you, now?" she asked, embarrassed.

He shook his head against her. "You'll never be ugly."

She wished they could stay here, hiding from the world, with their child sleeping peacefully in the room next door.

Still damp, the cool of his skin against her, Serenity shivered.

"You're cold," he said, lifting his head, immediately concerned. He grabbed another towel from the rack and wrapped her up like a child.

"What do we do now?" she asked, unsure if she was talking about Jackson, or their relationship.

Nothing had changed. No, that was wrong. Something *had* changed. She had Elizabeth now. Years earlier, she had begged Sebastian to change her, but he'd refused, determined he would not turn her into a monster. She'd had nothing else in her life back then, no reason to want to stay human. But now she had Elizabeth and the little girl was Serenity's priority.

She wanted to stay with Sebastian, but only as a human. What happened in the future would have to be dealt with then. They had already wasted the last three four years. If he wanted to be with her then she wouldn't allow them to waste any more.

"You know I'm going to have to leave you here alone," he said. "I must try to find Jackson."

She nodded.

"He won't know to come here. He won't find you."

Serenity bit her lip. "I'm scared," she admitted. "I'm scared for all of us."

"Don't be," he said, bending his head to hers. "I swear I'll protect you—both of you."

Her heart swelled with love and she prayed he would be able to keep his word. Sebastian lowered his head to her once again, kissing her deeply. She returned the kiss without hesitation; wrapping her legs around the back of his, fitting herself into the hard, smooth curves of his body.

They made love again, this time gentle, full of the love that had been missing for so long.

Chapter Eighteen

Back in the bedroom, Serenity changed into clean clothes. The warm glow of sex surrounded her and she hugged the feeling to herself.

Still the darkness that had forced its way into her life reared its ugly head and thought she shouldn't be allowed this small shred of happiness. Her own internal guilt tried to crush the emotion like a drunk with a beer can.

A soft knock came and Sebastian poked his head around the door.

"You decent?" he asked, mindful of their sleeping child.

"Yes," she said, and then added, "Not that it isn't anything you've seen before." The remark revealed a cheeky, flirty side and she smiled.

He walked into the room wearing the same dark, button-up shirt and suit. The outfit was almost identical to the one he'd cast, soaking wet, to the bathroom floor. In fact, he had worn the same thing every time she'd seen him.

Serenity laughed, "Don't you own any different clothing?"

He shrugged. "After hundreds of years you tend to get a bit bored of fashion. I can't be bothered to think about what to wear every day. Every few years I change the wardrobe to fit in. Life's easier if I wear the same thing."

Serenity had never been someone who bothered to think about fashion. With her abusive stepfather and then husband, clothes had been something she used to hide under, not make herself more noticeable. Since Jackson's death, she'd tried to make more of an effort with the way she dressed, but old habits die hard. When she wore fitted clothing, she consciously forced herself not to tug at the material or cover her breasts with her arms. T-shirts, or sweaters combined with jeans, were about the only thing she felt comfortable in.

"Well I guess you look good," she said. "So why change?"

Sebastian crossed the room and gave her a smile that made her insides crumble. "Exactly," he said, and bent to give her a brief kiss on the tip of her nose. His eyes searched her face for a moment, a small smile playing on his lips, as though he couldn't believe he was looking at her. "There are only a few hours of night left," he said.

Immediately, her postcoital glow dissipated. They couldn't hide out in this house forever. A monster roamed outside the four walls—one who wanted her dead—and Sebastian was the only one capable of stopping him.

On the bed, Elizabeth stirred. "Mommy?" she said, a small frown on her face as though she didn't know where she was.

Serenity raced to her side. "It's okay, honey. I'm here."

Elizabeth sat up, her hair matted on one side where she'd slept. She rubbed her eyes with the back of her hand.

"Mommy, I'm hungry."

Shit.

Serenity had been in such a rush to get out of the house, she hadn't thought to pack any snacks for Elizabeth.

"I didn't bring anything to eat. I'm so sorry, honey. Maybe we could order something in?"

It was two-thirty in the morning and she flashed Sebastian an awkward grin, not knowing what else to suggest.

"Don't worry," Sebastian said. "I have things for her to eat."

"You have food in the house?" she said, curiously.

Being a vampire, Sebastian had no need for food. She remembered the last time she'd been here, how fully stocked the fridge had been, though obviously none of it had been touched.

"I employ someone to look after the house. I call him if I'm going to be in town and he opens everything up for me and restocks the pantry. I could tell him not to bother with the food, but it's part of the service and helps to make me appear human."

Human...

She still couldn't get her head around the idea of him being a vampire. So easily, she allowed herself to forget he was something that shouldn't really exist, but then he spoke of the realities of his existence and she found the shock hitting her, almost as fresh as the first time.

"And anyway," he continued. "You never know when the food may come in handy."

"When you have human guests, you mean?" She couldn't help the bitter dagger of jealously shooting through her. What was wrong with her? She'd spent most of her life trying to prevent and placate fights, but now every time she opened her mouth she seemed to start one.

Sebastian turned, his eyes focusing upon hers.

"You are the only human I have ever brought back here. I promise."

"It's none of my business what you do."

"Yes," he said. "Yes, it is."

They held each other's gaze and two hundred years of intensity passed from his eyes. He couldn't glamour her, but he seemed to convey his emotions through stare alone.

"Mommy?" Elizabeth tugged on her hand, breaking her from the moment. "I'm still hungry."

Serenity flashed a bright smile. "Hey, you know what? Me too. Shall we see what we can find?"

"Can I have French toast?" she asked, scrambling off the side of the huge bed.

Serenity laughed. "I don't know, honey. We'll have to go check what's in the fridge."

Together, they climbed back down the huge staircase to the kitchen. The scene looked strangely like a normal family, except for the late hour and the fact one of them was a vampire.

Elizabeth's eyes were bloodshot and the little girl kept hiding wide yawns behind the palm of her hand. They had missed dinner and Serenity couldn't expect Elizabeth to sleep on an empty stomach. Besides, Serenity was hungry herself; ravenous, in fact.

As Serenity rummaged through the fridge, pulling out a carton of eggs, strawberries, and syrup, Sebastian stood close behind her.

"I must leave now," he spoke against her ear.

She tilted her head backward, nuzzling her cheek against his. "Be careful," she said, her heart tightening in her chest.

She couldn't bear to lose him, not again.

Sebastian turned to leave and a small hand slipped into his. He looked down to find Elizabeth's dark eyes staring up at him.

"I tasted the dirt and heard the wind in the trees," she said. "It's in the ground."

Sebastian frowned, "What is?"

"The thing you're looking for."

He crouched down. "How do you know that?"

"When I was asleep, I saw him sleeping too."

Sebastian glanced up at Serenity and she gave a small shrug. "Sometimes Elizabeth knows things—things she shouldn't. She has a way of knowing what others are thinking and she has dreams and often they come true."

Sebastian crouched to Elizabeth's level. "Did you see anything else?" he asked. "Hear anything else?"

She shook her head, her dark curls bouncing around her face. "No, but he felt happy. Like he was home."

Sebastian dropped a kiss on top of the little girl's head. A wave of nostalgic memory washed over him, so strong he had to stop himself stumbling back.

"Thank you, Elizabeth," he said. "Now I know where to start."

He stood and leaned over to Serenity, wrapping his arms around her. "I'll find him," he said. "You'll be safe here."

Mindful of the child watching them with wide, curious eyes, Sebastian gave her a simple, firm kiss on the mouth before reluctantly letting go.

Serenity drew Elizabeth toward her so mother and daughter stood together, Elizabeth's back pressed up against her legs, watching him leave.

Sebastian left the house and closed the front door behind him, turning to the night.

He didn't want to leave his family but had no choice. If he waited until Jackson found them, Jackson might turn up in daylight and Sebastian would be in the coma-like sleep he had no control over. Jackson would slaughter them while he lay in the next room.

His family.

He hardly believed he had a family again.

Fear at being close to humans again clutched his heart. Their humanity and fragility meant only one thing for him— loss. Their lives were fleeting and already in his mind, he raced through the years while they grew old and died, leaving him alone once again.

The thought brought back memories, a stab of remorseful pain. He once had another daughter, many years before. She hadn't been much older than Elizabeth when he'd been taken. Her name had been Isabelle. She had lived a long and happy life; though to Sebastian, she died on the day he'd been turned.

He forced himself not to think of the future. The past few years had been wasted in misery and loneliness, and he wouldn't allow himself to put any of them through that again. He wasn't being fair on either himself or them. He had no idea how things would work with Elizabeth but, if his instincts could be trusted, he thought she would prove herself to be more than human as well.

Serenity said Elizabeth 'had a way of knowing what others were thinking', but he thought it might be more. Elizabeth was special. She obviously had some kind of precognitive ability or telepathy, and she was still so young. He couldn't imagine what kind of woman she would become when she reached adulthood. Puberty could turn whatever talents she had now into something spectacular. If that happened, much of the world's supernatural side would be open to her, and that her father was a vampire would simply be accepted as part of who she was.

Did her precognitive abilities have something to do with her part vampire DNA? Though it seemed none of his vampire traits had passed through, some of the supernatural still made up her blood.

Though part of him hated the idea of his daughter never having a 'normal' life, another part was thrilled by the possibilities. That she was something special, not only as her own person—but as something supernatural—made an exciting prospect. She was his child, but in years to come she would also be his companion. A whole other world had suddenly opened up before him.

Sebastian moved quickly through the Los Angeles streets. Even in the middle of the night the city was never deserted, but fewer people were around than early evening.

Where are you, you son-of-a-bitch?

If Sebastian believed Elizabeth, Jackson had gone back to ground. He would be back in the forest, where he'd been turned. But the Angeles Forest covered thousands of acres with all types of different terrain—from ancient redwood forests to pine and fir covered mountaintops. Even with his sharpened senses, it was unlikely he would simply run across Jackson's trail. He'd already been back to the one place he thought Jackson might be and found nothing. Wherever Madeline took Jackson to turn him, it had been far away from where Sebastian buried his body.

Where to start?

One place made sense to Sebastian. Jackson had been shot at the airport—shot twice—and would be injured. If the injury meant spilled blood, he'd leave a trail.

Though Sebastian suspected Jackson healed quickly, just as he himself did, being shot would still weaken him. He'd need to rest and to feed to build back his strength. That would be his reason for heading back to the forest, so he could go back to the place he'd been turned.

A wave of purpose built inside Sebastian. With Jackson weakened, Sebastian wouldn't find a better time to locate Jackson and kill him.

He moved like a ghost through the night, only noticed by the chill he left on the warm autumn air. Drivers saw him as a flash across their windscreens as he crossed the road in front of them. For those on the street, he was something that caught their eye for the briefest of moments, except when they turned to look they found nothing. He was a chill against the back of the neck, the feeling they were not alone.

Some people blamed the fearful sensation on the presence of ghosts—but Sebastian had never seen such an entity. In his mind, most of the supernatural humans blamed on other things resided with his kind—the werewolves, the ghosts, the poltergeists. Most started with a vampire.

Since the days since Jesus walked the earth, his kind roamed among them. After all, hadn't Christ told his disciples to drink of his blood and eat of his flesh? Hadn't Jesus re-risen three days later?

Stories of his kind were everywhere. They linked back to every supernatural myth humans believed in. Werewolves were those vampires who fed only from other animals, never giving into the compulsion to consume human blood. Poltergeists were those unable to stay away from their human families after they had been turned, moving about the homes at night, trying to recapture their human lives. Angels were those vampires, who, protective of their human families, even after many generations, still guarded them and saved them from harm.

Then there were those who acted exactly how vampires should—killing to survive, terrifying humans and enjoying it.

At this time of night, with the noise abatement procedures to keep the rest of the city sleeping, the airport was quieter than in the middle of the day. Sebastian headed straight to terminal eight, knowing this was where Jackson attacked Serenity's friend and had been shot.

Passengers lay scattered around the terminal, stretched awkwardly across hard plastic chairs, or lying on the floor, heads rested on their bags. Middle of the night traveling might be in a vampire's regime but for humans, they still tried to sleep.

He moved quickly and quietly among them. A couple raised their heads, sensing him pass but for the most part he went unnoticed. He had no interest in the travelers.

Instead, he remained alert for Jackson's scent and it didn't take him long to find it.

At first a faint stench, just a whiff of something putrid on the already stale air, reached his sensitive nose. It was enough for Sebastian to follow and the scent quickly grew stronger. Within moments, the reek of death overwhelmed him and he knew he'd found the source. Sebastian looked up. Three sets of doors barred his way, small figures marking each of them.

He stood outside the bathrooms.

Though the spilt blood had long since been cleaned up, just the essence, a few missed drops, created the abhorrent smell, threatening to bring Sebastian to his knees and vomit.

Sebastian had come across spilt vampire blood before, but this was not the same. Vampires consumed live blood—the fluid created their very life-force and smelled as such; fresh and intoxicating. This scent of blood was rotten, like three-day-old meat left in the sun or road kill left to decompose on the side of the road.

Unconsciously, Sebastian put his hand over his nose and mouth.

He wanted to get away from the stench but he needed to follow the trail. He hated the idea of tracking this scent for miles but he had no choice.

The scent led out past gate eighty-three, out of the big glass doors and onto the runway. In the open space, the smell grew fainter, but Sebastian had no trouble detecting it. Jackson must have continued to bleed as he ran; leaving tiny splattered drops across the runway.

Sebastian's feet hit the tarmac, his long legs and strength carrying him across with supernatural speed.

Luckily Sebastian did not tire, but he had a long distance to cover between the airport and the forest, even at his breath-taking speed. Sebastian's main enemy was the sun and the passage of night happened all too quickly. He needed to find Jackson before the morning came.

He crossed through downtown Los Angeles and then through the city's boroughs. The houses came to an end and Sebastian entered the forest. All at once, calm settled over him. Something about being with nature spoke to him. Twigs cracked beneath his feet. All around, animals rustled in the bushes for their meals. They froze as soon as they caught Sebastian's scent, or dived and scurried away. He heard ferns curling, like the fingers of the dead, and the leaves on the trees opening, catching carbon dioxide in their pores. Beneath the putrid scent of Jackson's blood, the earth released its musty, damp odor.

The moon hung high above his head, embedded in the inky black of the sky. Somewhere in the distance came the sharp screech of an owl.

Jackson's scent was growing fainter. Jackson had probably started healing by this point, stopping the blood loss.

Sebastian pushed through shrubs and undergrowth. Branches whipped back at him, lashing at his face and legs.

He froze.

The scent suddenly powered over him in a tidal wave, almost knocking him backward. To his ears came the sounds of an animal feeding; slurping, chewing, gnawing.

With an extra burst of speed, he broke through another line of brush.

Jackson stood over his dirt grave. A young girl dangled by the throat, clamped in his jaws like a hyena having just scavenged its prey. The scent of blood made every sense in Sebastian's body scream. The girl would have barely been out of her teens—a young life cut short by this animal. Blood matted her long blonde hair and it hung down, almost brushing the ground. Her head lolled back, her eyes staring blankly at the night's sky.

A rush of hatred and revulsion toward Jackson washed over Sebastian. Yet his loathing went unfounded. He was a killer too. Just because he didn't prey on pretty young girls, didn't make him any less of a monster.

Jackson lifted his mouth from the girl's throat, using his hands to support her body. The blood coating the lower half of his face appeared black in the moonlight.

"Have you come to join me for supper?" he grinned.

Sebastian snarled, "I will never feed with you."

Jackson's head cocked to one side. "You're one of them, aren't you? You're like the one who made me?"

"I'm here to kill you, not converse with you."

Jackson let go of the girl and she hit the floor with a wet crunch. His eyes narrowed, a faint frown on his hideous face.

"Kill me? Why would you want to kill me?"

"I won't let any harm come to Serenity."

Jackson laughed; barking like a fox in the still night. "So the bitch has taken up with a vampire!"

Sebastian had done enough talking. With a growl, he leapt at Jackson, his fangs lengthened, arms outstretched. But

Jackson was faster than Sebastian gave him credit for. Jackson's fingers wrapped around Sebastian's forearm and he threw him.

Sebastian hit the ground with force and the impact jarred his whole body. The move had taken him by surprise, but it was the last time he intended for Jackson to have the upper hand.

Leaping back to his feet, Sebastian rushed him again. This time Sebastian was ready for Jackson. The monster counter-attacked, the two beings colliding in mid-air. But Sebastian managed to wrap his hands around Jackson's putrid throat and they landed, Sebastian on top of Jackson.

Beneath him, Jackson snarled, snapped like an animal and Sebastian growled in return. Jackson's hands grabbed Sebastian's shoulders but he couldn't budge the robust vampire.

The sound of fighting filled the forest, silencing all other creatures around them. Roosting birds burst from the tops of trees, rabbit scurried back to their burrows, deer ran for cover.

Sebastian's hand tightened around Jackson's neck. He would have to tear the beast's head off with his bare hands; he couldn't stand the thought of sinking his teeth into that abhorrent flesh.

But Sebastian felt something within him, the internal warning telling him morning was coming. He glanced towards the east and saw the faint lightening of the sky—the back turning to a deep indigo blue as the sun began its daily climb.

A low growl emitted from deep in his chest and automatically his hands loosened from around Jackson's neck. No longer in control, he rose to his feet and Jackson too, looked up at the sky.

Jackson jumped to his feet, crowing with laughter. "Run away! You are weak—pathetic. You will never beat me. See, not even the sun will kill me. I'm a higher form of life than you, more evolved. I am everything you are only better."

Sebastian's legs were already stepping away. He walked backward, his body on auto drive to get to his sleeping place before the sun rose. He was programmed to do this. Only in the most dire of circumstances—where his own life was under immediate threat—would his body not take him home.

Jackson jumped up and down, punching the air, whooping with laughter like a hideously overgrown and deformed schoolboy.

Furious, Sebastian could only watch as his body took him home.

Chapter Nineteen

After Sebastian left, Serenity made Elizabeth some French toast with berries and plenty of syrup. Elizabeth's eyes dropped as the little girl chewed her food. Once finished, Serenity dumped the dishes in the sink and they both went back up to bed.

Serenity tucked Elizabeth into the big bed and climbed in beside her. She snuggled behind her daughter, trying not to think the bad thoughts threatening to run rampage through her brain. She was worried about Sebastian and terrified that Jackson would somehow find them. Convinced she wouldn't be sleeping that night, she only closed her eyes to rest them. Within minutes, she was dead to the world.

Serenity woke, wondering what time it was. Blackout shutters had been fitted in the windows so no daylight poured through.

She sat up and glanced over at Elizabeth. Her daughter slept soundly, her mouth wide open. Serenity smiled. It wasn't the most fetching expression.

Sitting still, she tried to get a sense of Sebastian's presence in the house. She hoped desperately he was here. Where would he be sleeping?

Four years ago, she'd never figured out if he slept in one of the bedrooms, on a bed like a normal person, or in a coffin in the basement. The blackout shutters made her think he slept in a bedroom—he didn't seem like the type of person who would ever sleep in the dirt.

Should I go and check the other rooms? She wondered.

She paused awkwardly. She didn't want to disturb him but needed confirmation of his safety. Had he even found Jackson? Dear God, she hoped Sebastian had killed him. She wanted him to finally be out of their lives forever.

Carefully, Serenity slipped off the bed, not wanting to wake Elizabeth. After making a quick trip to the bathroom, she cracked open the door and peered out. As she had expected, everything was quiet.

Serenity padded along the hallway, her feet silent on the plush cream carpet. She reached the first door and paused outside. There was no indication of anyone inside. Nerves buzzed through her. How would he look? She had seen Madeline—Sebastian's maker—in a type of sleep, but she'd appeared to be in more of a trance and had woken every time Serenity moved.

She peered into the dark and waited for her eyes to adjust. No body lay lumped up beneath the sheets on the king-sized bed, so she backed away and closed the door. Serenity worked her way along the corridor, checking each of the rooms. Two of them were bathrooms and the other three were more bedrooms; all were fruitless. Maybe Sebastian slept underground after all? Maybe he rested in some special room designed with no chance of daylight getting in while he slept?

Light filtered up from the ground floor and a tall window on the staircase. None of these windows had been fitted with blinds; at least they hadn't been pulled down.

She headed down the staircase.

Something wasn't right. Serenity screwed up her nose. A smell wafted up to her, like trash left out in the sun too long.

She rounded the curve of the staircase. At the kitchen island, where she and Elizabeth had eaten their midnight breakfast not so many hours ago, sat a man. He stared at the ground, his too-long, greasy dark hair hanging in his face.

Her heart clambered into her throat. Tears of fear pricked the backs her eyes. All of the strength rushed out of her arms and legs.

Very slowly she turned back around, intending to run, but as soon as she moved, so did he.

The man lifted his face.

Serenity felt as though she'd been plunged right into the middle of a nightmare.

Jackson sat before her, but not at she remembered him. The creature in front of her looked as though it had ripped off Jackson's face and now wore it as a mask. The white skin was dull and she could make out every scar on his face. His dark eyes embedded deep in his skull, hollow rings served to deepen them. When he looked up, milky clouds fogged his irises, she couldn't tell if he stared directly at her or if he was blind and watched her from the afterlife.

"Hello, Serenity," he rasped, as though he had to force the voice out of dead lungs.

A strange choked sound came from her throat. Her head swam, the world blurred at the edges. She grabbed hold of the staircase banister and dragged herself back to reality.

He grinned at her. Instead of the lethally sharp, yet somehow graceful fangs she'd seen before on Sebastian and Madeline, all of Jackson's teeth seemed to have been filed down to points, as though part of a tribe from the Amazon.

"Aren't you going to come and give your husband a kiss?" His lips pulled back in a snarl that might have been a smile. A fat, black tongue darted out, past those small, sharp teeth, and lapped at his lips.

"Come give Daddy a kiss!"

There were stains of something around his mouth and on his chin. The stains appeared black against his pale, pale skin. His tongue flicked out again, smearing the black with saliva, and the stains turned red. With horror, Serenity realized the marks were dried blood.

She shook her head back and forth, over and over. Her foot reached backward, colliding with the rise of the stair. She stumbled, clutching at the banister.

In an instant, Jackson was in front of her on the staircase, his horrific face only inches from her own. His putrid breath washed over her, the force of it knocking her head back. He hissed and flecks of stinking spit hit her face, revealing those freakish teeth and black tongue. His body loomed over hers, oppressive, and she cringed back into the staircase, hoping to disappear.

Help Sebastian, she screamed in her head. *He's here! Help me!*

She hoped desperately he would hear her, but daylight streamed in through the windows and she knew even if he did, his helping would be impossible.

A terrifying thought occurred to her, one that hurt her even more than the abomination leering over her:

What if he never made it back? What if Jackson killed him?

Elizabeth's presence still sleeping upstairs worried her more. Did Jackson even know about her? Serenity would gladly let Jackson kill her if it meant he would leave before learning of Elizabeth's existence. Her heart broke at the thought of never seeing her daughter again, never kissing her skin or stroking her hair, but she would gladly give up her life for Elizabeth. She just hoped Jackson would take her body with him.

Her eyes filled with tears at how scared and alone Elizabeth would be, how she wouldn't know what to do or where her mommy had gone. But surely that would be better than her coming down to find her mother's body?

Jackson lowered his head and sniffed his way down the side of her face, her throat and down to her breasts. He licked his lips again.

"You got fat," he sneered. "Let yourself go a bit, didn't you, *Serenity*?" The way he said her name was like spitting a curse.

A tear ran from her left eye and down her cheek.

Years of abuse and torture flooded back to her. Though now he looked like a monster, even when he'd been human he'd had the heart of one.

"What do you want from me?"

He laughed. "What do you think, Serenity? Let me see..." He pretended to think for a minute, tapping one filthy nailed finger on the dead flesh of his lips. "Now could it be something to do with the last memory I have? Possibly the memory of you stabbing me with a fucking knife?" He shouted the words in her face and she squeezed her eyes shut, trying to get her face away from him.

She whined in fear. "Please..." she said, not knowing what she was going to say. "Please..."

"Please, please, please," he mimicked her in a high-pitched voice. "What are you asking me for, huh? Are you begging for me to take my conjugal rights as your husband?"

He grabbed both of her thighs and pulled her down toward him. She dropped two steps, and a small cry escaped her throat, the breath thumping out of her on each step. She ended up with Jackson between her legs.

"Well, look at that," he leered. "You can't keep away. I bet I can fuck you better than your pretty-boy who is scared of the light."

Her heart leapt at the mention of Sebastian.

"Where is he?" she said. She wanted to sound brave and defiant, despite her dominated position, but her voice came out whiny and begging. "What did you do to him?"

A horrible sick sensation tightened at the back of her throat and her stomach balled and coiled like a pit of worms.

Jackson leaned down, his face only inches from hers.

"He was damn easy to kill," he grinned. "I just held him down until the sun came up, and then—poof! He went up like a puff of smoke. Well, a puff of smoke that screams in agony of course."

Serenity moaned, her head falling to one side. How could this happen? She had only just found Sebastian and now she'd lost him again. The pain in her heart was too great for her to deal with right now. She couldn't let it overwhelm her. If she gave in, she was as good as dead.

"Is that the best you could do after you killed me?" Jackson sneered. "Some freaking vampire? Don't tell me you were screwing him? That's just gross."

"You don't know anything about him".

"You do realize you're still married, Serenity. You're a fucking adulteress. I think that's grounds for divorce."

"You're dead."

He bent down and his mouth closed hard over hers. Serenity screamed, the sound muffled as his revolting tongue pushed into her mouth like a cold, hard slug.

He broke away, laughing, and she burst up as though he'd been holding her underwater, gagging and gasping for breath. That moment would haunt her nightmares for years to come, should she survive this. She gagged at his rancid breath, the taste of him on her tongue like she'd swallowed sewage.

Jackson grinned down at her, exposing his pointed teeth. "Do I feel fucking dead, sweetheart?"

"Fuck you!" she spat.

His vacant, strange eyes went hard. All of the sarcastic humor left him and his face turned to stone. Jackson pulled his arm back and slapped her.

Serenity's head slammed backward, her ear ringing. Her eyes rolled. Her world started to close in and she fought against the darkness, struggling to stay conscious.

A large part of her wanted to give in. She just wanted this all to be over. She had been fighting her entire life and she was tired. If she gave in and let Jackson kill her, at least she would finally be at peace.

Yet she couldn't do it.

Perhaps if she were alone, then yes, she would simply give in and let Jackson do what he liked. But she was a mother and she had a daughter who needed her.

Serenity clutched to the last vestiges of light, mentally pulling her conscience toward them. She blinked hard, though her vision blurred and her ear still rang from the blow.

Jackson's face—hazy and distorted, but no less horrific—still hung only inches from hers.

"You can kill me if you want," she managed to say. "But you'll always be a monster."

Jackson opened his mouth to laugh at her but something stopped him. He glanced up the stairs behind her.

"Mommy?"

The sound of Elizabeth's voice calling down the stairs terrified her more than when she had first seen Jackson. Tears filled her eyes and she thought her heart would break in fear. Desperately, she'd hoped Jackson would leave Elizabeth unharmed, if he never found out about her, her life would be safe.

She'd been foolish to think such a thing possible. When had life ever been kind to her?

"Mommy?" Elizabeth's voice came again. From the pitch Serenity could tell she had descended the first couple of stairs and stopped, knowing something wasn't quite right.

"Go back upstairs, Elizabeth." Serenity called back up to her. Her own voice sounded surprisingly even.

"Someone's here, Mommy." Elizabeth's voice was so small, as though she was a long way away.

Serenity glanced back at Jackson. He stared back at Serenity, his eyes narrowed in concentration, a small frown of confusion creating lines between his already ragged eyes.

"It's nothing for you to worry about. Now do as I tell you and go back to bed."

"I can't, Mommy. I'm scared. Someone bad is here. I can smell him."

Serenity looked back at Jackson, waiting for him to leap off her and race up the stairs in triumph, to take the person Serenity loved most in the world. Yet Jackson still hadn't moved. Instead, he put one gnarled, filthy hand to his temple, and shook his head as though trying to clear water out of his ears.

"What is that?" he growled.

Serenity froze, not answering him. She heard the sound of small, bare feet padding in her two-footed steps, *thu-thunk,* as Elizabeth started to make her way further down the stairs.

"Stay where you are," Serenity called out, panic rising once again, like a shark out of the depths of an ocean. "Stay right where you are or I'm going to be very angry with you!"

205

Jackson climbed off Serenity and backed away. He put his hands out in front of him, his head craned back as though someone was shining an industrial flashlight in his face.

"What *is* that?" Genuine fear tainted his voice. "I can't see! What is it?"

Serenity risked a glance back. Elizabeth stood at the top of the stairs, small and defenseless, dwarfed by the grandeur of the staircase. Her face carried no expression, her young features smooth and vacant. She looked the same as she had a few nights earlier, when Serenity found her sleepwalking.

"Mommy?" she said again, though her face remained blank.

Serenity didn't want to attract Jackson toward her daughter, but she also didn't want to leave her standing at the top of the stairs. If Elizabeth was sleepwalking, she might just as easily miss her footing and fall down. However deadly Jackson might be, Serenity couldn't ignore the normal dangers presented to a small child.

Anyway, Jackson didn't look like he was going to hurt anyone anytime soon.

The freak he had become stumbled away from the staircase, his arms raised as though to protect his eyes. Serenity couldn't be certain, but the cause of his fear and discomfort seemed to be Elizabeth.

Slowly, Serenity started to edge her way backward up the staircase, toward her daughter.

"You won't get away with this," Jackson snarled. "Whatever trick you're pulling, I will figure it out and destroy you."

He turned and, so fast it seemed he simply vanished, he left the house, the big front door slamming in his wake.

Hardly daring to believe he'd gone, Serenity sobbed in relief. She turned and ran up the stairs and scooped her child up in her arms. Elizabeth's small arms wound around her neck, her legs straddling her waist, exactly the same as any other time Serenity found her out of bed.

Serenity held her close, her face buried in her daughter's soft hair.

Grief swamped her relief at still being alive.

Sebastian was dead. That monster had killed him.

The loss she thought she'd gotten over all those years ago returned with renewed force. It swelled up inside of her, like a balloon threatening to pop, and she wanted to scream with the injustice. What had she done to deserve this? How could something she thought she'd lost be given back to her for such a brief time, only to be snatched away.

She still had Elizabeth. Her daughter was alive and that was the most important thing. Yet even these thoughts made her cry harder. She hadn't even realized it until now, but deep down, part of her had hoped Sebastian would be in their lives once more. Now, of course, that was never going to happen.

It was all so final.

Serenity cried into Elizabeth's soft dark curls, her mind turning over the events of the last ten minutes.

What had just happened? Jackson fled all because of Elizabeth. Somehow her presence had hurt him. Serenity couldn't explain it, but she knew one thing with certainty.

Elizabeth had saved both of their lives.

Chapter Twenty

What was she supposed to do now?

Serenity didn't want to leave. Some sad, desperate part of her hoped Jackson had been wrong and Sebastian had survived. Though the house always felt utterly devoid of his presence, to walk away as if he never existed seemed like such a final act.

But she couldn't stay, not now that Jackson knew where to find her. It would only be a matter of time before he came back and killed her. But Jackson also knew where she lived. Nowhere was safe.

A horrible sickness gripped her stomach. He would always find her. She should have learned that by now. During their marriage, Jackson always promised if she ever tried to leave him, he would track her down and kill her.

It seemed, even after death, Jackson stayed true to his word.

Beside her, Elizabeth blinked and stretched, rubbing her eyes. They sat together on the stairs, Serenity's arm around Elizabeth's shoulders.

"I didn't like that man, Mommy," Elizabeth said; staring up at her with big, wet eyes. "He scared me."

"Me neither, sweetheart," she said, pressing Elizabeth against the side of her body. "He scared me too."

Heartbroken, Serenity struggled to control her emotions. Sebastian was dead and he'd taken a part of her heart with him. Over the years, she had somehow found peace, knowing Sebastian survived in the world somewhere. Now he no longer existed, he was nothing more than a pile of ash. Maybe she was in denial, but she couldn't bring herself to believe he was no longer a part of this world. He'd been her guardian angel and with him gone she felt exposed and vulnerable.

Beneath the grief, she was also terrified. Jackson might come back at any moment.

Rage bubbled beneath the grief; furious that Jackson could still do this to her, that he could come back into her life and rip everything she had ever worked for to shreds.

She wanted to cry. She wanted to grieve for Sebastian, for all the dreams she'd allowed herself to imagine—if only for the briefest of moments—but she needed to stay strong for Elizabeth.

Serenity lifted her head and took a wet, nasally breath. Her jaw tightened in fierce determination.

She would stop Jackson; whatever it took. She would kill him again, and again, and again, if she had to. She would kill the creature that took away the only man she had ever really loved.

Serenity had killed before. She'd murdered both Jackson and the vampire, Madeline. She was stronger than she gave herself credit for. She'd experienced more blood and violence at her own hands, then most people who still walked the streets. She'd murdered people, even though, technically, Jackson came back and Madeline was dead to start with.

Except now she had a weakness. Her recklessness had been easy to ignore when she only had her own life to worry about. Now she needed to think about Elizabeth as well.

The moment of power flaring within her quickly died.

In truth she only had two options. Stay and fight, or run.

Did Jackson even work by the same rules as the vampires? Silver and sunlight killed Madeline, but Jackson did not seem to have such weaknesses. He'd appeared here in the daylight

He held Sebastian down as the sun came up...

She pushed the thought away. Being overcome with loss at this point wouldn't help either her or Elizabeth. Not thinking about Sebastian's death was the only way she would be able to function.

But if sunlight did not harm Jackson, she had no way of knowing if any of the other 'traditional' vampire methods would either.

What the hell had Madeline created?

She would be laughing right now, Serenity thought. *Whatever hell the bitch existed in right now, she would be laughing her ass off.*

Jackson's return was the ultimate revenge.

If she didn't know how to fight him, her only other option was to run.

The thought of being on the run weighed down on her as if the devil himself clung to her back. To run would mean no end to this hell.

Serenity found herself plunged back into the torment of her previous life. Back then, she'd been terrified of leaving him and now she felt as though she were back in the same situation. The same fears encompassed her; if he found her what would he do to her? She could never live a simple life; she would forever be looking over her shoulder, expecting him to be there.

Then she had Elizabeth to consider. Would her daughter ever be able to lead a normal life? If they were constantly on the move she would never get the chance to settle down, go to school, or make friends of her own.

Jackson would always be there.

He would be the movement caught from the corner of her eye. He would be the shape standing in the shadows as she crossed the street. He would be the feeling that she wasn't alone when it was late at night and she was tucked up in bed.

Elizabeth would be better off if I was dead.

Depression that had haunted her for many years crept up. Like hands reaching from a grave, the fingers of despair clawed up at her, threatening to pull her down back beneath the earth.

The feeling terrified her almost as much as the knowledge of Jackson rising from the dead. After all, she might be able to run from Jackson. If she fell back into the helpless depression that had dominated her life for so many years, she couldn't run from herself.

"We need to go, sweetheart," Serenity said, making a decision.

Elizabeth looked up at her, "Where are we going?"

"To the airport. We're going to go on an airplane."

Immediately, Elizabeth's shoulders stiffened. "Are you coming too?"

"Yes, darling. I'm coming as well."

"And Sebastian?" she said. "Is my daddy coming?"

Serenity's heart twisted in pain. "No. Not this time."

"Why not?"

She couldn't tell her. She just couldn't. "Just do as I say, Elizabeth. We don't have time for a hundred questions."

"But Mom!" she protested. "He won't know where we are. He'll wake up and..."

"That's enough," she snapped, and Elizabeth fell silent.

They hadn't even had the chance to unpack yet. Their bags still sat at the bottom of the staircase.

There was nothing else she needed to do. She just had to pick up the bags and leave.

Serenity grabbed the keys from where Sebastian had dropped them on the hall console. The big electric gates barring the house from the road were controlled by a fob on the keychain and also from a panel on the inside of the door, but she thought she shouldn't leave the house unlocked.

With a tight, painful lump in her throat, Serenity picked up their bags and took Elizabeth's hand. They left the big house and Serenity pulled the heavy front door shut behind her. Sebastian's car sat in the driveway, but she didn't want to take the vehicle. It felt too much like stealing.

Together they walked down the gravel driveway, the small stones crunching beneath their feet, and Serenity pushed the button on the key-fob. Slowly the gates opened up in front of them.

Serenity glanced back at the house.

I'm so sorry, Sebastian, she spoke out to him mentally. She hoped wherever he was—whatever happened to his kind after they passed—he would hear and forgive her for bringing Jackson into his life. Her vision blurred with tears and she bit them back, pressing her lips together hard, fighting the hard lump in her throat.

They stepped onto the quiet street. Most of the people who lived in this area lived secretive lives and liked their privacy. No one hung out on the street corners in this neighborhood. People either rode in their cars or stayed in their homes.

Except today was an exception. As the gates closed and they started down the street, a car pulled alongside them.

"Mrs. Hathaway?"

She slowed her walk, groaning internally. She glanced to one side at the driver of the standard issue Chevrolet Impala Police Cruiser.

Detective Gingham—the detective who had questioned her down at the station.

Daylight shone through his thinning hair, the dyed black color appearing faker than ever. He still wore the stiff grey suit she'd seen him in at the station. His arm rested on the outside of the car door, the window wide open.

"I wasn't expecting to see you in this neighborhood, Mrs. Hathaway," he said. "Not your local neighborhood stroll?"

Serenity tightened her grip on Elizabeth's hand and kept walking. "I was visiting a friend."

Still crawling along beside her, he glanced up at the opulent houses, or at least the high walls and gates surrounding them. "Friends in high places, huh?"

Serenity stopped walking. "I wasn't aware that who my friends were was any business of yours, Detective."

"We've had reported sightings of the man we were discussing the other day in this area," he said, choosing his words carefully because of the presence of the child. "We're making inquiries in case anyone might have something else to tell us."

"I don't have anything else to tell you," she said, deliberately.

The car continued to drive alongside, its speed matching her pace. She continued to walk.

"No?" he said, his voiced raised. "Are you sure?"

"Totally."

"It's a bit of a coincidence, don't you think?" he continued, without even blinking. "That everywhere this man turns up, there you are as well?"

"Yes, it is a coincidence." She tried to keep her voice level.

"You see, that just doesn't sit right with me, Mrs. Hathaway. And I have really good instincts on these things. They got me where I am today. You understand, don't you?"

Serenity glanced down at Elizabeth. "This really isn't the time or the place, Detective."

"Then why don't you come back down to the station? I'm sure one of our operators can take care of your little girl while you help us out?"

Elizabeth looked up her. "What does the man want, Mommy?"

"He's a policeman, like your Uncle James. He thinks I can help him find someone."

"Yeah?" Her small face lit up. "Like someone on the television."

It briefly crossed Serenity's mind to wonder exactly what her daughter had been watching, but she went for the easy option.

"Yeah, honey. Like on the television."

Detective Gingham pulled the car over. Serenity sighed and pulled open the back door. With a heavy heart, she helped Elizabeth climb in the back seat and got in after her. What options did she have? She would rather she cooperated than have the detective find a reason to arrest her. She couldn't risk being separated from Elizabeth.

Serenity was getting to know the inside of the Los Angeles Police Department far more than she would have liked. She felt like she was experiencing déjà-vu as she followed the detective through the corridors, toward the room where he intended to interrogate her yet again.

Elizabeth had been happy to stay with one of the phone operators, bribed with the promise of hot chocolate and cookies. How well Elizabeth took things in her stride never failed to amaze Serenity. Something that left Serenity shaken and haunted, Elizabeth brushed off within an hour.

The door had a different number on the front, but otherwise the room was identical to the one she had been in yesterday.

Yesterday—had it really only been yesterday?

With the attitude of a sulky teenager, she sank into the plastic chair across the table from the detective. She slouched low, not making eye contact with the sharp blue eyes of the law officer. Guilt stirred in her gut, making her feel as though she were the criminal instead of the victim.

Technically she was a criminal—she had murdered Jackson to start with. But the secrets she held were secrets from most of mankind.

Detective Gingham sighed and leaned across the table toward her.

"So, Mrs. Hathaway, are you going to be straight with me now?"

"I don't know what you mean?"

"Don't bullshit me! Your husband is murdering people and everywhere he is spotted either has some connection to you or else there you are. If you're not protecting him, then why haven't you contacted me? You can't tell me there have been numerous sightings in this area and yet you haven't seen him?"

Serenity stared at the ground.

"What possible reason could you have for keeping his presence a secret?" the detective continued. "He is a dangerous man."

Serenity's head snapped up. "Do you think I don't know that?"

His eyes narrowed. "Is he threatening you? Is he threatening you and you daughter? If you talk to the police..."

Serenity laughed. "He wouldn't give a damn about me talking to you. He wouldn't even think of you as a threat."

Detective Gingham leaned on his forearms and repeated the question. "Is he threatening you?"

"My husband has always threatened me, Detective. From the moment I married him, his presence alone has been enough of a threat. But if you are asking me if I am helping him in any way, then no, Detective, I am not. I hate him more than any other being on the planet." Her voice shook with emotion. "And if I could do or say something that would make him disappear from my life forever, then I would do it."

"Mrs. Hathaway? Do you know where your husband is?"

"No, Detective." Her voice rose in anger. "For the last time, I honestly do not know where he is. Do I think he'll come after me again? Yes, I do. The whole reason he's back in this city is to torture me."

He sat back in his seat and some compassion leaked into the sharpness of his blue eyes.

"Then we'll set up a twenty-four hour surveillance. We'll surround you with police so he won't be able to get within a hundred yards of you."

Serenity shook her head. "It won't do any good. He'll kill your men."

Gingham raised his eyebrows in disbelief. "My men are trained professionals," he said. "They know how to take care of themselves."

"I don't want any more people to die."

"Then you and I want the same thing."

216

Serenity sighed and sat back in her seat. It didn't matter what she said. This man had his own agenda. What more could she do? If she told him the truth they would lock her up and probably take Elizabeth away from her.

She would have to disappear. She had no idea how to accomplish such a thing—especially with a small child in tow. If she were in a movie right now, she would know some dodgy guy who would be able to provide them with a fake passport, or other identity. As it was, she didn't know anyone like that, and the people she did know had either been attacked or murdered. Simply knowing her was likely to get someone killed.

"You'll understand if I ask you not to go anywhere, won't you, Mrs. Hathaway," he said, glancing down at her bags. "You need to stay close in case I have any more questions to ask."

"So you keep me close, surround me with officers, and when Jackson comes to kill me and my daughter, you try to arrest him."

The detective held her eye. "If he comes anywhere near you or your daughter, we will make sure he is apprehended."

Serenity snorted air out through her nose. "You just don't get it, do you? We're little more than bait to you."

"I assure you that's not true," he said, hurriedly.

"He'll kill your officers and then he'll kill me." She remembered Jackson's earlier reaction to Elizabeth. "If I am lucky, he'll, at least, let my daughter live."

"No one will come to any harm. I assure you of it."

"You can assure me all you want, Detective. But the truth is that Jackson isn't... normal."

"I'm aware of that. I've witnessed the autopsies of the people he has murdered." For once the incredibly controlled officer seemed to lose some of his composure. He stuttered

217

over his words and Serenity witnessed a slight shiver to his shoulders. "I've seen what he is capable of."

"That isn't what I mean..." She trailed off. What was she supposed to say? It wasn't as if she could tell him the truth. There was no chance in hell this man would believe her.

"Do whatever you need to do. There's nothing more I can say."

Chapter Twenty-one

Detective Gingham instructed two of his men to take Serenity and Elizabeth back to her apartment.

Serenity had no intention of staying there. As soon as the officers dropped them off, she ran inside, grabbed some more items of clothing and called a cab. She didn't want to be here, she only wanted to be with Sebastian. Of course, what she wanted was impossible, but at least being around his things gave her some comfort.

Both she and Elizabeth were exhausted. They'd experienced several nights of broken sleep and had suffered some serious emotional trauma. Serenity wanted to sleep but not there.

An unmarked car containing two officers followed the cab. Normally Serenity would have worried about leading them back to Sebastian's house, worried she would be creating problems for him, but none of that mattered anymore. They could ask all the questions they wanted. All she would be able to tell them was his name and that he was a friend. Nothing she said could hurt him now.

Back at the house she locked all the doors and windows, and double-checked them. Automatically, she took Elizabeth back to the room she'd come to think of as 'their' room. They were both beat and Elizabeth had even stopped asking questions, though the girl seemed happy to be back in the house, more relaxed.

Despite the fear surrounding them, they both needed to rest. The blackout shutters in the bedroom made the room as dark as if it were the middle of the night, it was easy to climb into the big bed and pretend it was.

The certainty that someone else was in the room hit her before she was even awake.

Serenity burst from sleep, her heart pounding, sick with fear.

Someone—a man—stood over her, his shape dark and looming in the poor light.

Serenity didn't even have time to scream, she just grabbed Elizabeth, pulling them both to the other side of the bed. Elizabeth, startled from sleep, started to cry. Serenity clutched her daughter to her body, terrified at this sudden intrusion.

Jackson was back. It had to be him!

"Wait," the man's voice said and immediately she knew it wasn't Jackson. "It's all right. It's only me."

Her head swam with confusion. Was she dreaming? This wasn't real—it couldn't be real. Sebastian couldn't be standing by her bedside, talking to her. It was impossible!

"He's been here, hasn't he?" the man beside her bed continued, his voice fired with anger. "I can smell him!"

Serenity couldn't speak.

The man reached over and flicked on the bedside lamp. A soft yellow light flooded the room and Serenity blinked at its sudden brightness. Sebastian was standing there, as real and solid as he'd ever been.

Elizabeth's tears quickly subsided. "Mommy, you scared me. It's only Sebastian, you big silly."

Serenity heard the pleasure in her daughter's voice and Elizabeth untangled herself from her mother's arms and half bounced, half scrambled across the bed toward him. Serenity made an attempt to grab her back again but her brain didn't seem to be talking to the rest of her body. Her arms remained useless and impassive by her sides.

"What's happened, Serenity?" Sebastian said. "Did he hurt you?"

She opened her mouth to tell him 'no', but her reply came out as only a squeak and she shook her head in response.

Instead, her daughter filled in her words. "The bad man told Mommy you were gone and you weren't coming back again."

Elizabeth's arms were wrapped around Sebastian's waist, his arm around her shoulders. The scene looked so natural she couldn't stand not to be part of it, however much she doubted her own eyes.

With trembling limbs, she crawled across the bed. Her hand shook as she reached out and touched his pale face. She almost expected her hand to pass right through him, but his skin felt as smooth as ice beneath her touch. Her thumb traced his full mouth, her palm cupping his cheek.

"I thought…" She couldn't manage any more. Her voice vanished as her throat closed over with emotion.

He took hold of her hand, holding it against his face. "Everything is okay. I'm here."

"Jackson said you were…" she tried again. This whole thing was all so overwhelming. How had he survived? Jackson said he'd held him down in the sunlight. He said Sebastian was nothing more than a pile of ash. Could he have regenerated? Was this some kind of vampire thing she knew nothing about?

Then reality sank in and she groaned.

It was so obvious! Jackson had lied—of course he had lied! It's not as if he'd ever been honest when he was alive.

Elizabeth still clung to Sebastian's side. Serenity collapsed against Sebastian, crushing them both against his solid chest. His fingers laced in her hair, his cool mouth pressed on the top of her head. She shook violently in his arms.

"Are you crying?" he asked her, trying to raise her head away from his chest.

She shook her head against him, not allowing him to move her.

Crying? No, she was laughing bitterly.

Why the hell had she believed Jackson so readily? When would she learn? She might have done something—given up even—thinking Sebastian was dead. Jackson knew her so well. He'd hoped she'd do exactly that.

"I should have sensed him here and felt your fear," Sebastian said, his muscles tensed around her. "I should have come out."

"It was daytime," she said. "The sunlight would have killed you."

Sebastian growled; a low rumbling deep inside his chest. "I would have taken Jackson down first."

Except they both knew those were just words. The sun was the one thing he couldn't fight.

"How did he even discover where I was?" said Serenity. "How did he find out about this place?"

Sebastian's hand went to his forehead and he shook his head. "I brought him here. He followed me back." Sebastian released his hold on them and spun away. He lashed out, his fist making contact with a wall, his knuckles mashing right through the plaster. "God damn it! I led him right to you!"

"Hey!" Serenity leapt to her feet. "Quit it, right now. There are some things we have no control over, this just happens to be one of them." She grabbed his hand and raised it to her lips, her eyes locking with his. "No more violence," she said. "Not when it isn't needed, and especially not when Elizabeth is around."

His eyes lifted to Elizabeth, who sat huddled on the bed. "I'm sorry."

The little girl gave a small smile.

"Let's get you back to bed," said Serenity to Elizabeth. "The grownups need to talk."

She settled Elizabeth back under the covers. "Leave the light on, Mommy," said Elizabeth.

"Sure thing, honey." Serenity stroked her daughter's hair until her breathing evened and she dropped back into sleep.

Slowly, Serenity got to her feet and walked over to where Sebastian still stood. Not wanting to leave Elizabeth alone, she grabbed his hand and tugged him into the adjoining bathroom. She closed the door and the latch engaged with a slight click. Finally afforded some privacy, Serenity threw herself into Sebastian's arms, crushing her mouth against his.

"I thought I'd lost you again," she said, between kisses. "I couldn't stand it, to think I finally had you back, only to be taken away from me again."

He kissed her back, their tongues dancing in ferocious passion. "I'm not going anyway," he told her, breaking the kiss.

223

"Do you promise me? Promise we won't be apart again. I can't bear the thought of spending any more of my life without you in it."

"Oh Serenity," he breathed. "I can't go back to existing without you in my life. I was in hell. I don't care what happens, I'll be right here, with you."

"And Elizabeth," she said. "Promise me you'll take care of her too. She's the most important thing in the world. I'd die myself before I let anything happen to her. A world without her in it wouldn't be a place I'd want to live in."

"Hush, don't talk about dying. I don't want to hear such things."

"I mean it though," she said, pulling away from him slightly so she could look up at him, directly in the eye. "Promise me you'll take care of her above all else."

"I promise, Serenity," he said, lowering his head and capturing her mouth in another sweet, intense kiss. She melted against him, her tongue brushing the smooth planes of his teeth, their tongues entwining in slips of cool and heat. She pressed her body up against his and his hands found her shirt, pulling at the material.

She wanted to feel his skin against hers, meld herself against him. She wanted him to encompass her, to fill her completely and stay that way forever. How had she gone so many years without feeling this way? Without wanting to be possessed fully by another person? To put herself in his hands and trust him not to hurt her?

With no inhibitions, Serenity tore at his shirt, popping open buttons to get to his beautiful, hard chest. Her mouth left his and worked along his cool shoulder, down across the firm curve of his pectoral, finally closing around the small nub of his nipple. Above her, Sebastian gasped, his fingers knotted in her hair as she circled his nipple with her tongue before repeating the action to its partner.

Sebastian pulled her back up, and now it was his turn to rid her of her clothes, pulling her t-shirt over her head, allowing her dark curls to tumble down her naked back. He reached around and unhooked her bra. Serenity slipped the straps from her shoulders, allowing the lace to fall to the floor, her full breasts exposed to him.

Sebastian popped the button of her jeans and she stepped out of them before shedding herself of her panties, so they pooled around her feet. Naked before him, his eyes roved her body, his full lips slack with a combination of lust and love.

Before, Serenity's insistence on being turned had marred their love making. Now, with the existence of Elizabeth, Serenity becoming like him was no longer on the table and they could lose themselves in each other without worrying about second agendas.

With urgency, Sebastian pulled off his own shirt, revealing the solid curve of his bicep, his graceful, strong forearms. Serenity stepped forward, into the circle of his arms, and finally rid him of the last of his clothes.

Overcome with desire, she wrapped her arms around his neck, fitting her body into his. Using his speed and strength, he whisked her around, her back slamming up against the wall.

"I don't want to live without you," she told him, between frantic kisses.

"Oh, Serenity," he gasped as he pushed her up against the wall, his cold fingers reaching between her thighs, slipping into her molten heat. "Let me show you how much I love you."

Jackson was livid. Had this kind of rage been inside him when he had been human? Red-hot fury burned through every part of him, firing his muscles, pounding on the backs of his eyeballs like a migraine that wouldn't let up. He couldn't keep still, he couldn't contain the anger inside of himself. Irrationally, he was terrified the rage would encompass him, explode from his body and spontaneously combust.

Instead he was reduced to pacing back and forth, pulling at his hair and railing at the world.

He was back in the forest again. All around him the debris of his fury lay like fallen angels. Small shrubs had been ripped up by their roots, bark shredded from the trees, low hanging branches torn away from the trees they had sprung from. Deep grooves were gouged from the soft earth, leaving the ground open and bleeding.

What was that thing at the house?

Something protected Serenity and as long as she kept it close, he was all but helpless. He was almost certain it was a person he was dealing with. The question was *who?* It couldn't be the vampire she was screwing. The daylight put an end to that possibility.

When the person was around he couldn't think, his muscles hurt, his vision was distorted. He shouldn't have spent so much time fucking around with Serenity. He should have killed her there and then, or grabbed her and brought her back to the depths of the forest.

Instead he had toyed with her and loved every second of it, right up until he had sensed that being. The strange black hole hovering above him.

When he had glanced up toward it, he felt as though he'd been blinded by the flash of a camera or looked directly at the sun. His hearing buzzed, like a terrible case of tinnitus, deafening him. Deaf and blind, he'd had no option other than to retreat—to leave the bitch until the next time.

The only thing left to do now was find out what—or who—was affecting him so badly. Now Serenity wasn't his only enemy. The person she kept with her would also pay. No one got away with doing that to him. He was stronger than anyone else and he would show them.

He'd have to go back. He'd have to watch and wait; learn who and what this adversary was.

But for now he needed to recuperate. Digging himself back into the soil, buried within its soft folds, he settled himself down. He would recover from the effects of the thing like sleeping off a bad hangover.

When he woke, he would seek his revenge.

Chapter Twenty-two

Sitting behind the wheel of his car, Detective Gingham drove up the wide street, toward the house where Serenity Hathaway had sought refuge. He wondering what types of people lived behind the high walls and huge gates towering over him on both sides. Who blocked themselves off from their neighbors like that?

Rich people—that's who.

Gingham frowned. What business did a woman like Serenity have with someone who could afford to live in one of these houses?

As soon as the call came in that she'd taken a cab to one of these homes, he did a search on the address. The house belonged to a Sebastian Bandores. Other than a name, he found no other information on the man. He held no mortgages, loans or credit cards registered to the property. Gingham only found utilities and a property management company linked to the address.

He made a mental note to send someone down to the management company and do some sniffing.

Sebastian Bandores didn't have a driver's license, a birth certificate or a passport. The man was like a ghost. No, worse—more like he never existed.

Gingham ran all the possibilities through his head. Could the name be an alibi for Serenity's husband? Were Jackson Hathaway and Sebastian Bandores the same man?

The detective's mind ran wild with possibilities. Perhaps Jackson had made a fortune over the time he'd been missing and bought the house? But the dates didn't line up. Whoever Sebastian Bandores was, he'd purchased the house more than fifty years ago. Had Jackson been involved in something big before he went missing? Drug dealing, people trafficking, weapons? All of the things that made people this kind of money, without leaving a paper trail. Was Sebastian Bandores a rich relation, involved in such things, and had gotten Jackson involved?

Still something didn't feel right.

The modest three-bed duplex the couple originally lived in didn't have the grandeur he would expect from a drug lord or weapons runner. From his profile, Jackson Hathaway wasn't blessed with the brains to keep that kind of double life going.

Gingham didn't put the lights on the top of the unmarked vehicle, but he drove too fast, pushing the speed limit as much as he dared.

He had no intention of letting this one go. He'd given two young officers strict instructions to follow Serenity wherever she went and to keep him informed. Gingham wasn't going to leave this assignment to junior officers.

Where he'd find the woman, so he'd find the murderer.

The detective had seen what this monster had done to his innocent victims—young women, an elderly couple sleeping in their bed. The bodies looked as though they'd been the victims of an animal attack. The teeth marks showed the jaw shape of a human, but the actual teeth marks themselves were wrong. Their pathologist theorized the murderer filed his own teeth down to points, or else sharp veneers had been attached to his own teeth.

What kind of person would do that?

Detective Gingham intended on being around when the bastard showed up.

He hadn't told the two young officers he was on his way. He didn't want it to look like he didn't trust them. If they noticed him, his excuse would be that he needed to check something out about the house.

The street was surprisingly empty. Street lamps lined the sidewalk, throwing circles of light on the tarmac. Ahead, he saw the shape of the patrol car parked on the side of the street. The headlights were out, the interior of the car in darkness.

Gingham frowned. The officers weren't undercover. Serenity was aware of them. In fact, their presence was supposed to be a deterrent. They didn't need to be sitting in the dark.

He picked up the radio, "Call back, Unit six."

Only the crackle of static came back to him, so he tried again.

Nothing.

His jaw hardened, his fingers tightening around the steering wheel. This didn't feel right. Had they gone inside the house? He struggled to believe they would disobey direct orders, but perhaps she had invited them in for coffee and they figured they could just as easily keep watch from inside the house.

Gingham pulled up his vehicle behind the patrol car. He opened the door and climbed out. His hand rested on his hip, his fingertips touching his .45 Smith and Wesson. Every sense fired on high alert. Cautiously, he approached the vehicle.

In the small amount of light the streetlamps offered, he made out the dark shapes of the police officers still sitting in their seats. Whatever was going on, they were still in the car.

He reached the driver's window and peered inside.

Only his professionalism stopped him from reeling back in shock.

Officer Phillips' head lolled against the back of the seat, his throat torn out. Only a small amount of remaining flesh and his spinal column connected his head to his body.

Officer Drew's head flopped to one side. Claw marks slashed down his face, shredding his cheeks to ribbons. His eyeball had been caught and ripped from the socket, the remaining hole wide and black with blood. The eyeball was nowhere to be seen.

"Jesus Christ," Gingham muttered below his breath. He quickly glanced from side to side, checking the street remained empty.

The car's radio was still intact so he leaned in to pick up the handset. A cold chill brushed against the nape of his neck and he froze. He suddenly became aware of the horrific smell filling the car. His first reaction was to get out—get away from the putrid, cloying stench and into the fresh air—but as his foot stepped back out of the car, a hard, clawed hand reached from behind and grabbed him by the shoulder. With insane strength, something yanked out of the vehicle and slammed him up against the side of the car. His solar plexus met with the metal roof, bursting the air from his lungs, leaving him gasping and coughing.

A voice spoke in his ear. "You gotta answer me some questions."

His balls tightened up into his body, and at that moment he was thankful he had no family to think of. No wife to worry about how she would cope alone, no child to worry about growing up without a father.

He didn't need to ask who held him in their horrific grasp. There was no mistaking the wounds on the cops. He'd seen it all before, lying on slabs in the mortuary.

"What do you want?" Gingham managed, his voice hoarse.

"You saw what I did to your guys. Tell me what I want to know or you're going to end up the same way."

"Are you going to tell me what you want or just keep threatening me?" His bravado desperately tried to mask the fear ebbing from his pores.

"The woman—Serenity—has something or someone with her all the time. Tell me what it is and I'll let you live."

His mind whirred, terror confusing him. What the hell was he talking about?

This murderer. Slaughterer. Madman.

"She has someone with her," the man growled. "Someone else is always there."

The words slipped from Gingham's mouth before he even thought them. "What? You mean Elizabeth—her daughter?"

Beside his ear came a sharp intake of fetid breath. Unmistakable surprise.

The moment the words left his lips, regret filled him. What had he done? That he might have put that little girl in danger tore him in pieces.

He had no family of his own; had he just condemned someone else's?

"No, sorry, I'm wrong. I think she was looking after the girl for a friend." He knew he was grasping at straws, trying to make the man believe something else, but he couldn't think of anything else he could do.

Jackson laughed in his ear and it sounded like death crying. "Nice try," he said. "But really, you can't go back on something as big as that."

Gingham's head fell forward, his forehead pressing against the cool of metal of the car roof. His hand still rested on his gun. Let the bastard think he'd won; let him think he'd given up. The minute the son of a bitch made his move, Gingham would shoot him.

He felt Jackson lean in and inhale sharply, taking in the line of his neck. If he didn't know differently, he would have thought the man found him attractive.

"Get the hell away from me," Gingham growled.

Jackson laughed again and Gingham cringed. He only wanted to get away from this revolting creature, but if he tried to run he was as good as dead.

Hoping to catch the monster by surprise, Gingham flipped his gun from its holster.

"Fuck you!" he yelled as he spun around, firing the weapon.

But Jackson was fast and darted out of the way. Instead of the bullet making contact with his attacker's chest, it caught him on the neck.

The thing roared and leapt at the detective, slamming into him. Excruciating pain ratcheted through his body as teeth sank into his throat.

One last thing passed through Gingham's mind. *'It's not human. Whatever it is, it's not human.'*

Jackson didn't know whether to be elated or furious at his discovery.

The detective's blood rushed through his veins, lifting him up on a high like a drug. The blood was clean and strong, and Jackson felt as though he'd ingested some of what made the man himself.

He knew someone would notice the two cars containing the mutilated bodies very soon. But he wasn't worried about getting caught. Nothing could contain him.

The wound in his neck burned. Someone shooting him again was almost laughable. When would they realize they could do nothing to stop him? He was invincible now: immortal, untouchable.

Only one thing stood in his way and his mind turned to the new information the detective had unthinkingly given him.

Serenity had a daughter.

The possibility of the child being his flashed through his mind. He dismissed the idea almost instantly. He would have known. He'd not fucked Serenity for several months before she killed him—several other women took care of that side of things. Any further along in her pregnancy, he would have noticed. Jackson always kept a sharp eye for any extra weight she packed on. He never liked women who let themselves go; too easy a slide to take.

Besides, the useless bitch had never been good for much, including never being able to do what a woman was designed for—to carry their husband's children. God, knows, they'd tried enough. Jackson would never have admitted to anyone, but that part of his life hurt. Losing all of those babies hurt him in a place he'd not even known existed, and made him resent and hate Serenity even more.

So to whom did the child belong? And why did the girl have such an effect on him? Why hadn't he been able to see her?

There must be some 'otherness' about the child. Some kind of supernatural property he hadn't banked on.

The thought popped in his head as though someone placed it there.

Surely the child wasn't the vampire's baby?

Anger fired within him together with another emotion, one he'd only pretended to acknowledge before.

Jealousy.

How had that dead thing managed to achieve what he had only failed at—impregnating Serenity with a child she managed to keep until term? Of course he could be wrong. Maybe the child was the result of a one-night stand? But Jackson knew in his cold, dead heart the vampire was the father. His certainty came from two reasons; Serenity wasn't the type for one-night stands, and the child was not one hundred percent human.

Chapter Twenty-three

Wrapped within the embrace of Serenity's arms, surrounded by her scent, the taste of her on his tongue, Sebastian at first missed the unmistakable aroma of spilled blood in the air. Beneath the aromatic fragrance seeped something else. Something rotten.

They lay curled together on a bed of soft towels on the bathroom floor, bundled after their lovemaking. Sebastian lifted his face from the warm crook of Serenity's neck, his body stiff with tension.

"What's wrong?" Serenity hissed, her own body stance instantly matching his.

Despite their involvement in each other, neither had forgotten the danger threatening them.

"Wait here," he said, jumping to his feet and throwing his clothes back on. "Something's happened outside."

"Oh God, it's him, isn't it?"

Sebastian nodded, "Lock these doors after me. Stay in the bedroom with Elizabeth. Don't come out until I come back." Serenity opened her mouth to speak, her face a mask of concern, but Sebastian cut her off. "Don't worry. I *will* come back."

Serenity stood on tiptoes and planted a kiss on his lips. "Be careful."

Sebastian returned the kiss, pressing her hard against him before forcing himself to release her. He gave her a tight smile and whisked from the room.

Using his speed, he raced down the stairs. He burst through the front door but forced himself to stop to lock the door behind him, hoping to give Serenity and Elizabeth that small-added protection. His feet barely made a sound on the gravel as he flew across the driveway and vaulted over the high stonewall.

Sebastian landed on his feet on the sidewalk, silent and alert.

Before him, two cop cars were parked at the curb. One of the vehicle doors stood open, spilling the stench of blood from the vehicle's innards. The power of the smell hit Sebastian like a tidal wave, almost bringing him to his knees. His jaw morphed and protruded, his fangs elongated, protruding from his upper lip. Sebastian couldn't see himself but he knew his eyes would be burning yellow in the darkness.

Forcing down his natural instincts, he approached the car emitting the worst of the stench.

The inside of the car was a slaughterhouse. Two cops still sat in their seats, obviously apprehended so fast they'd not even had the chance to pull their weapons or climb from the car. Across their laps, another man, wearing plain clothes but with a holster around his waist, lay with his throat torn out. Blood smeared the man's face, his eyes wide open, his mouth contorted in a scream of horror. More blood soaked into the fabric of the seats and had spilled in the foot well. If Sebastian had stepped into an abattoir, he'd have seen less blood.

Sebastian guessed the third man had arrived in the second vehicle. He must have been checking on the other two men when Jackson attacked.

Yet, something wasn't right.

Sebastian stepped back, trying to take in the scene with new eyes. The plain-clothed police officer's gun was discarded on the curb and the scent of Jackson's rotten blood lingered beneath that of the cops.

How had this other officer managed to pull his weapon before Jackson killed him?

If Jackson had wanted the man dead immediately, he would have slain him. The plain clothed policeman had been kept alive for a reason—at least long enough to get his weapon pulled and a shot fired.

Who was this man? Sebastian wondered. *What had Jackson wanted from him?*

Sebastian growled and slammed the palms of his hands against the car roof, the metallic clang ricocheting in the still night.

This would only bring trouble. Three dead policemen outside his front door weren't going to be a good thing.

Again, the stench of Jackson's blood, combined with the acrid tang of gun powder, wafted over him. The monster had been hurt again; the officer's shot must have made contact. His injury had its benefits. Jackson would need to recuperate, buying them some time.

Whatever happened now, he needed to get Serenity and Elizabeth away from the house. The dead officers would quickly be tracked down and the police would pull Serenity in for yet more questions. The fact the monster had managed to murder armed men, yet left Serenity unharmed, would raise their suspicions. They'd think Serenity to be involved, that she was protecting Jackson or had something to do with the men's deaths.

Not wasting any more time, Sebastian turned from the crime scene. From a crouch, he sprung at the tall wall surrounding his property, alighting briefly on the top before jumping to the ground. He raced back to the room Serenity and Elizabeth were locked in.

"It's me," he called through the thick wood. "Open up."

Movement came from the other side and Serenity's face appeared in the gap, peering out.

"He's not here," he said. "One of the police officers shot him again and he's run off. But we've got three dead cops outside and can't stay here. The rest of the force will be here any minute."

She opened the door fully and threw a glance back at their daughter, still asleep on the bed.

"What are we going to do?" she asked. "Where are we going to go?"

He chewed on his lower lip, "I'm not sure yet, but we need to get away from here. Away from Los Angeles."

"I'm not going to run," she said. "I can't keep running. Not from him."

"That's a crazy thing to say," he said. "What about Elizabeth? You're putting her safety at risk."

"Seems to me Elizabeth is Jackson's one weakness."

Sebastian frowned. "What do you mean?"

"When she came down the stairs and Jackson was all over me, he grabbed his head and started yelling '*what is it?*' And then he backed right out of here."

"Then we need to go somewhere where we're on an equal footing. If I can't kill him before the sun comes up, both of you will be in danger again. I can't spend another whole day asleep when you could both be murdered," said Sebastian, after he stored the nugget of information.

"What can we do?"

His thoughts went back to the caves and tunnels where he'd lived in Turkey—to the absolute darkness and impenetrable sunshine. If he could get Jackson to Goreme, Jackson wouldn't stand a chance. The only thing the monster held over him was his ability to walk in the light. In that domain, Jackson would have nothing.

In reality, he couldn't just put them all on a plane and head to Turkey. His mind whirred. Surely there must be somewhere close he could take them? Somewhere he could hide Serenity and Elizabeth and be able to take on Jackson on a level footing?

An idea, a possibility came to mind. The Angeles Forest used to be mined for gold, though the mines were long since abandoned. The dangerous ones had been sealed up by the Forestry department, but the ones considered safe were often roamed by hikers. They would be safe enough for Serenity and Elizabeth to hide in, but deep enough to prevent the appearance of the sun affecting him, forcing him to withdraw and leave them vulnerable.

Come the day, the place would attract hikers, but Sebastian hoped this thing wouldn't take that long. Jackson was strong, fast and increasingly smart, but Sebastian had two hundred years on him and, with the sun taken out of the equation, he was sure it wouldn't take long to outsmart and outfight the hideous Jackson.

But the plan meant taking them both to somewhere potentially dangerous for them, and not just because of Jackson's proximity. He didn't know if they would be forced to go deeper than where the normal tourists roamed.

He wished he could get Jackson down to the mines without taking Serenity and Elizabeth with him. But Jackson wanted Serenity.

If Serenity wasn't with him, Jackson wouldn't be there either.

This felt like he was using her as bait.

Maybe he could convince Serenity to leave Elizabeth somewhere—with her friends? But if Elizabeth was the thing protecting Serenity—the thing that had stopped Jackson from slaughtering her—he didn't want to risk them being separated.

"I need to take you both where the sunlight isn't going to affect me. When the sun rises, you need to be somewhere safe, somewhere I can protect you. We need to even the tables."

She was naturally cautious. "Where?"

"In the abandoned mines in the Angeles Forest."

Her face blanched.

"A few of them are opened to hikers now. They're safe."

She looked up at him, her dark eyes large and fathomless.

"I trust you," she said. "Whatever you think we need to do to stop Jackson once and for all, I am behind you."

Her trust hurt him in some deep, inexplicable way. Her life, and that of their daughter, was in his hands.

"Serenity…" he started to say, suddenly unsure of himself, but a shake of her head stopped him.

"I can't explain how having you back in my life has made me feel," she said. "It's as though something has been missing this whole time. Now you're here, I'm better. I'm calmer; I'm stronger. My heart isn't searching anymore."

He bent his head, her words resonating with his own emotions.

"You are strong," he said, quietly. "Look at everything you've done, everything you've coped with your whole life. You're stronger than I'll ever be."

Tears filled her eyes as he wrapped his arms around her, pulling her close.

"So what now?" she asked. "When do we leave?"

"Now," he said. "It needs to be tonight. I can't risk leaving you both alone for another day."

These weren't romantic words. He was being practical. The thought of spending another whole day expecting Jackson to show up while he slept on, helpless, was terrifying.

"So you need Jackson to come for us once we're in the tunnels?" she said. "You need us as bait to draw him to you?" Sebastian nodded, unable to vocalize the brutality of his plan. "How will he know where to find us?"

"He needs to follow our trail."

"Jeez, when I said about us being used as bait, I didn't think I'd end up feeling like a piece of dragged meat."

He cast his eyes down, "I don't know any other way."

"So you're going to have to wave me under his nose and then run?"

"I'm a fast runner."

"Yeah, I know, but carrying both me and Elizabeth? Are you sure you're still going to be faster than Jackson?"

"I'm hundreds of years older than he is," he growled. "I'll be faster."

"You'd better be," she warned.

"My love for you is stronger than his hatred—that's enough to make me faster."

"His hatred brought him back from death."

They locked eyes, frozen in the moment, of the dangers of their situation.

"I don't know any other way, Serenity," Sebastian said eventually. "He slaughtered three armed police officers out there. He's going to come for you eventually."

As though the mention of the men outside conjured their colleagues, the wail of sirens filtered through the thick walls of the house, Sebastian's sensitive ears picking up on them first.

"The police are on their way," he told her. "We need to get out of here fast. They know those officers were supposed to be protecting you. If they find you here unharmed, they're going to have plenty of questions."

At the mention of the police, Serenity's mind went to James Bently, of the danger she'd put him and his family in. She'd not heard from him since leaving her apartment and she hoped both he and his family remained safe. Amy and Noah were at least far away with Amy's mother but James had insisted on staying in the city.

As the siren's grew loud—and close—enough for her to hear, she wondered if James would be among the officers sent to investigate.

A longing to say goodbye to her old friend clutched her heart. If something should happen, she hated that James would never know what became of her. Of course Sebastian would take care of Elizabeth now, but should something happen to all of them she didn't want James to think he could have done more.

"I know we need to go," she said. "But can we just hide a couple of streets down for the moment and see if my friend, James is among the officers?"

"Why?"

"James might be able to help."

His jaw tightened. "It's my job to make sure you're safe."

"This isn't about you. James has been there for me over the past four years and I won't just give up on his friendship because you're back in my life. I love you but I've loved James as well, as a friend. If something should happen to us, I want him to have some idea about where to look for a body."

Sebastian's whole body went rigid at the word, "Don't talk like that!"

"Be practical, Sebastian. Anything could happen. A roof might cave in and trap us. I might break my leg and be unable to get out."

"I'd carry you out," he growled.

"And if something happened to you? What then? There's nothing wrong with having backup, Sebastian. It's not a failure to ask for help. I don't want James anywhere near Jackson but the future is unpredictable for us right now."

"Okay," he said, relenting. "But we need to move now or it's going to be too late."

Miraculously, Elizabeth had slept through the whole conversation. Now they needed to rouse her so she wouldn't wake later, not know what was happening or where she was, and be terrified.

Together, they crouched at her bedside and Serenity gently shook her shoulder. Elizabeth raised her head and blinked a couple of times.

"We need to go now, honey," Serenity said. "We're going on an adventure."

Elizabeth pulled herself to sitting and rubbed her eyes with the back of her hand. "What kind of adventure?"

"One out in the forest. Sebastian is going to take us."

"Yeah?"

Sebastian nodded. "That's right. I'm going to carry you there and it will be like you're flying."

The little girl's eyes widened, all sleepiness falling away. "Real flying? Like fairies?"

"Pretty much," said Serenity.

"We're going to move really fast now," he told her. "So hold on tight, okay?"

He swept them both up in his arms, Elizabeth in one arms, her arms loosely wrapped around his broad neck, and Serenity in the other.

"We're not going straight there, though," Serenity said to Sebastian. "We need to see if James is with the other officers first."

"Fine, but only for a minute. We don't have time to waste."

With Serenity and Elizabeth clutched to his body, cradled around each other, Sebastian ran. Serenity gasped in surprise and Elizabeth let out a little squeal of excitement.

She'd forgotten how it felt to move this way, with such speed, her hair whipping from her face, her skin pulled back as though experiencing g-force. Within moments, they'd burst from the house and Sebastian leaped over the tall walls. The motion snatched the breath from her lungs as they passed the car containing the murdered men. Serenity only caught a glimpse of swirling blue lights, the shapes of figures stood in the street and more vehicles creating a roadblock.

Sebastian stopped several blocks away and set them down. Serenity's feet touched the ground and she swayed slightly, motion sickness caused her head to swim. She glanced down at her daughter but Elizabeth grinned back up.

"That was fun!" the girl laughed.

Serenity smiled and ruffled her dark hair. Turning her attention back to Sebastian she asked, "Did you see him?"

He nodded, "Yeah, I'm pretty sure he was there."

Serenity raised her eyebrows and he sighed.

"Wait here," he told them and disappeared before their eyes.

Within seconds, Sebastian reappeared and deposited a man, kicking and yelling back on the street.

"Uncle James!" Elizabeth cried in delight.

The little girl's voice snatched the man out of the confused fear created by Sebastian's movement.

"Jesus, Serenity," said James, his eyes widening at the sight of her. "What the hell's going on? This jerk grabbed me off the street and moved like... like... I don't know what. I can't even describe it. I thought your ex-husband had me."

"I'm so sorry, James. I didn't mean to frighten you but I needed to talk to you and this was the only way."

"I only just heard you were the one being staked out at this house. I was already planning on coming to see you before we got the call about Detective Gingham and the other two officers."

Serenity gasped. "Detective Gingham was one of the men killed?"

"Yes, I assumed you knew."

"No, why would I?"

Sebastian turned to Serenity, "So you knew one of the men?"

"Yes, the detective. He'd called me in a couple of times for questioning now. The last time, he picked me and Elizabeth up down the street from your house."

"So he knows about you," Sebastian said. "He knows about Elizabeth."

Alarm jarred through her. "Yes, why are you saying all this?"

"Jackson let the man live for a short period of time, unlike the other two police-officers, who he murdered immediately. I think Jackson was trying to get information out of him. I've got a feeling it was to do with Elizabeth."

"Shit."

James turned to Sebastian, taking the man in properly for the first time. "So this is the one you've been telling me about," he said, not addressing Sebastian. "Elizabeth's father."

"It's a good thing I've already told her," Serenity snapped.

"Sorry, I wasn't thinking. I've just never met a..."

"Vampire," Sebastian finished for him, and grinned wickedly, flashing a glimpse of the fangs normally hidden further back in his jaw.

James didn't rear back, but held both his position and eye contact.

"Listen," Serenity said, placing a hand on James' forearm, pulling his attention back. "We don't have time for small talk. We're going to go and hide at a mine in Angeles Forest." She looked at Sebastian for the name.

"Dawn Mine," said Sebastian. "Two miles up Millard Canyon in Altadena."

James nodded, "I know it."

"Sebastian will take care of Jackson while we hide."

He shook his head. "The police should be there."

"Don't start. You've seen what he did to your men. I'm only telling you this so you know what's happening. If you don't hear from me within twenty-four hours then you can come looking. Agreed?"

"I don't like this, Serenity."

"Please, trust me." She stepped forward and placed a kiss on his cheek, his stubble grazing her lips. "And thank you for everything, James. You've been a better friend to me than I ever deserved."

He stared at her. "Why do I feel like you're saying goodbye?"

Chapter Twenty-four

James retreated back to his colleagues and Sebastian refocused on the dangerous task ahead. He planned to head back to where he'd encountered Jackson the previous night. Though he didn't want Jackson to challenge him with Serenity and Elizabeth in his arms, he needed to get close enough for Jackson to become aware of their presence.

Elizabeth held onto his neck, her small legs wrapped around his waist. Her tiny body weighed nothing to him, but he wrapped one arm around her for support. Serenity's weight was negligible but her adult size made running more awkward so she clung to his back, her face buried in a combination of his neck and her daughter's arm.

His companions only slowed Sebastian's speed by a fraction. As soon as he'd grown accustomed to his slight change in balance, he flew across the city, not much slower than normal. The lights of the city became a blur at his speed, the roar of traffic, and wail of sirens and car alarms quickly left behind.

Within minutes, he'd left the city and entered the steep, gravel pathways of the hills before these too, gave way to thicker bush and boulders. This time, Sebastian would have no trouble finding Jackson. Firstly, he knew the location of Jackson's lair. Secondly, the stench of Jackson's blood hung on the air like smoke in a bush fire. The shot Detective Gingham managed to squeeze off must have caught an artery, as the blood flow was even stronger than at the airport.

Both Serenity and Elizabeth hid against him, protecting their faces from the whipping branches and the wind as he tore along. Their warm bodies snuggled against his body gave him a strength and purpose. He'd spent so many years wandering aimlessly, going from one place to another with nothing to ground him, yet now he held his family in his arms and he didn't intend on letting them go.

As he entered the depths of the forest, tree trunks rising on every side, he closed the gap between them and their foe. Sebastian slowed to human pace and Serenity unraveled herself from him.

"Are we close?" she asked, keeping her voice low.

"Yes." The stench of Jackson's rotten blood filled his nostrils and the back of his throat as though he were drowning in it.

Would Jackson even be strong enough to follow them?

If he was badly injured, perhaps he would be buried beneath ground and pay no attention to Serenity's presence. If Jackson didn't know Serenity was there, he'd not know to follow them to the mines.

Elizabeth piped up. "Are we there yet?"

"Shhh," Serenity said, placing her finger against her own lips.

249

"Everyone needs to be quiet," said Sebastian. "I need to listen."

"What are you—"

"Hush, Elizabeth," Serenity cut her off and the little girl fell silent.

The three of them stood together, the sounds of the forest moving around them. Wind rustled the leaves of the trees, small animals scurried in the bushes, and larger mammals cracked twigs beneath their feet. But Sebastian listened past all these noises, primed for the movement of the monster Jackson had become.

Then, in the distance, came the increasingly familiar sound of slurping, grunting and chewing.

"Wait here," he told Serenity. "I'm pretty sure he's up ahead."

Serenity nodded and reached down, grasping Elizabeth's hand. Though the moon was almost full, allowing them enough light to see, being alone in the middle of the forest at night was always going to be scary for a human, never mind with something like Jackson after them.

Sebastian stepped forward and cupped her cheek in his palm. "I'll be fast," he told her.

She pressed her face against his hand, her eyes closing for a moment. She jerked away, as if forcing herself from him. "Okay, go."

He gave her a brief nod and darted through the trees, knowing he'd only appear a blur before their eyes, if they saw him at all.

Sebastian got close and slowed. He peered through the trees into a small clearing. Jackson was hunched over the sleek, brown body of a deer. The animal's legs kicked feebly as Jackson chewed his way through the deer's throat. Blood matted its fur, spilling down Jackson's chest and covering his hands. The deer clung to the last sparks of life but as Jackson fed, so the animal's motions grew weaker.

Jackson must have needed the blood to recuperate, but had been unable to find a human victim quickly enough. Seeing him feed from an animal didn't make Sebastian feel any better. From his own experience, when he'd first been turned and tried to live from the blood of animals, he'd soon discovered he needed human blood to keep his mind clear. Feeding on animal blood would only make Jackson more animalistic and Sebastian didn't think he needed any help in that area.

Jackson's involvement in his meal left him unaware of his surroundings. He still hadn't noticed he had company.

Sebastian spoke out loud, raising his voice to be heard. "I've got something you want."

The monster that had once been Serenity's husband lifted his face from the now dead deer. He gave a smile that looked more like a sneer and the corners of his mouth lifted to reveal his bloodied, pointed teeth.

Like an animal himself, Jackson sprang at Sebastian.

Serenity stood in the middle of the forest, unable to keep the trembles of fear from her body. She willed herself to get a hold for Elizabeth's sake but her body had a mind of its own and the shivering continued.

"Don't be scared, Mommy," came Elizabeth's thin voice. "Sebastian will take care of us."

Serenity suddenly realized Elizabeth may know more than she was letting on. It wouldn't be the first time her daughter predicted the future.

She crouched to her daughter's level. "Do you know what's going to happen, honey?" she asked. "Have you seen what's going to happen to us and the bad man?"

Elizabeth pressed her lips together. "I can only see the dark, Mommy. It's dark and cold, and we're hiding."

"Are you scared?" Serenity asked.

"A little. But I can't see any other way, Mommy. There's nowhere else to go."

Serenity thought she understood what Elizabeth was trying to tell her. The route they were taking was the only one open to them. They were all out of options.

Still, her stomach churned with nerves, every muscle and sense wound tight enough to break.

Suddenly Sebastian's arm wrapped around her waist and lifted her from her feet. Serenity let out a shriek and Elizabeth whooped in delight. Serenity's body pressed against his strong, hard torso as he ran, not even pausing to adjust his hold on them.

His speed and urgency terrified her. There was only one reason for him to run like this—because Jackson was chasing them. If Sebastian hadn't found Jackson, he would have stopped to discuss their next move.

Sebastian ran, covering miles of forest until finally reaching the dark, wooded area of Millard Canyon. A fifty-f00t waterfall rushed nearby, the water churning. Tirelessly, he climbed over numerous rock falls and boulders as he navigated the gorge. His feet splashed in stream after stream, ice-cold water dashing up his legs, soaking into his shoes. If Jackson hadn't been so hot on their heels, Sebastian would have worried about the number of waterways washing away their trail.

But Jackson *was* on their heels.

With Sebastian's superior speed, he'd been able to get a head start on the monster, but now with Elizabeth and Serenity slowing him slightly, their paces were dangerously matched.

In his arms, both the woman he loved, and his daughter, had fallen silent. Though he was aware how disorientating traveling at this sort of velocity was for a human, he hoped neither of them—but particularly Elizabeth—suffered. Elizabeth's small, more fragile body left her defenseless to motion sickness and he didn't know how her internal organs would cope with the g-force of their movement. He hoped her half-vampire genetics would protect her against such things.

Sebastian followed the trail route, a steep, narrow dirt path along the rim of the canyon. Jackson's stench followed and Sebastian heard the monster's snuffled breaths as he gave chase.

He crossed over and ducked under fallen tree trunks, careful to hold his two charges close. Blackened tree roots covered in white rocks protruded from the earth. The terrain grew rougher. The dried up streambeds became a boulder field, causing him to leap from one rounded rock to another.

He passed a huge tree whose branches rustled and swayed above. Before him, the open yawn of the mine entrance was partially hidden behind some rusted pieces of machinery.

Sebastian allowed himself to pause outside the entrance and set Serenity and Elizabeth down. Elizabeth gave him an uncertain smile, but otherwise seemed unaffected by the race through the night. Serenity's skin glowed pale in the moonlight, her dark eyes rolling. She stumbled and he reached out and caught her.

"Are you okay?" he asked.

"Just dizzy. We need to go in, don't we?"

"Yes, and fast. He's nearly here."

A tremor wracked through her body, shuddering beneath his touch.

"It's dark in there, Mommy," said Elizabeth, tugging on her mother's shirt. "I can't see, and it's cold and wet."

"I know, sweetheart, but we'll be safe."

Elizabeth didn't answer.

The sounds of Jackson crashing through the brush grew closer, the stink of death he carried with him increased in intensity.

"Are you ready?" he asked Serenity.

She nodded and he lifted them both in his arms once again.

Wooden struts supported the entrance to the mine. Sebastian ducked beneath and entered the cold, dark tunnel. The moonlight did little to penetrate the absolute black, but Sebastian's specialist eyes meant the darkness appeared as shades of gray instead of the nothingness Serenity and Elizabeth would be experiencing.

"We need to go down to the second level," he said. "You're going to experience a drop so hold on tight."

Being deeper in the earth meant when the sun did rise, he would be sheltered and wouldn't need to leave Serenity and Elizabeth unprotected. They only had an hour or so now before morning dawned. Being below ground was imperative.

Just inside the entrance, a pit led to the next level. Sebastian held them close and stepped off the edge, plummeting twenty feet or so down to the rock bed. He landed lightly, his lower body acting as a shock absorber, cushioning the impact for his family.

The roof changed in height, so Sebastian ducked in places as he navigated the tunnel, narrowly escaping catching his head on the jagged rock roof. His feet splashed through freezing puddles and ahead came the sound of muffled, rushing water. The numerous streams and waterfall of the area didn't stop simply because they were below ground. An old dammed waterfall fell ahead, and to their right, a fathomless pit filled with water lay as still, silent, and black as ice at night.

"Be careful," he told them. "There's deep water to the right."

He didn't want to take them toward more danger, so instead he turned left.

Sebastian wanted to take them to the end of the mine. With the tunnels being so narrow, if he positioned himself between them and Jackson, Jackson would literally need to step over him to get to them.

Sebastian had no intention of allowing such a thing to happen.

Smaller offshoots of tunnels opened out on both sides, but Sebastian ignored these and took them to the furthest end where solid rock blocked their way and curved up around their heads. He set them down gently.

Serenity's eyes were wide with fear in the darkness, her pupil huge and staring. Her eyes didn't focus on his face, unable to see him. Her hands grasped Elizabeth's shoulders, pressing the little girl against her body, her knuckles white. Sebastian knew she wouldn't be able to see a thing, the darkness as absolute as anything she might have experienced before. This in itself would be terrifying for her, without the horror that was Jackson also coming for them.

"You need to stay here," he instructed. "Don't move, okay?"

She gave small laugh, "I don't think you need to worry about that. I can't see a God damned thing."

Through the tunnel came a roar of rage, echoing in the narrow confines. Dirt and small rocks crumbled from the walls and roof, making Serenity cringe.

"He's here," she whispered.

Sebastian reached out both hands and cupped her face. He dipped down and kissed her mouth, imprinting the sensation on his mind. Then he dropped to his knee and kissed the top of Elizabeth's head.

"I love you," he said. "Both of you."

"Be safe," she said. "We need you."

Sebastian tore himself away, leaving them huddled together against the damp cold and the fear.

Jackson's scent grew stronger, filling the narrow passages with all of its filth and repugnance. In the passage above, the roar reduced to a low growl, its tremors reverberating around the confines. Footfalls scuffed the fallen rubble and lighter, more hollow ones followed as Jackson leapt between the fallen wooden struts. Yet the beast had not yet entered the lower level, perhaps scoping the upper tunnels before jumping down. Maybe the creature realized this could be some sort of trap and was alert for danger.

I'll give him danger, Sebastian thought, anger firing through his body. *I'll tear his head from his neck and his heart from his body.*

He couldn't help his own low rumble of rage vibrating deep in his chest. Above him, the sound of movement stopped as Jackson picked up the sound and paused.

Sebastian froze, ear cocked for Jackson's next movement. To a human, the creature would move almost silently but to a vampire, his movements were as loud as anything else.

Above him, Sebastian heard Jackson retrace his steps. He knew the creature stood at the pit, deciding his next move. Sebastian didn't need to wait long.

Jackson dropped through the hole in the roof, landing on the ground in front of Sebastian, and rose from a crouch. The hideous creature, his face pale and cracked, looked Sebastian up and down and smiled.

"Did you think luring me into the dark would somehow give you an advantage?" He laughed. "I thrive in the dark!"

"You're here so I can finish you off. You're halfway to death already."

Jackson held his arms out either side. "I am death and I'll deliver you into its arms—you, your bitch and her daughter."

Sebastian snarled. "Don't even mention them."

With a roar, he launched at Jackson and slammed into the monster's body. They both flew backward, landing with Sebastian on top, Jackson pinned beneath. Sebastian's jaw realigned, his fang protruding from his upper mouth. In the pitch-black, his blazing yellow eyes cast an eerie glow across Jackson's face.

Jackson snarled and lashed his head from side to side, snapping his pointed teeth at Sebastian's hands and arms, which held down his shoulders. But the creature was still strong, even with the recently healed wound. Sebastian hadn't fed for several nights and Jackson had plenty of fresh blood—that of the deer and the murdered police officers—racing through his veins, evening the tables.

Jackson's back bucked, dislodging Sebastian's hold. Sebastian fell back, his hands hit the rough stone bed of the mine. In an instant, he flipped himself back upright again but so did Jackson, so they stood facing one another like two wrestlers in a ring.

"You're going down, freak," Sebastian snarled.

Jackson titled his head and gave a snide smile. "The only thing I'll be going down on is Serenity."

"You'll never lay a finger on her. I'll make sure of it."

Jackson laughed, a cold sound. "You have no idea what you're dealing with, pretty-boy."

Unable to listen any more, Sebastian attacked again, his hands wrapping around Jackson's throat.

A swath of flashlights suddenly cut through the total darkness

"Freeze! Police!" The yell came from the opposite end of the mine.

Damn!

Sebastian never thought to consider the possibility of a second entrance to the mine on the lower level.

The distraction gave Jackson the moment he needed, and the creature sank his foul, pointed teeth into Sebastian's neck.

Sebastian roared.

Huddled together in the darkness, Sebastian's roar of pain cut through the still tunnel air. Serenity's heart broke at the sound, a sob of fear for him echoing back.

"Sebastian!" Elizabeth cried out, struggling against Serenity's hold. "The bad man is hurting him!"

With a sudden burst of strength, the small girl slipped from Serenity grasp. In the absolute darkness, with only touch as sight, Elizabeth vanished in the black.

Terror clutched her soul. "Elizabeth!" Serenity screamed, scrambling to her feet. She stumbled back down the tunnel, arms outstretched, fingers scraping against the rough walls as she tried to navigate her way. "Elizabeth, where the hell are you?" Serenity caught her foot on something solid and fell, smacking her knees against a fallen strut. Pain shot up her legs making her eyes water but the physical sensation was nothing compared to the total panic and fear she felt for the safety of her daughter.

"Oh, God, Elizabeth. Where are you?"

A hollow splash came from down the cave and a helpless cry followed. "Mommy!"

The water!

"Sebastian!" Serenity screamed, knowing he was preoccupied but unable to think around it. "Help her!"

In the far distance, pinpricks of flashlights lit the total darkness of the tunnel. The growls and snarls of the fighting creatures still filled the mine and she had no idea if Sebastian had even heard her or if he knew Elizabeth was in danger.

As Jackson's teeth sank into Sebastian's neck, sending blinding pain spearing through his body, three police officers rounded the corner of the tunnel, their weapons drawn and pointed.

At the sight of the guns, Jackson leapt from Sebastian, leaving his throat bitten and torn. Sebastian raised a hand to his injury, fearing that the creature's bite may have been infected, but the skin meshed and healed beneath his palm.

"Freeze! Police!" One of the officers called again.

"Help her!" Serenity's cry filled the tunnel, snatching Sebastian's attention.

Elizabeth!

The little girl must have taken the other passage, the one leading to the water filled crevasse. Otherwise she'd have run right into them.

With Jackson suddenly gone, Sebastian ducked out of the beam of the officer's flashlights and ran to save his daughter's life.

Serenity stumbled around in the dark, blind and helpless. She walked into a wall and hit her head against a jagged piece of rock. Her head spun and she put out her arms to steady herself.

Sebastian brushed past. "I'll get her," he said, before disappearing into the dark again.

"She's fallen in the water!" Serenity cried after him.

Within a second, she heard a second splash and she knew Sebastian had gone in after Elizabeth.

"Oh God," she cried. "Please let her be all right."

Total fear encompassed her heart at the thought of losing her daughter and made her completely forget about Jackson.

A cold arm wrapped around her waist and a dead hand pressed against her mouth, stifling her scream.

"Finally," Jackson breathed putrid air in her ear. "I've got you alone."

With ferocious strength, he dragged her backward, her heels scraping the ground, bumping against the fallen wooden struts and rock falls. Serenity struggled against him, but his hold was like two iron bands wrapped around her chest and face, leaving her helpless.

Just please let Elizabeth live…

Chapter Twenty-five

Sebastian dived in the ice-cold, black water, the water rushing past his face, submerging his body. Through the water, he picked up on Elizabeth's thrashing as she sank beneath the surface, creating a disturbance in the otherwise still surroundings. The little girl's heartbeat thundered; the sound carried in the closely compressed molecules.

He powered through the water, whole body and head submerged, his feet kicking a beat. The icy temperature didn't affect him, but he dreaded to think how Elizabeth's fragile body was coping with the shock.

With arms outstretched, he reached for her, his fingertips catching her clothing. He kicked again, propelling himself close enough to wrap an arm around her.

Panicked, Elizabeth fought against him but he was far too strong. Sebastian changed direction and swam up. They broke through the surface and Elizabeth gasped in air.

Beams of light cut across the black surface. Figures stood on the edge.

Sebastian swam toward them.

"Someone help them!" A voice shouted.

Sebastian lifted a shivering, wet Elizabeth from the water, setting her on the edge, and then hauled himself out. Water ran from his clothing, but he paid no attention.

"Serenity?" he yelled. "Serenity, where are you?"

A police officer put a hand out, touched his arm. "The suspect has fled," he said. "You're both safe now."

Sebastian shook him off. "Where's her mother?" he said. "She was here when Elizabeth fell in."

He shook his head. "There's no one else here."

Making sure Elizabeth was being wrapped in one of the officer's jackets, Sebastian ran up the tunnel, checking each offshoot passage. The mine was empty.

A roar of rage burst from his chest and he punched the wall, causing mini landslides to trickle down.

"Serenity" he yelled again, his heart breaking. He knew exactly what had happened to her.

Jackson.

Sebastian contained his fury and went back to where Elizabeth was being warmed back up. The little girl shivered, her large dark eyes peering up at him.

"Wait here," he told Elizabeth, and faced the officer. "Take care of her, okay?"

"You can't leave the scene, Sir. We need to ask you some questions," the officer said.

"If you want your guy, and don't want another death on your hands, you'll let me go."

Sebastian's eyes flashed yellow and the officer fell silent.

"I'll be back," he said, before spinning away.

Jackson must have taken Serenity back up to the upper level and escaped that way. He couldn't have gone out the lower entrance—the police officers blocked that exit. Sebastian crouched beneath the yawning hole in the roof and sprang back up the pit. He landed with both feet on the floor of the upper tunnels and raced from the mine, bursting back out into the night.

Using his speed, he took after Jackson. His wet clothes slapped around his body but he ignored the discomfort. Following the lingering scent of the monster on the night, he leapt back over the boulders and fallen trees. He picked up no scent of Serenity; Jackson's odor of death had completely masked her trail. But as he'd feared on the way up, the numerous waterways gradually wiped out Jackson's scent. If only Jackson had still been injured, he'd have left a strong enough scent to track, even through the streams.

Sebastian reached the bottom of the fifty-foot waterfall and stood, uncertain, as the water thundered before him. He had no idea which way Jackson went and the creature had enough of a head start to have put miles between them.

Sebastian lifted his face to the moon and cried. "Serenity!"

Only the sounds of the forest came back to him and he fell to his knees in anguish. He'd failed her. He'd promised to protect her and he'd let her down. Wanting to rip his own heart out, he forced himself to make his way back to the mine. At the bottom entrance, the one he'd missed, James stood with Elizabeth and a number of other officers.

As Sebastian approached, his jaw rigid, his fists balled at his sides, both James and Elizabeth looked up.

"Where's Serenity?" James demanded as soon as Sebastian was close enough to hear.

"She's gone."

James launched himself at Sebastian, grabbing him by the collar. "Where the hell is she?" He yelled, trying to shake an immovable force.

"I don't know. Jackson took her."

"You son of a bitch! You were supposed to protect her. You were supposed to kill Jackson."

"Something happened. Elizabeth fell into deep water. What would you have done? Protected Serenity at all costs and let Elizabeth drown?" James flinched at his words but Sebastian continued. "Serenity once told me that I should protect Elizabeth; that she wouldn't want to continue to live in a world where Elizabeth didn't exist."

Dawn was coming and Sebastian glanced up at the sky.

"Sebastian's going to find her again."

Elizabeth's tiny voice broke through the two males' fight and they glanced down. The miniature version of Serenity peered back up at them.

"I will," Sebastian said and bent to scoop Elizabeth up in his arms. He buried his face in his daughter's soft dark curls.

"I tried to tell Mommy," Elizabeth said, starting to cry. "I told her it was too dark for me to see and I was wet, but she didn't understand."

Elizabeth couldn't predict the future this time, he realized. She didn't see it because she physically wasn't able to see what happened. Her own presence in the situation must have blinded her third eye or whatever sense it was she used to visualize events.

"Hush," Sebastian rocked his daughter as she sobbed in his embrace. "This isn't your fault."

The only one who failed her is me.

"I can feel Mommy," Elizabeth said, with tiny hitching sobs. "She's scared and cold, and she's thinking about me."

"What else?" Sebastian asked, his heart hitching in hope. "Can you see where she is?"

"No, but the bad man has her. He's going to bite her and make her forget us."

Sebastian gritted his teeth, trying to contain the anger building within him. The thought of that creature so much as touching Serenity made him want to rage at the world, to scream his fury at the night and tear up trees by their roots. Jackson had tortured her during his lifetime and now he continued his reign of terror as part of the undead. Sebastian didn't know what would happen to Serenity if Jackson repeatedly fed from her without killing her. For vampires, the victim would eventually turn, but Jackson was some kind of half-breed and Sebastian couldn't predict the effect on Serenity.

I'll find her before that happens, he vowed.

He had a daughter now; a half-vampire child whose powers he suspected would only grow stronger with each passing year.

He would keep his promise to Serenity and take care of Elizabeth. He wasn't sure how it would work—with him only living at night—but she was his child. Anyway, he reminded himself, Elizabeth was half-vampire. She would never be able to live a normal life, not while her mother was missing. Not while she lived catching glimpses of her mother's pain.

He put Elizabeth down and crouched to her level. "You know I'm your daddy, right?" he asked her. Elizabeth nodded her head in response. "Well I'm going to take care of you and we're going to find Mommy, okay. I'll spend every moment I have searching for her until I bring her back to us."

"Promise?" she asked.

"I promise."

Sebastian would keep his promise to Serenity but he'd also keep his promise to Elizabeth. He'd never stop looking. One day, with Elizabeth's help, he would find her again.

BURIED

About the Author

Marissa Farrar is a multi-published horror and paranormal author. She was born in Devon, England, loves to travel and has lived in both Australia and Spain. She now resides in Devon with her husband, two children, a crazy Spanish rescue dog and four hens. She has a degree in Zoology, but her true love has always been writing.

Her dark take on a vampire romance, Alone, was first published in 2009 and has now being re-launched, together with the next books in what is now the 'Serenity' series.

Her short stories have been accepted for a number of anthologies including, Their Dark Masters, Red Skies Press, Masters of Horror: Damned If You Don't, Triskaideka Books; and 2013: The Aftermath, Pill Hill Press.

If you want to know more about Marissa, then please visit her website at www.marissa-farrar.blogspot.com or her facebook page at www.facebook.com/marissa.farrar.author.

MARISSA FARRAR

THE DARK ROAD

What starts as an adventure for Sasha Mills turns into a terrifying fight for survival...

Emotionally blackmailed by the cold-footed fiancé she hasn't seen in a year, Sasha abandons her life in London to track him in Siem Reap, Cambodia, where he's teaching.

While in Bangkok, locals react strangely to her request to travel the following day, insisting it is a not a good day to travel despite numerous posters advertising buses running every day. Ignoring the warnings, Sasha assumes some kind of bank holiday and offers a large amount of money. She secures a seat on the solitary bus heading for Siem Reap.

Thrown together with a random group of international backpackers, including the handsome Josh, Sasha is no longer certain of what lies ahead as they cross the Cambodian border and the roads turn into dirt tracks.

Soon after, a storm like none she's ever witnessed before descends upon them. When one of their group disappears off the side of the road, Sasha realizes she has more than just the warnings of land mines to worry about.

One by one, the travelers lose their minds as they are plunged into the terrifying secrets of the Dark Road.

www.ingramcontent.com/pod-product-compliance
Lightning Source LLC
Chambersburg PA
CBHW050020180626
46810CB00002B/510